John Oldham, Robert Bell

The Poems of John Oldham

John Oldham, Robert Bell

The Poems of John Oldham

ISBN/EAN: 9783337406745

Printed in Europe, USA, Canada, Australia, Japan

Cover: Foto ©Andreas Hilbeck / pixelio.de

More available books at **www.hansebooks.com**

POETICAL WORKS

OF

JOHN OLDHAM

THE POEMS OF

JOHN OLDHAM

EDITED WITH A MEMOIR

BY

ROBERT BELL

LONDON

CHARLES GRIFFIN AND CO.

STATIONERS' HALL COURT.

CONTENTS.

iv CONTENTS.

JOHN OLDHAM.

1653—1683.

SOME student, curious in the lore of old book-stalls, .may chance to have lighted upon a stout little volume of poems, printed in the seventeenth century, and bearing the name of John Oldham. Unless he happened to be familiar with the history of the period, he might never have heard the name before, and would, probably, conclude that Oldham was one of the swarm of scurrilous doggrel-mongers who abounded in those days of literary anarchy and licentiousness, and who, like other ephemera, perished as soon as they were born. The inference would be natural enough. Nearly a hundred years have elapsed since the publication of the last edition of these poems; and in the interval they have gone down into oblivion. To the present generation of readers they are almost unknown. Yet they obtained considerable celebrity in the lifetime of the author, and present legitimate claims to a place in every complete collection of English poetry. As a satirist, Oldham possesses incontestable merits of a high order. His subjects, like those of all writers who have lashed the vices of their day, are for the most part temporary; but the spirit, point, and freedom of the treatment inspires them with permanent interest. His Satires throw a flood of light on the politics, morals, and manners of the Restoration, and are everywhere marked by the broad hand of vigorous and original genius. Nor is this his greatest excellence. Throughout the whole of his writings he displays a courage and independence which honourably distinguish him in an age of corruption and servile adulation; and the few incidents of his life with which we are acquainted bear practical testi-

mony to that love of liberty, and scorn of the slavery of
patronage, which are energetically asserted in his poems.
By the force of these qualities he won his reputation,
and rose from a position of obscurity to the companionship
of men of rank and letters, and the intimate friendship of
Dryden.

John Oldham was the son of a nonconformist minister
who had a congregation at Nuneaton. He was born at
Shipton, near Tedbury, in Gloucestershire, on the 9th August,
1653; and, after having received the rudiments of his education at home, was placed at Tedbury school, where he remained for two years. He was indebted for this step in his
preliminary career to an alderman of Bristol, who had a son
at the school, and was anxious that the boy should have the
advantage of reading with young Oldham—from which it
may be inferred that the latter had already shown more than
average diligence and capacity. Oldham made a rapid progress at Tedbury; and in June, 1670, was entered at Edmund
Hall, Oxford, where he was assisted in his studies by the
Rev. Mr. Stephens, who early discovered the tendency of his
genius. Here he soon distinguished himself by his mastery
of Greek and Latin. His favourite authors were the poets,
and the success with which he cultivated them is shown in
his subsequent translations and imitations. The love of
poetry manifested itself strongly at this period, and at last
took complete possession of his time and thoughts. Later
in life, when opportunities were thrown open to him of
embarking in more profitable pursuits, he confessed that his
efforts in every other direction were fruitless, and that the
Muse, his 'darling sin,' still drew him back to the inveterate
habit of his youth:

> In vain I better studies there would sow;
> Oft have I tried, but none will thrive or grow.

In May, 1674, he took his degree of B.A.; shortly after
which, much against his own wishes and remonstrances, he
was summoned home by his father, who, probably, could not
afford the expense of a more prolonged residence at the Uni-

versity. No definite scheme of life appears to have been marked out for him; and to a mind impatient of idleness and dependence, the short time he remained in Gloucestershire, especially if his sketch of an 'ugly old priest' may be accepted as a sample of the people by whom he was surrounded,* must have been intolerably irksome. In the following year, the small-pox, so frequently the subject of poetical lamentations, carried off his close companion, Mr. Richard Morwent, and Oldham expressed his grief at the loss of his friend in a Pindaric Ode, which displays much tenderness of feeling and variety of illustration. This is the only poem he is known to have written during that interval; but it is not unlikely that he found ample employment in planning some of the longer poems he afterwards produced. To this period may, probably, be assigned the germs of the Satires against the Jesuits. Living in a society of nonconformists, he was at least in a position to hear religious and sectarian topics discussed with zeal and bitterness, and may have been, to some extent, led to the consideration of the subject by surrounding influences. But the intercourse with these people was, in other respects, dreary and uncongenial, and he was glad to make his escape from them when a prospect of settling in the neighbourhood of London was offered to him, although connected with a drudgery he disliked. The situation, that of

---

* This satire, entitled *Character of a certain ugly old Priest*, is in prose, and was written in 1676, two years after Oldham returned home. It is so offensively coarse that there is some difficulty in believing the traditional story that he designed it as a portrait of his father. Its exaggerations of personal ugliness are grotesque and preposterous, and look more like a hideous conception of the writer's fancy than a picture drawn from real life. The priest is described as a solecism in nature, with a foul skin, a yawning mouth, and a monstrous nose; a gruff voice that has preached half his parish deaf; a prodigious skull that would furnish a whole regiment of round-heads; and a pair of ears of a length so inordinate that he binds them over his crown at night instead of quilt night-caps. Had Oldham meant to gibbet his father in this outrageous caricature, he would, in all probability, have touched upon some of the points of temper or disposition which may be presumed to have provoked so graceless a satire; but there is not a single allusion throughout the whole that warrants such a supposition.

usher at the free school of Croydon, in Surrey, was not very tempting. The stipend was trifling, and the labour monotonous and oppressive. But it possessed the greatest of all attractions for Oldham, because, inconsiderable as it was, it secured occupation and independence.

The duties of this employment, involving meaner responsibilities than those of tuition, left him little time for poetry; he made, notwithstanding, so profitable a use of his scanty leisure that he produced several pieces, some of which, obtaining circulation in MS., found their way into the literary coteries, and rendered their unknown author an object of curiosity to the town wits and critics. Oldham, shut up in his school-room, entirely unconscious of the sensation he had created in the great world of Fops'-alley and the coffee-houses, was one day surprised, in the midst of his tasks, by a visit from Rochester, Sedley, and Dorset, accompanied by other persons of celebrity, into whose hands his verses had fallen. Mr. Shepherd, the worthy master of the school, seeing Lord Rochester's card, and thinking it quite impossible that such a mark of distinction could be intended for his obscure assistant, took the whole credit of the compliment to himself, and, after carefully arranging his toilet, went to receive his visitors. The scene that followed might have been put into one of Shadwell's comedies. The old gentleman had prepared a speech for the occasion, expressing his high sense of the honour conferred upon him, and modestly deprecating his claims to so extraordinary a condescension; when Lord Dorset good-naturedly interposed, and informed him that the motive of the visit was to see his usher. By this time Mr. Shepherd had got into a little confusion in his speech, and was probably not unwilling to make his retreat, confessing, frankly enough, that he had neither the wit nor learning to qualify him for such fine company. How it fared with the poet when he was summoned to their presence is not related. But no immediate consequences followed the visit. It was Oldham's first experience of courtiers and patronage, and his manner of receiving his visitors may not have been calculated to propitiate their favour.

It is certain, at least, that whatever impression he made upon them, they left him in the situation in which they found him, and that he still continued to drudge at a toil from which his taste revolted, and which yielded him scarcely a bare subsistence. In one of his Satires, evidently alluding to his own case, he deplores the position of a man who is thus compelled to 'beat Greek and Latin for his life,' and whose rewards are inferior to those of a dancing-master:—

> But who would be to the vile drudgery bound
> Where there so small encouragement is found?
> Where you for recompense of all your pains
> Shall hardly reach a common fiddler's gains?
> For when you've toiled, and laboured all you can,
> To dung and cultivate a barren brain,
> A dancing master shall be better paid,
> Though he instructs the heels, and you the head.

This thankless occupation was relieved by the secret work in which he delighted; and if the unexpected recognition of his talents had no other effect, it seems at all events to have stimulated him to more constant and systematic efforts. He tells us that he could not resist the infatuation of making verses; and that even when he said his prayers, he could scarcely refrain from turning them into rhyme.

After he had passed three years at Croydon, he was fortunate enough, in 1678, to obtain the appointment of tutor to the two grandsons of Sir Edward Thurland, a judge, residing in the neighbourhood of Reigate. This situation was procured for him through the interest of his friend, Mr. Harman Atwood, a barrister, whose death he afterwards lamented in an elaborate ode. It was during this period he composed those famous invectives against the Jesuits, which, appearing at a moment when the discovery of the Popish plot predisposed the public to receive such writings with avidity, at once established his reputation. Oldham remained in Judge Thurland's family till 1680; and afterwards became tutor for a short time to the son of Sir William Hicks, who lived nearer to London. At this gentleman's house he formed an acquaintance with Dr. Richard Lower, a physician and

medical writer, celebrated amongst his contemporaries by a con-
troversy in which he was engaged on the theory of the transfusion of the blood.* Lower appears to have infected Oldham
with his enthusiasm, and to have induced him to devote his
unoccupied hours to the study of medicine, which, with the
caprice of a new passion, he followed sedulously for a whole
year, and then abandoned to return to his first love.

At the close of Oldham's engagement, Sir William Hicks
proposed that he should accompany his son on his travels into
Italy.   But, eager to test his powers in a different arena,
Oldham declined the offer. The success of his poems made him
anxious to escape from the bondage of tuition; and his literary ambition naturally led him to settle in London.   Here
Rochester, Sedley, and the rest renewed their acquaintance
with him; and through their introduction he became personally
known to Dryden, who discerned in him a genius kindred to
his own. A close and warm friendship grew up between
them.   Dryden was bringing out his *Religio Laici*, and his
opinions had not yet undergone that change which might
have placed an insuperable barrier between him and the
author of the *Satires on the Jesuits*.

Oldham was now in the midst of that brilliant society which,
fixing its centre at Will's Coffee-house, radiated to all the
points of dissipation and gaiety in the metropolis. It was a

---

* Lower, in his *Tractatus de Corde, item de motu et calore Sanguinis,
et Chyli in eum transitu*, published in 1669, maintained the doctrine of
the transfusion of blood from the vessels of one living animal to those
of another, which he had experimentally demonstrated at Oxford in
1665, and afterwards upon an insane person before the Royal Society.
He claimed the merit of the discovery, which was disputed by Francis
Potter, a native of Wiltshire, but which really belonged to neither of
them, having been pointed out half a century before in a work published at Frankfort by Libavius, a German physician and chemist.
The faculty took a great interest in the discussion, and it ended in the
explosion of a theory found to be practically attended with the most
pernicious consequences. Lower enjoyed a high reputation in his
profession, and was considered one of the ablest physicians of his
time. Unfortunately, he laboured under the disadvantage of being a
Whig, and when the Popish plot was discovered, he got into discredit
with the Court party, and lost the greater part of his practice.

scene of novel excitement to one whose life had hitherto been passed in retirement and wearisome routine; but its attractions were soon exhausted. The social moralist was not to be bribed or corrupted by these dangerous pleasures, and he saw in the profligacies of the town only fresh subjects for indignant satire. Had he been disposed to minister to the vanity and vices of the fashionable world, the seductions that were thrown in his way were sufficiently numerous and flattering. Admitted to a familiar intercourse with many distinguished persons, he was particularly noticed by the Earl of Kingston. That nobleman pressed him to accept the office of private chaplain to his household, which promised a more secure provision for the future than could be hoped for from the precarious profession of authorship; but Oldham preferred his liberty, with all its risks and hardships. His proud and manly nature resented the degradation to which clergymen in such situations were subjected; who for

Diet, a horse, and thirty pounds a-year,

were treated more like menials than gentlemen. In his Satire addressed to a friend about to leave the University (published after this offer had been made to him), he draws a striking picture of the humiliations and indignities heaped upon the unhappy private chaplain, who, after many years of servitude in a noble family, might consider himself fortunate to be preferred to some slender benefice, on condition of his marrying his lady's cast-off waiting-woman. The sketch is curious as an illustration of the domestic life of the period.

The Earl of Kingston, finding he could not prevail upon Oldham to enter his house as a dependent, invited him as a guest on a visit to his seat at Holmes-Pierpont, in Nottinghamshire. Oldham accepted the invitation, and was received with a kindness and consideration as creditable to his lordship as to the poor struggling poet who had so honourably vindicated the dignity of his calling. About this time Oldham published a volume of poems and translations, in the advertisement to which he took occasion to assert his independence of the kind of patronage which, in those days, reduced the profession of literature to a level with the livery of the servants' hall. This volume, contrary to the prevailing custom, but like every other work published by Oldham, appeared without the name of a patron. Not content with merely discountenancing the practice, he could not resist the opportunity of exposing the system of egotism and servility which was countenanced by the example of the most celebrated authors. He promises his readers that, should his book ever reach another edition, it shall come out with all due pomp of venality and affectation : ' By that time belike the author means to have ready a very sparkish dedication, if he can but get himself known to some great man that will give a good parcel of guineas for being handsomely flattered. Then likewise the reader (for his farther comfort) may expect to see him appear with all the pomp and trappings of an author ; his head in the front very finely cut, together with the year of his age, commendatory verses in abundance, and all the hands of the poets of quorum to confirm his book, and pass it for authentic. This at present is content to come abroad naked, undedicated, and unprefaced, without one kind word to shelter it from censure ; and so let the critics take it amongst them.'

Oldham had not long enjoyed the seclusion and hospitalities of Holmes-Pierpont, when he was seized by an attack of small-pox, which terminated in his death on the 9th December, 1683, in the thirtieth year of his age. His life closed in the lap of luxuries that presented a strange contrast to the obscurity in which the greater part of it had been passed ; and the honours paid to his memory may be accepted without suspicion as evidence of the respect in which he was held, since no man certainly ever took less pains to cultivate favour or flattery. The Earl of Kingston attended as chief mourner at his funeral, and afterwards erected a monument over his grave. When his *Remains* were collected and published in 1684, they were accompanied by tributes to his memory from Dryden, Flatman, Tom D'Urfey, Gould, and

others. Testimonies of this description are generally of
little value; but Dryden's lines on this occasion form a
remarkable exception in the strict justice of their sentiments,
and the reality of their pathos.

The notices that have been preserved of Oldham's personal
appearance describe him as having the aspect of a student
and a close observer. He was tall and slender, with disagree-
able features, a long face, a prominent nose, and a sarcastic
expression in his eyes. His constitution betrayed symptoms
of consumption; and we gather from numerous passages in
his works that the life of London was less congenial to his
tastes and habits than the repose and elastic air of the
country. Granger says that he was of a very different turn
from his father, and that he appears to have been no enemy
to the fashionable vices; but this assertion should be received
with caution in reference to a writer who literally made a
crusade against the licentiousness of the town. If he fell
into the excesses of the company with which he mixed during
the short term of his residence in London, there is no doubt
that he speedily abandoned and renounced them.*

We have it on Spence's authority that Pope considered
Oldham a very indelicate writer, admitting, at the same time,
that he had strong rage, but that it was too like Billingsgate.
The criticism is true; but it is not the whole truth. There
were elements better and nobler than Billingsgate in Oldham
—masculine vigour, learning, variety and fitness of diction,

---

* A letter of Oldham's, preserved in the Bodleian Library, and
quoted in the last edition of Croker's Boswell, sufficiently confirms this
statement. It is addressed to one of his companions, and runs thus:—
' Thou knowest, Jack, there never was a more unconcerned coxcomb
than myself once; but experience and thinking have made me quit
that humour. I think virtue and sobriety (how much so ever the men
of wit may turn 'em into ridicule) the only measures to be happy, and
believe the feast of a good conscience the best treat that can make a
true epicure. I find I retain all the briskness, airiness, and gaiety I
had, but purged from the dross and lees of debauchery; and am as
merry as ever, though not so mad.' This passage acquires additional
force from the fact that Oldham died at an age when most men give
unrestrained indulgence to their love of pleasure. Nor are there
wanting other evidences of the serious change that passed over his

and a sententious strength which Pope entirely overlooked.
Dryden esteemed him as a satirist nearer to his own standard
than any other writer of his time ; a panegyric sustained by
the opinion of Mr. Hallam, who says that ' Oldham, far
superior in his satires to Marvell, ranks perhaps next to
Dryden.' The affecting lines in which Dryden deplores the
loss of the young poet, and indicates the prominent features
of his character, leave, indeed, little more to be added by
others :—

> Farewell, too little and too lately known,
> Whom I began to think and call my own ;
> For sure our souls were near allied, and thine
> Cast in the same poetic mould as mine.
> One common note on either lyre did strike,
> And knaves and fools we both abhorred alike ;
> To the same goal did both our studies drive,
> The last set out the soonest did arrive :
> Thus Nisus fell upon the slippery place,
> While his young friend performed and won the race.
> O early ripe ! to thy abundant store
> What could advancing age have added more ?
> It might (what nature never gives the young)
> Have taught the numbers of thy native tongue ;
> But satire needs not these, and wit will shine
> Through the harsh cadence of a rugged line :
> A noble error, and but seldom made,
> When poets are by too much force betrayed.
> Thy generous fruits, though gathered ere their time,
> Still showed a quickness ; and maturing time
> But mellows what we write to the dull sweets of rhyme.
> Once more, hail and farewell ! Farewell, thou young,
> But ah ! too short, Marcellus of our tongue ;
> Thy brows with ivy and with laurels bound ;
> But fate and gloomy night encompass thee around.

---

spirit after his brief experience of the dissipations of London. Amongst
his *Miscellaneous Remains* there is a paper written on the near prospect of death, in which the deep impressions made upon his mind are
earnestly expressed. In this penitential meditation, Oldham re-
proaches himself with the transgressions of the past ; but the language
of contrition employed on such occasions must not be taken at its
literal value. In moments of self-confession and religious reflection,
men usually exaggerate their former errors and omissions ; and when
Oldham alludes to his excesses and neglects, we may reasonably conclude that he magnifies them. As this paper is not only interesting
in itself as a pendant to the sketch of Oldham's character, but probably contains the last lines he wrote, it is inserted in full at the end
of the volume.

In the energy and volume of his writings, Oldham closely resembles Dryden. This resemblance, it should be observed, is exempt from a suspicion of imitation, as Oldham really preceded Dryden in the pieces in which it exists, the *Satires on the Jesuits* having been written two years before the appearance of *Absalom and Achitophel*, the first of Dryden's satires. Even were it otherwise, his vehemence betrays a temperament too eager of utterance to wait upon the study of models. Whatever is in him, therefore, of excellence or failure, has at least the merit of unimpeachable originality. The ruggedness of his versification—evidence alike of carelessness in art, and of the rude strength that resists restraints—did not escape the friendly criticism of Dryden, who excuses it under the plea that Satire does not need the refinements of skilfully-balanced numbers. Another apology for these pieces may be found in the nature of their subjects, and the disposition of the times to which they were addressed. Their boldness secured them immediate audience, and their ruggedness gave them a rougher edge, like that of a jagged hatchet that mangles its victims. But Oldham's indifference to the structure of his lines appears chiefly in the Satires where he is carried away by the impetuosity of his feelings. In two or three of his minor pieces he shows himself capable of a more melodious treatment.* It must be confessed, however, that the title bestowed upon him by Dryden of the

---

* Oldham was not insensible to the charge of metrical harshness, and in one of his prefaces he defends himself on the ground that he was more occupied with the argument than the vehicle. 'I confess,' he says, 'I did not so much mind the cadence as the sense and expressiveness of my words, and therefore chose not those which were best disposed for placing themselves in rhyme, but rather the most keen and taunt, as being the most suitable to my argument. And certainly no one that pretends to distinguish the several colours of poetry would expect that Juvenal, when he is lashing vice and villany, should flow so smoothly as Ovid or Tibullus, when they are describing amours and gallantries, and have nothing to disturb and ruffle the evenness of their style.' This vindication of his ruggedness reveals one of his most conspicuous merits—his choice of language, which is at once familiar and striking, and everywhere the faithful representative of impulsive ardour and strong convictions.

'young Marcellus of our tongue,' whatever he might have done to have earned it had he lived, less happily expressed his characteristics than that by which he was better known—the 'English Juvenal;' an appellation which is justified no less by the power and severity of his strictures, than by their animated portraiture of contemporary life and manners. In this latter point of view, his poems possess an obvious historical value.

During Oldham's life his Satires were received with great favour, and several times reprinted.* A third edition of the *Satires on the Jesuits* was published in 1685; and in 1686 his works were collected in a single volume by the publisher who had previously issued them separately. In 1710 they reached a seventh edition; and were republished in two volumes in 1722. The last edition, edited by Captain Edward Thompson, appeared in 1770.† They have never been included in any general collection of the English Poets; being denied admission as a whole, no doubt very

---

* Oldham had some admirers who considered him entitled to take rank amongst the first poets in the language. Winstanley says of him that he was 'the delight of the muses, and glory of these last times; a man utterly unknown to me, but only by works, which none can read but with wonder and admiration; so pithy his strains, so sententious his expressions, so elegant his oratory, so reviving his language, so smooth his lines, in translation outdoing the original, and in invention matchless.' Winstanley's critical opinion, it is scarcely necessary to say after this indiscriminate panegyric, is not worth much, but it indicates how highly Oldham was esteemed in some quarters by his contemporaries.

† Thompson, whose critical pretensions brought upon him the merciless ridicule of his critics, also edited the works of Marvell and Paul Whitehead. He belonged to the maritime service, and appears to have resorted to literature as a *pis aller* when the peace of 1762 threw him out of employment His first venture was a licentious poem called the *Meretriciad*, in which he celebrated the most notorious women of the town; this was followed by the *Courtezan* and the *Demirep*, the subjects of which may be inferred from their titles. He also published a sort of rambling account of his own life, called *Sailors' Letters*. In his professional capacity he acquired a more creditable reputation, and was considered a man of ability and courage. As a writer, the best things he produced were some sea-songs, excellent in their kind. 'The topsails shiver in the wind,' and a few others, still retain their popularity.

properly, in consequence of the coarseness objected to by Pope. It might be expected, nevertheless, that Oldham would have been recognised in the *Anthologies*, which, composed of picked specimens, afforded the means of bringing the public acquainted with him without compromising the taste of readers or editors. Yet here also he has been passed over in silence. If the principle of exclusion had been consistently acted upon in all instances, there would be less reason to complain of his rejection; but it is not easy to understand by what rule of taste or morality he was refused a place in collections that presented the public with the obscenities of Swift in full, suffering not a scrap to escape; nor is that fastidiousness very intelligible which saw no objection to confer on such men as Rochester, whose lives and writings were saturated with grossness, a distinction denied to a poet who dragged their delinquencies before the bar of public opinion.*

It must be admitted that Oldham wrote some pieces which deserve the obloquy they have incurred, and that there are expressions and allusions in his Satires which would be unpardonable in a writer of the nineteenth century. In this respect, however, he is not more open to censure than the most famous of his contemporaries : and, although such transgressions are not to be excused by examples, it would be obviously unjust to hold up to particular condemnation in him

---

* Amongst Oldham's poems there is a lamentation on the death of Rochester, imitated from a Greek pastoral, and conceived in the usual vein of extravagant panegyric. Rochester was the first man of rank or influence that noticed Oldham, who in these stanzas discharges the obligations he owed to his memory. No personal considerations for Rochester, however, restrained him during the lifetime of that distinguished profligate from exposing the vices he practised, or the social delinquencies of the order to which he belonged. Pope has instituted a comparison between Oldham, Dorset, and Rochester, as poets, which curiously exemplifies the special character of his own taste. Rochester, he says, had much more delicacy and knowledge of mankind than Oldham, and was the medium between him and Dorset, who was better than either. The regularity of Dorset, and the wit of Rochester, were, as might be expected, preferred by Pope to the rough energy of Oldham.

a corrupt taste which has not excluded the works of Dryden from general circulation. Indeed, making a reasonable allowance for the common language and usages of the period, Oldham is entitled to credit, not only for having written so little that is offensive in this way, but for the general tendency of his writings in an opposite direction. The end he had in view should be taken into account in forming an estimate of the means he employed. If he descended to coarseness it was not to stimulate a prurient or depraved appetite, but to turn against vice its own weapons. The licentiousness of the age, the servility of pandering authors, the neglect of literature, the pride and profligacy of the nobility, and the degradation of the lower orders of the clergy, are the topics upon which he gives free scope to his honest satire; and he knew that if he treated them with delicacy and reserve he must inevitably fail in making the impression he desired. He was too much in earnest to pick and choose his phrases, or trim his versification. He thought only of the matter, and was indifferent to the manner. As he has himself frankly acknowledged, the indignation is everywhere paramount to the art:—

> Nor needs there art or genius here to use,
> Where indignation can create a muse.

In the core of his bold and vehement Satires, there is a sound and permanent material which may be safely liberated from incidental impurities, and which it is the design of the present volume to preserve. The poems retained in this collection comprise the whole of his published works, with the exception of a few pieces which may be omitted with advantage to his fame, and would be productive of no pleasure to his readers. The principle upon which they have been excluded can hardly require any justification; but it is proper to add that no liberties have been taken with the poems, beyond the exercise of that discretion which has been found indispensable in the case of Rochester and others, and which is sanctioned by an evident necessity. The text, which in all former editions is full of errors and corruptions, has been carefully revised throughout.

The rank Oldham may be considered entitled to hold amongst English satirists must not be determined by a critical examination of the quality of his verse. He is not one of those writers who advanced the art of poetry, or whose example stimulated its cultivation. He abounds in faults of negligence, and wilful violations of metrical laws. Content with the condensed force he threw at the first heat into his lines, he took no further trouble about their structure. He was as indifferent to accuracy in his rhymes as to melody in his versification; and wounds the sensitive ear no less by such discords as 'give' and 'unbelief,' 'long' and 'gone,' than by the irregularity of his rhythm. His language, always nervous, and well suited to his purpose by its idiomatic freedom, is never governed in the selection by any consideration of euphony or purity of taste; and, giving way to the overwhelming rage that is the prevailing characteristic of his Satires, he frequently repeats the same terms of objurgation and obloquy, which might have been easily varied by the exercise of a calmer judgment. These faults lie upon the surface. They strike the most careless reader; who soon, however, begins to perceive that they are the faults of an impetuous temperament, and not of ignorance or incapacity, and that Oldham's merits must be estimated by a very different test.

Of all the fugitive writers on the Protestant side who contributed to foment the agitation produced by the revelations of Titus Oates, Oldham is the ablest and boldest. He is not merely the most honest representative of the spirit that actuated his party, at a period when the kingdom was convulsed by religious feuds, but the only one whose works, addressed to the passions of the hour, are worth reproduction. He belongs wholly to the terrible episode of the Popish Plot. The entire term of his literary life did not spread over more than four or five years; and throughout that time the public mind was absorbed by the topics upon which he has dilated with such zealous frenzy in his attack on the Jesuits. As Dryden, a little later, espoused the

2—2

interests of the Duke of York's adherents, so Oldham asserted
the views of their opponents; and in this aspect his Satires
possess a special interest, and supply an important deside-
ratum.   They exhibit at its height the fury that pervaded
the Protestant party, and enable us to balance the account of
violence between them and the Roman Catholics.   The
writings of Dryden have transmitted to posterity an impression, too hastily adopted by modern historians, that the
Tories immeasurably transcended the Whigs in malignity and
intemperance; but in the invectives of Oldham we find a
display of bitterness and rancour which even Dryden himself
has not surpassed.   The advantage of superior skill was
with the greater poet; but Oldham rivals him in the breadth
and torrent of his vituperation.

Nor are these Satires less curious as a picture of living
manners.   They reflect with minute fidelity the life of the
Restoration.   In his sketches of the modes and habits of
London, Oldham enters into a variety of particulars that
bear upon the moral and social attributes of the time.   The
panorama he thus brings before us is full of illustrative
details.   From the incidents of the streets, the slightness of
the house architecture, the frequency of fires, the insecurity
of passengers by night and day, and the exploits of scourers,
roarers, and padders, he ascends to the delinquencies of the
higher orders, the corruptions at court, the venality of authors
and parasites, the neglect of literature, and the servile
homage that was paid to wealth.   The vividness of his portraiture of the contemporary age, and the stern justice he
executes upon its vices, invest his Satires with a lasting
historical value that abundantly compensates for the ruggedness of his verse, and vindicates his right to a high place
amongst English satirists.

POEMS

OF

JOHN OLDHAM.

TO THE MEMORY OF MY DEAR FRIEND, MR. CHARLES MORWENT.*

A PINDARIC.

Ostendunt terris hunc tantùm fata, nec ultrà
Esse sinunt.   VIRG.

I

BEST Friend! could my unbounded grief but rate
    With due proportion thy too cruel fate;
Could I some happy miracle bring forth,
Great as my wishes and thy greater worth,
        All Helicon should soon be thine,
        And pay a tribute to thy shrine.
The learnèd sisters all transformed should be,
No longer nine, but one Melpomene:

---

* This is the earliest poem that can be traced to a date. It was
written in 1675, when Oldham was twenty-two years of age, and published in his *Remains*, four years after his death. It is carefully con-
structed on the models then in vogue, and shows considerable skill in
the exhaustive process of extravagant panegyric. The germs of future
excellence strike root boldly in this piece, which is remarkable for
variety and fertility of illustration, and has many passages of sweetness
and beauty. Pope considered this ode one of the best of Oldham's
compositions, and noted it on a fly-leaf of a copy in his possession, for
special commendation, together with the *Fourth Satire on the Jesuits*,
the *Satire on Virtue*, the translation of Horace's *Art of Poetry*, and the
Impertinent from Horace. This note of Pope's was communicated to
Captain Thompson by Mr. Wilkes.

Each should into a Niobe relent,
At once thy mourner and thy monument:
   Each should become
  Like the famed Memnon's speaking tomb,
   To sing thy well-tuned praise;
  Nor should we fear their being dumb,
Thou still wouldst make them vocal with thy rays.

2

O that I could distil my vital juice in tears!
  Or waft away my soul in sobbing airs!
    Were I all eyes,
   To flow in liquid elegies;
    That every limb might grieve,
   And dying sorrow still retrieve;
My life should be but one long mourning day,
And like moist vapours melt in tears away.
   I'd soon dissolve in one great sigh,
    And upwards fly,
Glad so to be exhaled to heaven and thee:
A sigh which might well-nigh reverse thy death,
And hope to animate thee with new breath;
Powerful as that which heretofore did give
A soul to well-formed clay, and made it live.

3

  Adieu, blest Soul! whose hasty flight away
   Tells heaven did ne'er display
  Such happiness to bless the world with stay.
  <u>Death</u> in thy fall betrayed <u>her</u> utmost spite, [white.
And showed her shafts most times are levelled at the
  She saw thy blooming ripeness time prevent;
She saw, and envious grew, and straight her arrow sent:
  So buds appearing ere the frosts are past,
   Nipped by some unkind blast,
  Wither in penance for their forward haste.
   Thus have I seen a morn so bright,
   So decked with all the robes of light,
   As if it scorned to think of night,

Which a rude storm ere noon did shroud,
And buried all its early glories in a cloud.
    The day in funeral blackness mourned,
    And all to sighs, and all to tears it turned.

4

But why do we thy death untimely deem;
        Or fate blaspheme?
    We should thy full ripe virtues wrong,
        To think thee young.
Fate, when she did thy vigorous growth behold,
    And all thy forward glories told,
Forgot thy tale of years, and thought thee old.
    The brisk endowments of thy mind,
    Scorning in the bud to be confined,
Out-ran thy age, and left slow time behind;
Which made thee reach maturity so soon,
And, at first dawn, present a full spread noon.
So thy perfections with thy soul agree,
Both knew no non-age, knew no infancy.
Thus the first pattern of our race began
His life in middle-age, at 's birth a perfect man.

5

So well thou actedst in thy span of days,
As calls at once for wonder and for praise.
    Thy prudent conduct had so learnt to measure
    The different whiles of toil and leisure,
No time did action want, no action wanted pleasure.
    Thy busy industry could time dilate,
        And stretch the thread of fate:
Thy careful thrift could only boast the power
To lengthen minutes, and extend an hour.
    No single sand could e'er slip by
    Without its wonder, sweet as high:
And every teeming moment still brought forth
    A thousand rarities of worth.
While some no other cause for life can give,
    But a dull habitude to live,

Thou scornedst such laziness while here beneath,
And livedst that time which others only breathe.

6

Next our just wonder does commence,
How so small room could hold such excellence.
Nature was proud when she contrived thy frame,
   In thee she laboured for a name:
   Hence 'twas she lavished all her store,
As if she meant hereafter to be poor,
    And, like a bankrupt, run o' th' score.
Her curious hand here drew in straits, and joined
All the perfections lodged in human kind;
    Teaching her numerous gifts to lie
    Cramped in a short epitome.
So stars contracted in a diamond shine,
    And jewels in a narrow point confine
    The riches of an Indian mine.
      Thus subtle artists can
Draw nature's larger self within a span:
A small frame holds the world, earth, heavens and all
Shrunk to the scant dimensions of a ball.

7

Those parts which never in one subject dwell,
But some uncommon excellence foretell,
   Like stars, did all constellate here,
   And met together in one sphere.
Thy judgment, wit and memory conspired
To make themselves and thee admired;
And could thy growing height a longer stay have known,
Thou hadst all other glories, and thyself out-done.
   While some to knowledge by degrees arrive,
    Through tedious industry improved,
   Thine scorned by such pedantic rules to thrive,
    But swift as that of angels moved,
And made us think it was intuitive.
Thy pregnant mind ne'er struggled in its birth,
But quick, and while it did conceive, brought forth;

The gentle throes cf thy prolific brain
    Were all unstrained, and without pain.
Thus when great Jove the Queen of Wisdom bare,
So easy and so mild his travails were.

8

Nor were these fruits in a rough soil bestown,
As gems are thickest in rugged quarries sown.
Good nature, and good parts, so shared thy mind,
    A muse and grace were so combined,
'Twas hard to guess which with most lustre shined. .
    A genius did thy whole comportment act,
    Whose charming complaisance did so attract,
       As every heart attacked.
Such a soft air thy well-tuned sweetness swayed,
As told thy soul of harmony was made;
All rude affections that disturbers be,
That mar or disunite society,
       Were foreigners to thee.
Love only in their stead took up its rest;
    Nature made that thy constant guest,
And seemed to form no other passion for thy breast.

9

This made thy courteousness to all extend,
And thee to the whole universe a friend.
Those who were strangers to thy native soil and thee,
    No strangers to thy love could be,
Whose bounds were wide as all mortality.
    Thy heart no island was, disjoined
(Like thine own nation) from all human kind;
But 'twas a continent to other countries fixed
As firm by love, as they by earth annexed.
Thou scornedst the map should thy affection guide,
Like theirs who love by dull geography,
Friends but to whom by soil they are allied:
    Thine reached to all beside,
To every member of the world's great family.
Heaven's kindness only claims a name more general,

Which we the nobler call,
Because 'tis common, and vouchsafed to all.

10

Such thy ambition of obliging was,
Thou seemedst corrupted with the very power to please.
    Only to let thee gratify,
At once did bribe and pay thy courtesy.
Thy kindness by acceptance might be bought,
    It for no other wages sought,
        But would its own be thought.
No suitors went unsatisfied away
But left thee more unsatisfied than they.
Brave Titus! thou mightst here thy true portraiture
    And view thy rival in a private mind.   [find,
       Thou heretofore deservedst such praise,
When acts of goodness did compute thy days,
Measured not by the sun's, but thine own kinder
    rays.
    Thou thoughtest each hour out of life's journal lost,
      Which could not some fresh favour boast,
And reckonedst bounties thy best Clepsydras.

11

Some fools, who the great art of giving want,
Deflower their largess with too slow a grant:
Where the deluded suitor dearly buys
       What hardly can defray
     The expense of importunities,
   Or the suspense of torturing delay.
Here was no need of tedious prayers to sue,
    Or thy too backward kindness woo.
    It movèd with no formal state,
Like theirs whose pomp does for entreaty wait:
    But met the swift'st desires half way,
    And wishes did well-nigh anticipate;
    And then as modestly withdrew,
Nor for its due reward of thanks would stay.

12

Yet might this goodness to the happy most accrue;
  Somewhat was to the miserable due,
    Which they might justly challenge too.
Whate'er mishap did a known heart oppress,
  The same did thine as wretched make;
  Like yielding wax, thine did the impression take,
And paid its sadness in as lively dress.
Thou couldst afflictions from another breast translate,
  And foreign grief impropriate;
Oft-times our sorrows thine so much have grown,
    They scarce were more our own;
  Who seemed exempt, thou sufferedst all alone.

13

Our small'st misfortunes scarce could reach thy ear,
    But made thee give in alms a tear;
  And when our hearts breathed their regret in sighs,
  As a just tribute to their miseries,
  Thine with their mournful airs did symbolize,
Like throngs of sighs did from its fibres crowd,
  And told thy grief for our each grief aloud:
    Such is the secret sympathy
We may betwixt two neighbouring lutes descry,
If either, by unskilful hand too rudely bent,
  Its soft complaint in pensive murmurs vent,
    As if it did that injury resent,
Untouched, the other straight returns the moan,
    And gives an echo to each groan;
  From its sweet bowels a sad note's conveyed,
    Like those which to condole are made,
As if its bowels too a kind compassion had.

14

Nor was thy goodness bounded with so small extent,
    Or in such narrow limits pent.
  Let female frailty in fond tears distill,
    Who think that moisture which they spill

Can yield relief,
Or shrink the current of another's grief,
Who hope that breath which they in sighs convey
Should blow calamities away;
Thine did a manlier form express,
And scorned to whine at an unhappiness;
Thou thoughtst it still the noblest pity to redress.
So friendly angels their relief bestow
On the unfortunate below,
For whom those purer minds no passion know:
Such nature in that generous plant is found,
Whose every breach does with a salve abound,
And wounds itself to cure another's wound.
In pity to mankind it sheds its juice,
Glad with expense of blood to serve their use:
First, with kind tears our maladies bewails,
And after heals;
And makes those very tears the remedy produce.

15

Nor didst thou to thy foes less generous appear,
(If there were any durst that title wear,)
They could not offer wrongs so fast,
But what were pardoned with like haste;
And by thy acts of amnesty effaced.
Had he who wished the art how to forget,
Discovered its new worth in thee,
He had a double value on it set,
And justly scorned the ignobler art of memory.
No wrongs could thy great soul to grief expose,
'Twas placed as much out of the reach of those,
As of material blows.
No injuries could thee provoke,
Thy softness always damped the stroke:
As flints on feather-beds are easiest broke.
Affronts could ne'er thy cool complexion heat,
Or chase thy temper from its settled state:
But still thou stoodst unshocked by all,

As if thou hadst unlearned the power to hate,
Or, like the dove, were born without a gall.

16

Vain stoics who disclaim all human sense,
And own no passions to resent offence,
May pass it by with unconcerned neglect,
And virtue on those principles erect,
Where 'tis not a perfection, but defect.
Let these themselves in a dull patience please,
  Which their own statues may possess, .
  And they themselves when carcasses.
Thou only couldst to that high pitch arrive,
To court abuses, that thou mightst forgive:
Wrongs thus in thy esteem seemed courtesy,
And thou the first was e'er obliged by injury.

17

Nor may we think these godlike qualities
  Could stand in need of votaries,
Which heretofore had challenged sacrifice.
  Each assignation, each converse
  Gained thee some new idolaters.
Thy sweet obligingness could supple hate,
And out of it, its contrary create.
Its powerful influence made quarrels cease,
And feuds dissolved into a calmer peace.
Envy resigned her force, and vanquished spite
  Became thy speedy proselyte.
Malice could cherish enmity no more;
  And those which were thy foes before,
  Now wished they might adore.
Cæsar may tell of nations took,
And troops by force subjected to his yoke:
We read as great a conqueror in thee,
Who couldst by milder ways all hearts subdue,
  The nobler conquest of the two;
Thus thou whole legions mad'st thy captives be,
And, like him too, couldst look, and speak thy victory.

18

Hence may we calculate the tenderness
　　　　Thou didst express
To all, whom thou didst with thy friendship bless.
To think of passion by new mothers bore
　　　　To the young offspring of their womb,
Or that of lovers to what they adore,
　　　　　　Ere duty it become:
　　We should too mean ideas frame,
　　　　Of that which thine might justly claim,
And injure it by a degrading name:
　　　　　　Conceive the tender care
Of guardian angels to their charge assigned,
　　　　　Or think how dear
　　To heaven expiring martyrs are;
　　These are the emblems of thy mind,
The only types to show how thou wast kind.

19

On whomsoe'er thou didst confer this tie,
　　　　'Twas lasting as eternity,
And firm as the unbroken chain of destiny.
Embraces would faint shadows of your union
　　　　show,
　　　　Unless you could together grow.
That union which is from alliance bred,
　　　　　　Does not so fastly wed,
　　　　Though it with blood be cemented:
That link wherewith the soul and body's joined,
Which twists the double nature in mankind,
　　　　Only so close can bind.
That holy fire which Romans to their Vesta paid,
　　Which they immortal as the goddess made,
　　Thy noble flames most fitly parallel;
For thine were just so pure, and just so durable.
Those feignèd pairs of faithfulness, which claim
　　　　So high a place in ancient fame,
　　　　Had they thy better pattern seen,

They'd made their friendship more divine,
And strove to mend their characters by thine.

20

Yet had this friendship no advantage been,
 Unless 'twere exercised within;
What did thy love to other objects tie,
 The same made thy own powers agree,
 And reconciled thyself to thee.
 No discord in thy soul did rest,
 Save what its harmony increased.
Thy mind did with such regular calmness move,
As held resemblance with the greater mind above.
 Reason there fixed its peaceful throne,
  And reigned alone.
The will its easy neck to bondage gave,
And to the ruling faculty became a slave.
 The passions raised no civil wars,
Nor discomposed thee with intestine jars:
  All did obey,
And paid allegiance to its rightful sway.
 All threw their resty tempers by,
  And gentler figures drew,
Gentle as nature in its infancy,
As when themselves in their first beings grew.

21

Thy soul within such silent pomp did keep,
As if humanity were lulled asleep;
So gentle was thy pilgrimage beneath,
 Time's unheard feet scarce make less noise,
Or the soft journey which a planet goes;
 Life seemed all calm as its last breath,
A still tranquillity so hushed thy breast,
 As if some Halcyon were its guest,
  And there had built her nest;
It hardly now enjoys a greater rest.
As that smooth sea which wears the name of peace,
 Still with one even face appears,

And feels no tides to change it from its place,
No waves to alter the fair form it bears:
As that unspotted sky,
Where Nile does want of rain supply,
Is free from clouds, from storms is ever free:
So thy unvaried mind was always one,
And with such clear serenity still shone,
As caused thy little world to seem all temperate zone.

22

Let fools their high extraction boast,   [cost;
And greatness, which no travail, but their mother's,
Let them extol a swelling name,
Which theirs by will and testament became—
At best but mere inheritance,
As oft the spoils, as gift, of chance;
Let some ill-placed repute on scutcheons rear,
As fading as the colours which those bear,
And prize a painted field,
Which wealth as soon as fame can yield;
Thou scornedst at such low rates to purchase worth,
Nor couldst thou owe it only to thy birth,
Thy self-born greatness was above the power
Of parents to entail, or fortune to deflower.
Thy soul, which, like the sun, heaven moulded bright,
Disdained to shine with borrowed light:
Thus from himself the eternal being grew,
And from no other cause his grandeur drew.

23

Howe'er, if true nobility
Rather in souls than in the blood does lie:
If from thy better part we measures take,
And that the standard of our value make,
Jewels and stars become low heraldry
To blazon thee.
Thy soul was big enough to pity kings,
And looked on empires as poor humble things;

Great as his boundless mind,
Who thought himself in one wide globe confined,
And for another pined;
Great as that spirit whose large powers roll
Through the vast fabric of this spacious bowl,
And tell the world as well as man can boast a soul.

24

Yet could not this an haughtiness beget,
Or thee above the common level set.
Pride, whose alloy does best endowments mar,
(As things most lofty smaller still appear)
With thee did no alliance bear.
Low merits oft are by too high esteem belied,
Whose owners lessen while they raise their price;
Thine were above the very guilt of pride,
Above all others, and thy own hyperbole:
In thee the wid'st extremes were joined,
The loftiest, and the lowliest mind.
Thus though some part of heaven's vast round
Appear but low, and seem to touch the ground,
Yet 'tis well known almost to bound the spheres,
'Tis truly held to be above the stars.

25

While thy brave mind preserved this noble frame,
Thou stoodst at once secure
From all the flattery and obloquy of fame,   [same:
Its rough and gentler breath were both to thee the
Nor this could thee exalt, nor that depress thee lower;
But thou, from thy great soul, on both lookedst down,
Without the small concernment of a smile or frown.
Heaven less dreads that it should fired be
By the weak flitting sparks that upwards fly,
Less the bright goddess of the night
Fears those loud howlings that revile her light,
Than thou malignant tongues thy worth should
blast,
Which was too great for envy's cloud to overcast.

'Twas thy brave method to despise contempt,
And make what was the fault the punishment,
What more assaults could weak detraction raise,
When thou couldst saint disgrace,
And turn reproach to praise.
So clouds which would obscure the sun, oft gilded be,
And shades are taught to shine as bright as he;
So diamonds, when envious night
Would shroud their splendour, look most bright,
And from its darkness seem to borrow light.

26

Had heaven composed thy mortal frame,
Free from contagion as thy soul or fame:
Could virtue been but proof against death's arms,
Thou hadst stood unvanquished by these harms,
Safe in a circle made by thy own charms.
Fond pleasure, whose soft magic oft beguiles
Raw inexperienced souls,
And with smooth flattery cajoles,
Could ne'er ensnare thee with her wiles,
Or make thee captive to her soothing smiles.
In vain that pimp of vice essayed to please,
In hope to draw thee to its rude embrace.
Thy prudence still that syren past
Without being pinioned to the mast:
All its attempts were ineffectual found;
Heaven fenced thy heart with its own mound,
And forced the tempter still from that forbidden
ground.

27

The mad Capricios of the doting age
Could ne'er in the same frenzy thee engage;
But moved thee rather with a generous rage.
Gallants, who their high breeding prize,
Known only by their gallanture and vice,
Whose talent is to court a fashionable sin,
And act some fine transgression with a jaunty mien,
May by such methods hope the vogue to win.

Let those gay fops who deem
Their infamies accomplishment,
Grow scandalous to get esteem,
And by disgrace strive to be eminent.
Here thou disdainest the common road,
Nor wouldst by aught be wooed
To wear the vain iniquities of the mode.
Vice with thy practice did so disagree,
Thou scarce couldst bear it in thy theory.
Thou didst such ignorance 'bove knowledge prize,
And here to be unskilled, is to be wise.
Such the first founders of our blood,
While yet untempted, stood
Contented only to know good.

28

Virtue alone did guide thy actions here,
Thou by no other card thy life didst steer:
No sly decoy would serve,
To make thee from her rigid dictates swerve;
Thy love ne'er thought her worse
Because thou hadst so few competitors;
Thou couldst adore her when adored by none,
Content to be her votary alone;
When 'twas proscribed the unkind world,
And to blind cells, and grottos hurled,
When thought the phantom of some crazy brain,
Fit for grave anchorets to entertain,
A thin chimera, whom dull gown-men frame
To gull deluded mortals with an empty name.

29

Thou ownedst no crimes that shunned the light,
Whose horror might thy blood affright,
And force it to its known retreat.
While the pale cheeks do penance in their white,
And tell that blushes are too weak to expiate;
Thy faults might all be on thy forehead wore,
And the whole world thy confessor.

3—2

Conscience within still kept assize,
　To punish and deter impieties:
　That inbred judge such strict inspection bore,
　　So traversed all thy actions o'er,
　　The Eternal Judge could scarce do more:
　　Those little escapades of vice,
　　Which pass the cognizance of most,
In the crowd of following sins forgot and lost,
Could ne'er its sentence or arraignment miss:
Thou didst prevent the young desires of ill,
　　And them in their first motions kill:
The very thoughts, in others unconfined
　　　　And lawless as the wind,
　　Thou couldst to rule and order bind;
They durst not any stamp but that of virtue bear,
And free from stain, as thy most public actions, were.
Let wild debauchees hug their darling vice,
　　And court no other paradise,
　　　Till want of power
　　Bids them discard the stale amour,
　　And when disabled strength shall force
　　　A short divorce,
Miscall that weak forbearance abstinence,
Which wise morality, and better sense,
Styles but, at best, a sneaking impotence.
　　Thine a far nobler pitch did fly,
'Twas all free choice, nought of necessity.
　　Thou didst that puny soul disdain
Whose half-strain virtue only can restrain;
　　Nor wouldst that empty being own,
　　Which springs from negatives alone,
But truly thoughtst it always virtue's skeleton.

30

Nor didst thou those mean spirits more approve,
Who virtue only for its dowry love;
Unbribed thou didst her sterling self espouse,
Nor wouldst a better mistress choose.

Thou couldst affection to her bare idea pay,
The first that e'er caressed her the Platonic way.
　To see her in her own attractions dressed,
　　　　　Did all thy love arrest,
　Nor lacked there new efforts to storm thy breast.
　　　　　Thy generous loyalty
Would ne'er a mercenary be,
But chose to serve her still without a livery.
　Yet wast thou not of recompense debarred,
　But countedst honesty its own reward;
Thou didst not wish a greater bliss to accrue,
For to be good to thee was to be happy too;
　　　　That secret triumph of thy mind,
Which always thou in doing well didst find,
Were heaven enough, were there no other heaven
　designed.

31

What virtues few possess but by retail,
　　In gross could thee their owner call;
They all did in thy single circle fall.
Thou wast a living system where were wrote
All those high morals which in books are sought.
　　　　Thy practice did more virtues share
Than heretofore the learnèd porch e'er knew,
Or in the Stagyrite's scant ethics grew:
Devout thou wast as holy hermits are,
Which share their time 'twixt ecstasy and prayer;
Modest as infant roses in their bloom,
　　　Which in a blush their lives consume;
　　　So chaste, the dead are only more,
Who lie divorced from objects, and from power;
　　　So pure, that if blest saints could be
Taught innocence, they'd gladly learn of thee.
Thy virtue's height in heaven alone could grow,
Nor to aught else would for accession owe:
It only now's more perfect than it was below.

32

Hence, though at once thy soul lived here and there,
   Yet heaven alone its thoughts did share;
   It owned no home, but in the active sphere.
Its motions always did to that bright centre roll,
   And seemed to inform thee only on parole.
Look how the needle does to its dear north incline,
   As, wer't not fixed, 'twould to that region climb;
            Or mark what hidden force
         Bids the flame upwards take its course,
         And makes it with that swiftness rise,
   As if 'twere winged by the air through which it
      flies.
Such a strong virtue did thy inclinations bend,
   And made them still to the blest mansions tend.
   That mighty slave, whom the proud victor's rage
         Shut prisoner in a golden cage,
         Condemned to glorious vassalage,
         Ne'er longed for dear enlargement more,
   Nor his gay bondage with less patience bore,
Than this great spirit brooked its tedious stay,
         While fettered here in brittle clay,
   And wished to disengage and fly away.
   It vexed and chafed, and still desired to be
Released to the sweet freedom of eternity.

33

   Nor were its wishes long unheard,
   Fate soon at its desire appeared,
   And straight for an assault prepared.
   A sudden and a swift disease
First on thy heart, life's chiefest fort, does seize,
And then on all the suburb-vitals preys:
   Next it corrupts thy tainted blood,
And scatters poison through its purple flood.
   Sharp achès in thick troops it sends,
And pain, which like a rack the nerves extends.

Anguish through every member flies,
And all those inward agonies
Whereby frail flesh in torture dies.
All the staid glories of thy face,
Where sprightly youth lay checked with manly grace,
　　Are now impaired,
And quite by the rude hand of sickness marred.
　　Thy body, where due symmetry
　　In just proportions once did lie,
　　Now hardly could be known,
Its very figure out of fashion grown;
And should thy soul to its old seat return,
　　And life once more adjourn,
'Twould stand amazed to see its altered frame,
And doubt (almost) whether its own carcass were the
　　same.

34

And here thy sickness does new matter raise
　　Both for thy virtue and our praise;
　　'Twas here thy picture looked most neat,
　　　　When deep'st in shades 'twas set,
Thy virtues only thus could fairer be
Advantaged by the foil of misery.
Thy soul, which hastened now to be enlarged,
　　And of its grosser load discharged,
Began to act above its wonted rate,
And gave a prelude of its next unbodied state.
　　So dying tapers near their fall,
When their own lustre lights their funeral,
Contract their strength into one brighter fire,
And in that blaze triumphantly expire;
　　So the bright globe that rules the skies,
　　Though he gild heaven with a glorious rise,
　　Reserves his choicest beams to grace his set;
　　　　And then he looks most great,
　　And then in greatest splendour dies.

35

Thou sharpest pains didst with that courage bear,
And still thy looks so unconcerned didst wear,
Beholders seemed more indisposed than thee;
 For they were sick in effigy.
Like some well-fashioned arch thy patience stood,
And purchased firmness from its greater load.
Those shapes of torture, which to view in paint
 Would make another faint,
Thou couldst endure in true reality,
And feel what some could hardly bear to see.
Those Indians who their kings by tortures chose,
Subjecting all the royal issue to that test,
 Could ne'er thy sway refuse,
If he deserves to reign that suffers best.
Had those fierce savages thy patience viewed,
 Thou'dst claimed their choice alone;
They with a crown had paid thy fortitude,
 And turned thy death-bed to a throne.

36

 All those heroic pieties,
Whose zeal to truth made them its sacrifice:
Those nobler Scævolas, whose holy rage
Did their whole selves in cruel flames engage,
Who did amidst their force unmoved appear,
 As if those fires but lambent were,
Or they had found their empyreum there;
Might these repeat again their days beneath,
They'd seen their fates out-acted by a natural death,
And each of them to thee resign his wreath.
In spite of weakness and harsh destiny,
To relish torment, and enjoy a misery:
 So to caress a doom,
As makes its sufferings delights become:
So to triumph o'er sense and thy disease,
As amongst pains to revel in soft ease:

These wonders did thy virtue's worth enhance,
And sickness to high martyrdom advance.

37

Yet could not all these miracles stern fate avert,
      Or make 't without the dart.
Only she paused awhile, with wonder strook,
Awhile she doubted if that destiny was thine,
    And turnèd o'er again the dreadful book,
        And hoped she had mistook;
    And wished she might have cut another line.
        But dire necessity
        Soon cried 'twas thee,
And bade her give the fatal blow.
Straight she obeys, and straight the vital powers grow
  Too weak to grapple with a stronger foe,
  And now the feeble strife forego.
  Life's sapped foundation every moment sinks,
  And every breath to lesser compass shrinks;
  Last panting gasps grow weaker each rebound,
  Like the faint tremblings of a dying sound:
  And doubtful twilight hovers o'er the light,
  Ready to usher in eternal night.

38

Yet here thy courage taught thee to outbrave
    All the slight horrors of the grave:
      Pale death's arrest
      Ne'er shocked thy breast;
Nor could it in the dreadfullest figure dressed.
That ugly skeleton may guilty spirits daunt,
Whom the dire ghosts of crimes departed haunt;
Armed with bold innocence thou couldst that mormo *
  dare,
      And on the barefaced King of Terrors stare,
As free from all effects as from the cause of fear.

---

* Bugbear.

Thy soul so willing from thy body went,
As if both parted by consent,
No murmur, no complaining, no delay,
Only a sigh, a groan, and so away.
Death seemed to glide with pleasure in,
As if in this sense too 't had lost her sting.
Like some well-acted comedy, life swiftly passed,
And ended just so still and sweet at last.
Thou, like its actors, seemedst in borrowed habit here
beneath,
And couldst, as easily
As they do that, put off mortality.
Thou breathedst out thy soul as free as common breath,
As unconcerned as they are in a feignèd death.

39

Go, happy soul, ascend the joyful sky,
Joyful to shine with thy bright company:
Go, mount the spangled sphere,
And make it brighter by another star:
Yet stop not there, till thou advance yet higher,
Till thou art swallowed quite
In the vast unexhausted ocean of delight:
Delight, which there alone in its true essence is,
Where saints keep an eternal carnival of bliss;
Where the regalios of refinèd joy,
Which fill, but never cloy;
Where pleasure's ever growing, ever new,
Immortal as thyself, and boundless too;
There mayst thou learnèd by compendium grow,
For which in vain below
We so much time, and so much pains bestow.
There mayst thou all ideas see,
All wonders which in knowledge be,
In that fair beatific mirror of the deity.

40

Meanwhile, thy body mourns in its own dust,
And puts on sables for its tender trust.

Though dead, it yet retains some untouched grace,
Wherein we may thy soul's fair footsteps trace,
Which no disease can frighten from its wonted place:
Even its deformities do thee become,
And only serve to consecrate thy doom.
Those marks of death which did its surface stain,
     Now hallow, not profane.
    Each spot does to a ruby turn;
       What soiled but now, would now adorn.
Those asterisks, placed in the margin of thy skin,
Point out the nobler soul that dwelt within:
Thy lesser, like the greater, world appears
All over bright, all over stuck with stars.
So Indian luxury, when it would be trim,
     Hangs pearls on every limb.
Thus, amongst ancient Picts, nobility
     In blemishes did lie;
Each by his spots more honourable grew,
And from their store a greater value drew:
Their kings were known by the royal stains they bore,
     And in their skins their ermine wore.*

41

Thy blood where death triumphed in greatest state,
Whose purple seemed the badge of tyrant fate,

---

* In this stanza, Oldham appears to have closely imitated Dryden's lines on the death of Lord Hastings. Thus Dryden:—

  'So many spots, like næves on Venus' soil,
  One jewel set off with so many a foil. . . . .
  Or were these gems sent to adorn his skin,
  The cabinet of a richer soul within?
  No comet need foretel his change drew on,
  Whose corpse might seem a constellation.'

It is not a little remarkable that this was also Dryden's first poem, written in his seventeenth year, on a similar occasion. Oldham appears to considerable advantage in comparison. His ode is a more elaborate and correct composition, abounding quite as much in conceits, but with this difference, that Dryden's are for the most part forced and preposterous, and huddled together, while Oldham's have a certain kind of dignity and appropriateness, and are usually kept clear of inconsistency and confusion. Dryden's versification suffers equally by contrast. Oldham seems to have taken particular pains with this piece.

And all thy body o'er
　　Its ruling colours bore :　　　　.
That which infected with the noxious ill,
　　But lately helped to kill,
　　Whose circulation fatal grew,
　　And through each part a swifter ruin threw,
　　Now conscious, its own murder would arraign,
　　And throngs to sally out at every vein.
Each drop a redder than its native dye puts on,
As if in its own blushes 'twould its guilt atone.
　　A sacred rubric does thy carcass paint,
　　And death in every member writes the saint.
　　So Phœbus clothes his dying rays each night,
And blushes he can live no longer to give light.

42

Let fools, whose dying fame requires to have,
　　Like their own carcasses, a grave,
　　Let them with vain expense adorn
　　　　　　　Some costly urn,
　　Which shortly, like themselves, to dust shall turn.
　　Here lacks no Carian sepulchre,
Which ruin shall ere long in its own tomb inter ;
　　No fond Egyptian fabric built so high
　　　　As if 'twould climb the sky,
　　　　And thence reach immortality.
　　　　Thy virtues shall embalm thy name,
And make it lasting as the breath of fame.
　　　　　　　When frailer brass
　　·　　Shall moulder by a quick decrease ;
　　　　When brittle marble shall decay,
　　And to the jaws of time become a prey ;
Thy praise shall live, when graves shall buried lie,
　　　　Till time itself shall die,
And yield its triple empire to eternity.

SOME VERSES ON PRESENTING A BOOK TO COSMELIA.*

G O, humble gift, go to that matchless saint,
   Of whom thou only wast a copy meant:
And all that's read in thee, more richly find
Comprised in the fair volume of her mind;
That living system, where are fully writ
All those high morals, which in books we meet:†
Easy, as in soft air, there writ they are,
Yet firm, as if in brass they graven were.
Nor is her talent lazily to know,
As dull divines, and holy canters do;
She acts what they only in pulpits prate,
And theory to practice does translate:
Not her own actions more obey her will,
Than that obeys strict virtue's dictates still:
Yet does not virtue from her duty flow,
But she is good, because she will be so:
Her virtue scorns at a low pitch to fly,
'Tis all free choice, nought of necessity:‡
By such soft rules are saints above confined,
Such is the tie, which them to good does bind.

---

* These verses were written in September, 1676; and the three
pieces immediately following these have reference, probably, to the
same person, and to the same period. They are the only ' love verses'
in the collection. The *Parting* seems to apply to Oldham's departure
for Croydon, which took place a short time before; and in the lines
complaining of absence, he directly alludes to the drudgeries in which
he is engaged, and which leave him few opportunities of seeing the
lady. Oldham's strength did not lie in pathos of tenderness; yet
there is much feeling and delicacy in these little pieces, and a purity
of sentiment very rare in the poetical love-making of the period.

† In this passage, and one or two others, Oldham appropriated, as
equally applicable to the lady, certain images he had already addressed
in the preceding (at that time unpublished) poem to the memory of his
friend Morwent. Thus, in the *Ode*:—
   ' Thou wast a living system where were wrote
    All those high morals which in books are sought.'

   ‡ Thine a far nobler pitch did fly,
   'Twas all free choice, nought of necessity.—*Ode.*

The scattered glories of her happy sex
Ja her bright soul as in their centre mix:
And all that they possess but by retail,
She hers by just monopoly can call;
Whose sole example does more virtues shew,
Than schoolmen ever taught, or ever knew.
No act did e'er within her practice fall,
Which for the atonement of a blush could call:
No word of hers e'er greeted any ear,
But what a saint at her last gasp might hear:
Scarcely her thoughts have ever sullied been
With the least print or stain of native sin:
Devout she is, as holy hermits are,
Who share their time 'twixt ecstasy and prayer;
Modest, as infant roses in their bloom,
Who in a blush their fragrant lives consume:
So chaste, the dead themselves are only more,
Who lie divorced from objects, and from power;*
So pure, could virtue in a shape appear,
'Twould choose to have no other form, but her;
So much a saint, I scarce dare call her so,
For fear to wrong her with a name too low:
Such the seraphic brightness of her mind,
I hardly can believe her womankind:
But think some nobler being does appear,
Which, to instruct the world, has left the sphere,
And condescends to wear a body here;
Or, if she mortal be, and meant to show
The greater art, by being formed below;
Sure Heaven preserved her, by the fall uncurst,
To tell how good the sex was made at first.

---

* Devout thou wast as holy hermits are,
  Which share their time 'twixt ecstasy and prayer;
  Modest as infant roses in their bloom,
    Which in a blush their lives consume,
      So chaste, the dead are only more,
  Who lie divorced from objects, and from power.—*Ode.*

THE PARTING.

TOO happy had I been indeed, if fate
 Had made it lasting, as she made it great;
But 'twas the plot of unkind destiny,
To lift me to, then snatch me from my joy:
She raised my hopes, and brought them just in view,
And then, in spite, the charming scene withdrew.
So he of old the promised land surveyed,
Which he might only see, but never tread:
So heaven was by that damned caitiff seen,
He saw't, but with a mighty gulf between,
He saw't, to be more wretched and despair again.
Not souls of dying sinners, when they go,
Assured of endless miseries below,
Their bodies more unwillingly desert,
Than I from you, and all my joys did part.
As some young merchant, whom his sire unkind
Resigns to every faithless wave and wind,
If the kind mistress of his vows appear,
And come to bless his voyage with a prayer,
Such sighs he vents as may the gale increase,
Such floods of tears as may the billows raise;
And when at length the launching vessel flies,
And severs first his lips, and then his eyes,
Long he looks back to see what he adores,
And, while he may, views the belovèd shores.
Such just concern I at your parting had,
With such sad eyes your turning face surveyed:
Reviewing, they pursued you out of sight,
Then sought to trace you by left tracks of light;
And when they could not looks to you convey,
Towards the loved place they took delight to stray,
And aimed uncertain glances still that way.

COMPLAINING OF ABSENCE.

TEN days (if I forget not) wasted are
  (A year in any lover's calendar)
Since I was forced to part, and bid adieu
To all my joy and happiness in you:
And still by the same hindrance am detained,
Which me at first from your loved sight constrained:
Oft I resolve to meet my bliss, and then
My tether stops, and pulls me back again:
So when our raisèd thoughts to heaven aspire,
Earth stifles them, and chokes the good desire.
Curse on that man whom business first designed,
And by't enthralled a freeborn lover's mind!
A curse on fate who thus subjected me,
And made me slave to any thing but thee!
Lovers should be as unconfined as air,
Free as its wild inhabitants from care:
So free those happy lovers are above,
Exempt from all concerns but those of love:
But I, poor lover militant below,
The cares and troubles of dull life must know;
Must toil for that which does on others wait,
And undergo the drudgery of fate.
Yet I'll no more to her a vassal be,
Thou now shalt make and rule my destiny:
Hence troublesome fatigues! all business hence!
This very hour my freedom shall commence:
Too long that jilt has thy proud rival been,
And made me by neglectful absence sin;
But I'll no more obey its tyranny,
Nor that, nor fate itself shall hinder me,
Henceforth from seeing and enjoying thee.

PROMISING A VISIT.

SOONER may art, and easier far, divide
  The soft embracing waters of the tide,
Which with united friendship still rejoin,
Than part my eyes, my arms, or lips from thine:
Sooner it may time's headlong motion force,
In which it marches with unaltered course,
Or sever this from the succeeding day,
Than from thy happy presence force my stay.
Not the touched needle (emblem of my soul)
With greater reverence trembles to its pole,
Nor flames with surer instinct upwards go,
Than mine, and all their motives tend to you.
Fly swift, ye minutes, and contract the space
Of time, which holds me from her dear embrace:
When I am there I'll bid you kindly stay,
I'll bid you rest, and never glide away.
Thither, when business gives me a release
To lose my cares in soft and gentle ease,
I'll come, and all arrears of kindness pay,
And live o'er my whole absence in one day.
Not souls, released from human bodies, move
With quicker haste to meet their bliss above,
Than I, when freed from clogs that bind me now,
Eager to seize my happiness, will go.
Should a fierce angel armed with thunder stand,
And threaten vengeance with his brandished hand,
To stop the entrance to my paradise,
I'll venture, and his slighted bolts despise.
Swift as the wings of fear shall be my love,
And me to her with equal speed remove;
Swift as the motions of the eye or mind,
I'll thither fly, and leave slow thought behind!

A DITHYRAMBIC.

A DRUNKARD'S SPEECH IN A MASK.*

'Ουκ ἐστὶ Διθύραμβος ἂν ὕδωρ πίνη.

I

YES, you are mighty wise, I warrant, mighty wise!
  With all your godly tricks and artifice,
Who think to chouse me of my dear and pleasant vice.
  Hence, holy sham! in vain your fruitless toil;
  Go, and some inexperienced fop beguile,
  To some raw entering sinner cant and whine,
Who never knew the worth of drunkenness and wine.
  I've tried, and proved, and found it all divine:
  It is resolved, I will drink on, and die,
  I'll not one minute lose, not I,
  To hear your troublesome divinity:
Fill me a top-full glass, I'll drink it on the knee,
Confusion to the next that spoils good company!

---

* Written in August, 1677. This characteristic delineation of the
mad valour of drink must be understood, like the *Satire against Virtue*,
to have been intended as a masked attack on one of the prominent
vices of the day. Etherege, Rochester, or Sedley might have sat for
the portrait, and were probably the actual originals from whom it was
drawn. They were as notorious for their excesses in this way, as
Dryden for his temperance, and Waller for water-drinking. It
would be absurd to suppose that this reeling dithyrambic was seriously
meant. The bombastic fury that pervades it is the very essence of
ridicule. Oldham, when he wrote it, was secluded at Croydon, and
neither in the disposition nor the circumstances to indulge in 'riotous,
guilty living.' His days and nights were given to labour and study,
and we have an evidence in the next poem, written in the following
month, that his thoughts were differently employed. The dithyrambic
is a singular example of premeditated extravagance. The end is
attained, not by peculiar felicity of diction, but by audacious hyperbole.
It does not bring out its effects by striking phrases, such as the 'plumpy
Bacchus with pink eyne' of Shakespeare, or Dryden's portrait of
Shadwell rolling home from a treason-tavern, 'liquored in every chink;'
but it hits the mark by its accumulation of daring images. The sub-
limity of the Ercles' vein is capitally sustained in the last stanza, where
the imperious roarer demands a deluge, with the ocean for his mighty
cup; calls for the Canary fleet, setting every man to empty a ship;
and finally desires the universe to be set a tilt, and the globe turned
up, that they may drain the world dry.

2

That gulp was worth a soul; like it, it went,
And throughout new life and vigour sent:
I feel it warm at once my head and heart,
I feel it all in all, and all in every part.
    Let the vile slaves of business toil and strive,
    Who want the leisure, or the wit to live;
    While we life's tedious journey shorter make,
    And reap those joys which they lack sense to take.
Thus live the gods (if aught above ourselves there be)
    They live so happy, unconcerned, and free;
    Like us they sit, and with a careless brow
Laugh at the petty jars of human kind below;
    Like us they spend their age in gentle ease;
Like us they drink; for what were all their heaven, alas!
If sober, and compelled to want that happiness.

3

Assist, almighty wine, for thou alone hast power,
      And others I'll invoke no more;
    Assist, while with just praise I thee adore;
    Aided by thee, I dare thy worth rehearse,
In flights above the common pitch of grovelling verse.
    Thou art the world's great soul, that heavenly fire,
    Which dost our dull half-kindled mass inspire.
We nothing gallant and above ourselves produce,
    Till thou dost finish man, and reinfuse.
Thou art the only source of all the world calls great,
Thou didst the poets first, and they the gods create;
    To thee their rage, their heat, their flame they owe,
    Thou must half share with art, and nature too;
They owe their glory, and renown to thee;
    Thou givest their verse and them eternity.
    Great Alexander, that biggest word of fame,
    That fills her throat, and almost rends the same,
    Whose valour found the world too strait a stage
    For his wide victories and boundless rage,

Got not repute by war alone, but thee,
He knew he ne'er could conquer by sobriety,
And drunk, as well as fought, for universal monarchy.

4

Pox o' that lazy claret! how it stays!
   Were it again to pass the seas,
   'Twould sooner be in cargo here,
'Tis now a long East-India voyage, half a year.
   'Sdeath! here's a minute lost, an age I mean,
    Slipped by, and ne'er to be retrieved again.
For pity suffer not the precious juice to die,
Let us prevent our own, and its mortality:
Like it, our life with standing and sobriety is palled,
And like it too, when dead, can never be recalled.
   Push on the glass, let it measure out each hour,
    For every sand a health let's pour,
    Swift as the rolling orbs above,
   And let it too as regularly move;
Swift as heaven's drunken red-faced traveller, the sun,
   And never rest till his last race be done,
   Till time itself be all run out, and we
   Have drunk ourselves into eternity.

5

Six in a hand begin! We'll drink it twice apiece,
   A health to all that love and honour vice!
Six more as oft to the great founder of the vine!
   (A god he was, I'm sure, or should have been)
   The second father of mankind I meant,
   He, when the angry powers a deluge sent,
   When for their crimes our sinful race was drowned,
   The only bold and venturous man was found,
Who durst be drunk again, and with new vice the world
      replant.
   The mighty patriarch 'twas of blessèd memory,
Who 'scaped in the great wreck of all mortality,
And stocked the globe afresh with a brave drinking
      progeny.

In vain would spiteful nature us reclaim,
Who to small drink our isle thought fit to damn,
   And set us out of the reach of wine,
In hope strait bounds could our vast thirst confine;
He taught us first with ships the seas to roam,
Taught us from foreign lands to fetch supply.
Rare art! that makes all the wide world our home,
Makes every realm pay tribute to our luxury.

6

Adieu, poor tottering reason! tumble down!
This glass shall all thy proud usurping powers drown,·
And wit on thy cast ruins shall erect her throne:
   Adieu, thou fond disturber of our life!
That checkest our joys, with all our pleasure art at strife:
   I've something brisker now to govern me,
   A more exalted noble faculty,
Above thy logic, and vain boasted pedantry.
Inform me, if you can, ye reading sots, what 'tis
   That guides the unerring deities?
   They no base reason to their actions bring,
   But move by some more high, more heavenly thing,
   And are without deliberation wise:
   Even such is this, at least 'tis much the same,
For which dull schoolmen never yet could find a name.
   Call ye this madness? damn that sober fool,
('Twas sure some dull philosopher, some reasoning tool)
   Who the reproachful term did first devise,
   And brought a scandal on the best of vice.
Go, ask me, what's the rage young prophets feel,
   When they with holy frenzy reel:
Drunk with the spirits of infused divinity,
   They rave, and stagger, and are mad, like me.

7

   Oh, what an ebb of drink have we,
   Bring, bring a deluge, fill us up the sea,
Let the vast ocean be our mighty cup,
We'll drink it, and all its fishes too, like loaches, up.

Bid the Canary fleet land here: we'll pay
  The freight, and custom too defray:
Set every man a ship, and when the store
Is emptied, let them straight dispatch, and sail for more.
  'Tis gone! and now have at the Rhine,
  With all its petty rivulets of wine:
The empire's forces with the Spanish we'll combine,
We'll make their drink too in confederacy join.
  'Ware France the next: this round Bordeaux shall
     swallow;
  Champagne, Langon, and Burgundy shall follow.
    Quick! let's forestall Lorraine;
  We'll starve his army, all their quarters drain,
And, without treaty, put an end to the campaign.
Go, set the universe a tilt, turn the globe up,
  Squeeze out the last, the slow unwilling drop:
A pox of empty nature! since the world's drawn dry,
    'Tis time we quit mortality,
    'Tis time we now give out, and die,
Lest we are plagued with dulness and sobriety.
  Beset with link-boys, we'll in triumph go,
A troop of staggering ghosts, down to the shades below:
  Drunk we'll march off, and reel into the tomb,
  Nature's convenient dark retiring-room;
And there, from noise removed, and all tumultuous
    strife,
Sleep out the dull fatigue, and long debauch of life.
          [*Tries to go off, but tumbles down, and
            falls asleep.*

DAVID'S LAMENTATION FOR THE DEATH OF SAUL AND JONATHAN, PARAPHRASED.*

ODE.

I

AH wretched Israel! once blessed and happy state,
    The darling of the stars, and heaven's care,
    Then all the bordering world thy vassals were,
    And thou at once their envy and their fear,
How soon art thou, alas! by the sad turn of fate
    Become abandoned and forlorn!
How art thou now become their pity, and their scorn!
Thy lustre all is vanished, all thy glory fled,
    Thy sun himself set in a blood red,
    Too sure prognostic! which does ill portend
    Approaching storms on thy unhappy land,
Left naked, and defenceless now to each invading hand,
    A fatal battle, lately fought,
    Has all these miseries and misfortunes brought,
    Has thy quick ruin and destruction wrought:
    There fell we, by a mighty overthrow,
    A prey to an enraged, relentless foe,
The toil and labour of their wearied cruelty.
Till they no more could kill, and we no longer die:
Vast slaughter all around the enlargèd mountain swells,
    And numerous deaths increase its former hills.

2

In Gath let not the mournful news be known,
    Nor published in the streets of Askalon;
    May fame itself be quite struck dumb!
Oh! may it never to Philistia come,
Nor any live to bear the cursèd tidings home!

---

* This piece bears the date of September, 1677. It is extremely unequal, and inferior, as a whole, to the paraphrases of the 137th *Psalm* and the *Hymn of St. Ambrose*; but the concluding stanzas, from the 7th to the close, are dignified and pathetic.

Lest the proud enemies new trophies raise,
And loudly triumph in our fresh disgrace:
No captive Israelite their pompous joy adorn,
Nor in sad bondage his lost country mourn:
No spoils of ours be in their temples hung,
No hymns to Ashdod's idol sung,
Nor thankful sacrifice on his glad altars burn.
Kind Heaven forbid! lest the base heathen slaves
Thy sacred and unutterable name,   [blaspheme
And above thine extol their Dagon's fame; .
Lest the vile Fish's worship spread abroad,
Who fell a prostrate victim once before our conquering
God:
And you, who the great deeds of kings and kingdoms
write,
Who all their actions to succeeding age transmit,
Conceal the blushing story, ah! conceal
Our nation's loss, and our dread monarch's fall:
Conceal the journal of this bloody day,
When both by the ill play of fate were thrown away:
Nor let our wretched infamy, and fortune's crime,
Be ever mentioned in the registers of future time.

3

For ever, Gilboa, be cursed thy hated name,
The eternal monument of our disgrace and shame!
For ever cursed be that unhappy scene,
Where slaughter, blood, and death did lately reign!
No clouds henceforth above thy barren top appear,
But what may make thee mourning wear:
Let them ne'er shake their dewy fleeces there,
But only once a year
On the sad anniverse drop a remembering tear:
No flocks of offerings on thy hills be known,
Which may, by sacrifice, our guilt and thine atone:
Nor sheep, nor any of the gentler kind hereafter stay
On thee, but bears and wolves, and beasts of prey,
Or men more savage, wild, and fierce than they;

A desert may'st thou prove, and lonely waste,
Like that our sinful, stubborn fathers passed,
Where they the penance trod for all they there trans-
      gressed:
Too dearly wast thou drenched with precious blood
Of many a Jewish worthy, spilt of late,
Who suffered there by an ignoble fate,
And purchased foul dishonour at too high a rate:
Great Saul's ran there amongst the common flood,
His royal self mixed with the baser crowd:
He, whom Heaven's high and open suffrage chose ·
The bulwark of our nation, to oppose
    The power and malice of our foes;
Even he, on whom the sacred oil was shed,
Whose mystic drops enlarged his hallowed head,
Lies now (oh Fate, impartial still to kings!)
Huddled and undistinguished, in the heap of meaner
      things.

4

Lo! there the mighty warrior lies,
With all his laurels, all his victories,
To ravenous fowls, or worse, to his proud foes, a prize:
How changed from that great Saul whose generous
A conquering army to distressèd Jabesh led,   [aid,
At whose approach Ammon's proud tyrant fled;
How changed from that great Saul whom we saw
     bring,
From vanquished Amalek, their captive spoils and king;
When unbid pity made him Agag spare:
Ah pity! more than cruelty, found guilty there:
Oft has he made these conquered enemies bow,
    By whom himself lies conquered now:
At Micmash, his great might they felt and knew,
    The same they felt at Dammin too.
Well I remember, when from Helah's plain
He came in triumph, met by a numerous crowd,
Who with glad shouts proclaimed their joy aloud;

A dance of beauteous virgins led the solemn train,
And sung, and praised the man that had his thousands
      slain.
   Seir, Moab, Zobah felt him, and where'er
     He did his glorious standards bear,
Officious victory followed in the rear:
Success attended still his brandished sword,
And, like the grave, the gluttonous blade devoured:
Slaughter upon its point in triumph sate,
And scattered death, as quick and wide as fate.

         5

Nor less in high repute and worth was his great son,
   Sole heir of all his valour and renown,
Heir too (if cruel fate had suffered) of his throne:
   The matchless Jonathan 'twas, whom loud tongued
   Amongst her chiefest heroes joys to name,   [fame
   E'er since the wondrous deeds at Seneh done,
Where he, himself a host, o'ercame a war alone:
   The trembling enemies fled, they tried to fly,
   But fixed amazement stopped, and made them die.
Great archer he! to whom our dreaded skill we owe,
Dreaded by all who Israel's warlike prowess know;
   As many shafts, as his full quiver held,
   So many fates he drew, so many killed:
Quick and unerring they as darted eye-beams flew,
   As if he gave 'em sight, and swiftness too.
Death took her aim from his, and by't her arrows threw.

         6

Both excellent they were, both equally allied
    On nature's and on valour's side:
   Great Saul, who scorned a rival in renown,
   Yet envied not the fame of 's greater son,
   By him endured to be surpassed alone:
   He, gallant prince, did his whole father show,
And fast as he could set the well-writ copies drew,
   And blushed that duty bid him not out-go:

Together, they did both the paths to glory trace;
  Together, hunted in the noble chase;
  Together, finished their united race;
  There only did they prove unfortunate,
    Never till then unblessed by fate,
    Yet there they ceased not to be great;
Fearless they met and braved their threatened fall,
And fought when heaven revolted, fortune durst rebel.
When public safety, and their country's care
Required their aid, and called them to the toils of war;
As parent eagles, summoned by their infants' cries, .
    Whom some rude hands would make a prize,
Haste to relief, and with their wings out-fly their eyes;
  So swift did they their speedy succour bear,
  So swift the bold aggressors seize,
So swift attack, so swift pursue the vanquished enemies:
  The vanquished enemies with all the wings of fear
     Moved not so quick as they,
  . Scarce could their souls fly fast enough away.
Bolder than lions, they thick dangers met,
Through fields with armèd troops, and pointed har-
    vests set,
Nothing could tame their rage, or quench their generous heat:
    rous heat:
Like those, they marched undaunted, and like those,
  Secure of wounds, and all that durst oppose,
So to resisters fierce, so gentle to their prostrate foes.

7

  Mourn, wretched Israel, mourn thy monarch's fall,
And all thy plenteous stock of sorrow call,
    To attend his pompous funeral:
  Mourn each, who in this loss an interest shares,
    Lavish your grief, exhaust it all in tears:
      Your Hebrew virgins too,
Who once in lofty strains did his glad triumphs sing,
Bring all your artful notes, and skilful measures now.

Each charming air of breath, and string,
Bring all to grace the obsequies of your dead king,
And high, as then your joy, let now your sorrow flow.
Saul, your great Saul is dead,
Who you with nature's choicest dainties fed,
Who you with nature's gayest wardrobe clad,
By whom you all her pride, and all her pleasures had:
For you, the precious worm his bowels spun,
For you, the Tyrian fish did purple run,
For you, the blest Arabia's spices grew,
And Eastern quarries hardened pearly dew;
The sun himself turned labourer for you:
For you, he hatched his golden births alone, [shone,
Wherewith you were arrayed, whereby you him out-
All this and more, you did to Saul's great conduct owe,
All this you lost in his unhappy overthrow.

8

Oh death! how vast a harvest hast thou reaped of late!
Never before hadst thou so great,
Ne'er drunkest before so deep of Jewish blood,
Ne'er since the embattled hosts at Gibeah stood,
When three whole days took up the work of fate,
When a large tribe entered at once thy bill,
And threescore thousand victims to thy fury fell.
Upon the fatal mountain's head,
Lo! how the mighty chiefs lie dead!
There my belovèd Jonathan was slain,
The best of princes, and the best of men;
Cold death hangs on his cheeks, like an untimely frost
On early fruit; there sits, and smiles a sullen boast,
And yet looks pale at the great captive she has ta'en.
My Jonathan is dead! oh dreadful word of fame!
Oh grief! that I can speak 't, and not become the
          same!   [gone,
He's dead, and with him all our blooming hopes are
And many a wonder, which he must have done,
And many a conquest, which he must have won.

They're all to the dark grave and silence fled,
And never now in story shall be read, ·
   And never now shall take their date,
Snatched hence by the preventing hand of envious fate.

9

Ah, worthy prince! would I for thee had died!
Ah, would I had thy fatal place supplied!
I'd then repaid a life, which to thy gift I owe,
Repaid a crown, which friendship taught thee to forego:
   Both debts, I ne'er can cancel now:
Oh, dearer than my soul! if I can call it mine,
 For sure we had the same, 'twas very thine,
 Dearer than light, or life, or fame,   [name.
Or crowns, or anything that I can wish, or think, or
 Brother thou wast, but wast my friend before,
 And that new title then could add no more:
Mine more than blood, alliance, nature's self could make,
  Than I, or fame itself can speak:
 Not yearning mothers, when first throes they feel,
To their young babes in looks a softer passion tell:
 Not artless undissembling maids express
 In their last dying sighs such tenderness:
Not thy fair sister, whom strict duty bids me wear
 First in my breast, whom holy vows make mine,
Though all the virtues of a loyal wife she bear,
  Could boast an union so near,
Could boast a love so firm, so lasting, so divine.
 So pure is that which we in angels find
 To mortals here, in heaven to their own kind:
So pure, but not more great must that blessed friend-
  ship prove   [remove)
(Could, ah, could I to that wished place, and thee
Which shall for ever join our mingled souls above.

10

Ah, wretched Israel! ah, unhappy state!
 Exposed to all the bolts of angry fate!
Exposed to all thy enemies' revengeful hate!

Who is there left their fury to withstand?
What champions now to guard thy helpless land?
Who is there left in listed fields to head
Thy valiant youth, and lead them on to victory?
  Alas! thy valiant youth are dead,
  And all thy brave commanders too:
Lo! how the glut and riot of the grave thus lie,
  And none survive the fatal overthrow,
To right their injured ghosts upon the barbarous foe!
Rest, ye blessed shades, in everlasting peace,
  Who fell your country's bloody sacrifice:
  For ever sacred be your memories,
  And oh! ere long may some avenger rise
    To wipe off heaven's and your disgrace:
  May they, these proud insulting foes,
Wash off our stains of honour with their blood:
May they ten thousandfold repay our loss,
For every life a myriad, every drop a flood!

UPON THE WORKS OF BEN JONSON.*

ODE.

I

GREAT thou! whom 'tis a crime almost to dare to
        praise,†
Whose firm, established, and unshaken glories stand,
        And proudly their own fame command,
  Above our power to lessen or to raise,   [bays;
And all, but the few heirs of thy brave genius, and thy

---

* Written in 1678, the year when Oldham left Croydon.
† The indifference, or worse, in which the Elizabethan poets were
held in the early part of the reign of Charles II., is evident from the
whole of this poem; but Oldham rather overstates the case in reference to Ben Jonson, who was generally considered a greater genius
than Shakespeare. About the time, however, when Oldham was writing this panegyric on Jonson, and condemning the age for its neglect
of him, the tide of opinion was beginning to turn, and Jonson and his
contemporaries were slowly coming into fashion again. It was in this
year Dryden produced his tragedy of *All for Love; or, the World Well*

Hail mighty founder of our stage! for so I dare
Entitle thee, nor any modern censures fear,
    Nor care what thy unjust detractors say;
They'll say, perhaps, that others did materials bring,*
    That others did the first foundations lay,
    And glorious 'twas (we grant) but to begin,
      But thou alone couldst finish the design,
All the fair model, and the workmanship was thine:
    Some bold adventurers might have been before,
    Who durst the unknown world explore;
By them it was surveyed at distant view,
And here and there a cape, and line they drew,
Which only served as hints, and marks to thee,
Who wast reserved to make the full discovery.
    Art's compass to thy painful search we owe,
Whereby thou wentest so far, and we may after go;
By that we may wit's vast and trackless ocean try,
    Content no longer, as before,
    Dully to coast along the shore,
But steer a course more unconfined and free,
Beyond the narrow bounds that pent antiquity.

Lost, written professedly in imitation of the 'divine Shakespeare' whom he had himself been mainly instrumental in bringing into neglect. But he made ample reparation afterwards, in the noble and comprehensive characters of him both in prose and verse.

  * This was one of the charges brought against Jonson by the Restoration critics—that he borrowed his materials. The most remarkable case was that of the *Alchemist*, which he was accused of having plagiarized from a play by a Mr. Tomkis, called *Albumazar*, produced at Cambridge in 1614. Dryden gave currency to the charge by repeating it in a prologue to *Albumazar* on its revival in 1668:

    'And Jonson, of those few the best, chose this,
      As the best model of his master-piece:
      Subtle was got by our Albumazar,
      The Alchemist by this Astrologer;
      Here he was fashioned, and we may suppose
      He liked the fashion well, who wore the clothes.'

In these lines we may see how Jonson was estimated in relation to the poets of his own time, Dryden setting him above them all. The charge of plagiarism, in the instance of *Albumazar*, is wholly set aside by the conclusive fact that it was not printed or acted till four years after the production of the *Alchemist*.

2

Never till thee, the theatre possessed
A prince with equal power and greatness blessed;
  No government, or laws it had
    To strengthen and establish it,
  Till thy great hand the sceptre swayed,*
But groaned under a wretched anarchy of wit:
  Unformed and void was then its poesy,
  Only some pre-existing matter we
      Perhaps could see,
    That might foretel what was to be;
  A rude and undigested lump it lay,
Like the old chaos, ere the birth of light and day,
Till thy brave genius like a new creator came,
    And undertook the mighty frame.
No shuffled atoms did the well-built work compose,
It from no lucky hit of blundering chance arose,
(As some of this great fabric idly dream)
  But wise, all seeing judgment did contrive,
    And knowing art its graces give:
No sooner did thy soul with active force and fire
    The dull and heavy mass inspire,
    But straight throughout it let us see
Proportion, order, harmony,
  And every part did to the whole agree,   [poetry.
And straight appeared a beauteous, new-made world of

3

Let dull and ignorant pretenders art condemn;
  (Those only foes to art, and art to them)

---

* Jonson himself asserted his claim to the honour of having been
the founder of the stage, and the first to give it laws. The passage
occurs in his well-known lines to Richard Brome:
    ' I had you for a servant once, Dick Brome,
      And you performed a servant's faithful parts:
    Now you are got into a nearer room
      Of fellowship, professing my old arts.
    And you do do them well; with good applause
      Which you have justly gained from the stage,
    By observations of those comic laws
      Which I, your master, first did teach the age.'

The mere fanatics, and enthusiasts in poetry,
(For schismatics in that, as in religion be)
    Who make 't all revelation, trance, and dream;
      Let them despise her laws, and think
      That rules and forms the spirit stint:
Thine was no mad, unruly frenzy of the brain,
      Which justly might deserve the chain,
    'Twas brisk, and mettled, but a managed rage,
Sprightly as vigorous youth, and cool as temperate age:
    Free, like thy will, it did all force disdain,
    But suffered reason's loose and easy rein,
      By that it suffered to be led,
Which did not curb poetic liberty, but guide:
    Fancy, that wild and haggard faculty,
    Untamed in most, and let at random fly,
    Was wisely governed, and reclaimed by thee;
    Restraint and discipline was made endure,
And by thy calm and milder judgment brought to
      lure;
    Yet when 'twas at some nobler quarry sent,
    With bold and towering wings it upward went,
      Not lessened at the greatest height,
Not turned by the most giddy flights of dazzling wit.

4

    Nature and art, together met and joined,
    Made up the character of thy great mind:
      That, like a bright and glorious sphere,
    Appeared with numerous stars embellished o'er,
And much of light to thee, and much of influence
      bore;
    This, was the strong intelligence, whose power
Turned it about, and did the unerring motions steer;
    Concurring both, like vital seed and heat,
    The noble births they jointly did beget,
      And hard 'twas to be thought,
Which most of force to the great generation brought.

OLDHAM.   5

So mingling elements compose our bodies frame,
  Fire, water, earth, and air,
   Alike their just proportions share,
  Each undistinguished still remains the same,
  Yet can't we say that either's here, or there,
But all, we know not how, are scattered everywhere.

5

Sober and grave was still the garb thy muse put on,
  No tawdry careless slattern dress,
   Nor starched, and formal with affectedness,
Nor the cast mode, and fashion of the court and town;
  But neat, agreeable, and jaunty 'twas,
   Well fitted, it sate close in every place,
And all became, with an uncommon air and grace:
  Rich, costly and substantial was the stuff,
Not barely smooth, nor yet too coarsely rough:
  No refuse, ill-patched shreds of the schools,
   The motley wear of read and learnèd fools,
No French commodity which now so much does take,
  And our own better manufacture spoil;
   Nor was it aught of foreign soil,
But staple all, and all of English growth and make:
  What flowers soe'er of art it had, were found
   No tinsel slight embroideries,
  But all appeared either the native ground,
Or twisted, wrought, and interwoven with the piece.

6

Plain humour, shown with her whole various face,
  Not masked with any antic dress,
  Nor screwed in forced ridiculous grimace
   (The gaping rabble's dull delight,
  And more the actor's than the poet's wit)
   Such did she enter on thy stage,
And such was represented to the wondering age:
  Well wast thou skilled and read in human kind,
In every wild fantastic passion of his mind,

Didst into all his hidden inclinations dive,
    What each from nature does receive,
Or age, or sex, or quality, or country give;
    What custom too, that mighty sorceress,
      Whose powerful witchcraft does transform
Enchanted man to several monstrous images,
    Makes this an odd, and freakish monkey turn,
    And that a grave and solemn ass appear,
And all a thousand beastly shapes of folly wear:
    Whate'er caprice or whimsey leads awry
    Perverted and seduced mortality,
      Or does incline, and bias it
From what's discreet, and wise, and right, and good
      and fit;
    All in thy faithful glass were so expressed,
    As if they were reflections of thy breast,
    As if they had been stamped on thy own mind,
And thou the universal vast idea of mankind.

7

Never didst thou with the same dish repeated cloy,
    Though every dish, well-cooked by thee,
    Contained a plentiful variety;
To all that could sound relishing palates be,
Each regale with new delicacies did invite,
    Courted the taste, and raised the appetite:
    Whate'er fresh dainty fops in season were,
    To garnish and set out thy bill of fare;
    (Those never found to fail throughout the year,
    For seldom that ill-natured planet rules,
    That plagues a poet with a dearth of fools)
    What thy strict observation e'er surveyed,
From the fine, luscious spark of high and courtly
      breed,
    Down to the dull insipid cit,
    Made thy pleased audience entertainment fit,
Served up with all the grateful poignancies of wit.

8

Most plays are writ like almanacks of late,
And serve one only year, one only state;
Another makes them useless, stale, and out of date;
  But thine were wisely calculated, fit
  For each meridian, every clime of wit,
  For all succeeding time, and after-age,
  And all mankind might thy vast audience sit,
  And the whole world be justly made thy stage:
  Still they shall taking be, and ever new,
Still keep in vogue in spite of all the damning crew;
  Till the last scene of this great theatre,
        Closed and shut down,
    The numerous actors all retire,
  And the grand play of human life be done.

9

Beshrew those envious tongues who seek to blast thy
        bays,
  Who spots in thy bright fame would find, or raise,
  And say it only shines with borrowed rays;
  Rich in thyself, to whose unbounded store
  Exhausted nature could vouchsafe no more,
Thou couldst alone the empire of the stage maintain,
  Couldst all its grandeur, and its port sustain,
  Nor needest others subsidies to pay,
Needest no tax on foreign, or thy native country lay,
  To bear the charges of thy purchased fame,
      But thy own stock could raise the same,
Thy sole revenue all the vast expense defray:
Yet, like some mighty conqueror in poetry,
      Designed by fate of choice to be
Founder of its new universal monarchy,
  Boldly thou didst the learnèd world invade,
  Whilst all around thy powerful genius swayed,
  Soon vanquished Rome, and Greece were made
  Both were thy humble tributaries made,   [submit,
And thou returnedst in triumph with her captive wit.

10

Unjust, and more ill-natured those,
Thy spiteful and malicious foes,
Who on thy happiest talent fix a lie,
And call that slowness, which was care and industry.
Let me (with pride so to be guilty thought)
Share all thy wished reproach, and share thy shame,
If diligence be deemed a fault,
If to be faultless must deserve their blame:
Judge of thyself alone (for none there were,
Could be so just, or could be so severe)
Thou thy own works didst strictly try
By known and uncontested rules of poetry,
And gavest thy sentence still impartially:
With rigour thou arraignedst each guilty line,
And sparedst no criminal sense, because 'twas thine:
Unbribed with labour, love, or self-conceit,
(For never, or too seldom we,
Objects too near us, our own blemishes can see)
Thou didst no small delinquencies acquit,
But saw'st them to correction all submit,
Saw'st execution done on all convicted crimes of wit.

11

Some curious painter, taught by art to dare,
(For they with poets in that title share)
When he would undertake a glorious frame
Of lasting worth, and fadeless as his fame,
Long he contrives, and weighs the bold design,
Long holds his doubting hand e'er he begin,
And justly, then, proportions every stroke and line,
And oft he brings it to review,
And oft he does deface, and dashes oft anew,
And mixes oils to make the flitting colours dure,
To keep 'em from the tarnish of injurious time
secure;
Finished, at length, in all that care and skill can do,
The matchless piece is set to public view,

And all surprised about it wondering stand,
          And though no name be found below,
Yet straight discern the inimitable hand,
And straight they cry 'tis Titian, or 'tis Angelo :
So thy brave soul, that scorned all cheap and easy ways,
          And trod no common road to praise,
Would not with rash, and speedy negligence proceed,
  (For whoe'er saw perfection grow in haste ?
  Or that soon done, which must for ever last?)
  But gently did advance with wary heed,
And shewed that mastery is most in justness read :
Nought ever issued from thy teeming breast,
But what had gone full time, could write exactly best,
And stand the sharpest censure, and defy the rigidest
    test.

12

'Twas thus the Almighty Poet (if we dare
Our weak, and meaner acts with His compare)
When He the world's fair poem did of old design,
(That work, which now must boast no longer date than
    thine,)
  Though 'twas in Him alike to will and do,
  Though the same Word that spoke, could make it too,
Yet would He not such quick, and hasty measures use,
Nor did an instant (which it might) the great effect
    produce;
  But when the All-wise himself in council sate,
  Vouchsafed to think and be deliberate.
When Heaven considered, and the Eternal Wit and
    Sense,
  Seemed to take time, and care, and pains,
          It shewed that some uncommon birth,
That something worthy of a God was coming forth;
Nought incorrect there was, nought faulty there,
No point amiss did in the large voluminous piece appear;
  And when the glorious Author all surveyed,
  Surveyed whate'er His mighty labours made,

Well pleased He was to find
All answered the great model and idea of His mind:
　Pleased at himself He in high wonder stood,
And much His power, and much His wisdom did applaud,
To see how all was perfect, all transcendent good.

13

Let meaner spirits stoop to low precarious fame,
　Content on gross and coarse applause to live,
　And what the dull and senseless rabble give;
Thou didst it still with noble scorn contemn,
　Nor wouldst that wretched alms receive,
The poor subsistence of some bankrupt, sordid name:
　Thine was no empty vapour, raised beneath,
　　　　And formed of common breath,
　The false and foolish fire, that's whisked about
By popular air, and glares a while, and then goes out;
But 'twas a solid, whole, and perfect globe of light,
　That shone all over, was all over bright,
And dared all sullying clouds, and feared no darkening
　　　　night;
　Like the gay monarch of the stars and sky,
　　Who wheresoe'er he does display
　His sovereign lustre, and majestic ray,
　Straight all the less, and petty glories nigh
　　　　Vanish, and shrink away,　　　　[day.
O'erwhelmed and swallowed by the greater blaze of
With such a strong, an awful and victorious beam
　Appeared, and ever shall appear, thy fame,
Viewed, and adored, by all the undoubted race of wit,
　Who only can endure to look on it;
　　The rest o'ercome with too much light,　　[quite.
With too much brightness dazzled, or extinguished
　Restless and uncontrolled, it now shall pass
　As wide a course about the world as he;
　And when his long-repeated travels cease,
　　Begin a new and vaster race,
And still tread round the endless circle of eternity.

A LETTER FROM THE COUNTRY TO A FRIEND IN TOWN,

GIVING AN ACCOUNT OF THE AUTHOR'S INCLINATIONS TO POETRY.*

AS to that poet† (if so great a one as he,
    May suffer in comparison with me)
When heretofore in Scythian exile pent,
To which he by ungrateful Rome was sent.
If a kind paper from his country came,
And wore subscribed some known and faithful name,
That, like a powerful cordial, did infuse
New life into his speechless gasping muse,
And straight his genius, which before did seem
Bound up in ice, and frozen as the clime,
By its warm force and friendly influence thawed,
Dissolved apace, and in soft numbers flowed;
Such welcome here, dear sir, your letter had
With me, shut up in close constraint as bad:
Not eager lovers, held in long suspense,
With warmer joy, and a more tender sense,
Meet those kind lines which all their wishes bless,
And sign and seal delivered happiness:
My grateful thoughts so throng to get abroad,
They overrun each other in the crowd:
To you with hasty flight they take their way,
And hardly for the dress of words will stay.
    Yet pardon, if this only fault I find,
That while you praise too much, you are less kind:
Consider, sir, 'tis ill and dangerous thus
To over-lay a young and tender muse:
Praise, the fine diet which we're apt to love,
If given to excess, does hurtful prove:

---

* Written in July, 1678. At this time Oldham had left Croydon, and was residing in the house of Judge Thurland, near Reigate. Notwithstanding the improved circumstances in which he was placed, we still find him lamenting the close constraint of his situation, and longing for freedom.　　　　† Ovid.

Where it does weak distempered stomachs meet,
That surfeits, which should nourishment create.
Your rich perfumes such fragrancy dispense,
Their sweetness overcomes and palls my sense;
On my weak head you heap so many bays,
I sink beneath 'em, quite oppressed with praise,
And a resembling fate with him receive,
Who in too kind a triumph found his grave,
Smothered with garlands, which applauders gave.
    To you these praises justlier all belong,
By alienating which yourself you wrong:
Whom better can such commendations fit
Than you, who so well teach and practise wit?
Verse, the great boast of drudging fools, from some,
Nay most of scribblers, with much straining come:
They void 'em dribbling, and in pain they write,
As if they had a stranguary of wit:
Your pen, uncalled, they readily obey,
And scorn your ink should flow so fast as they:
Each strain of yours so easy does appear,
Each such a graceful negligence does wear,
As shews you have none, and yet want no care;
None of your serious pains or time they cost,
But what thrown by, you can afford for lost.
If such the fruits of your loose leisure be,
Your careless minutes yield such poetry,
We guess what proofs your genius would impart,
Did it employ you, as it does divert:
But happy you, more prudent and more wise,
With better aims have fixed your noble choice.
While silly I all thriving arts refuse,
And all my hopes and all my vigour lose
In service on that worst of jilts, a muse,
For gainful business court ignoble ease,
And in gay trifles waste my ill-spent days.
    Little I thought, my dearest friend, that you
Would thus contribute to my ruin too:

O'errun with filthy poetry and rhyme,
The present reigning evil of the time,
I lacked, and (well I did myself assure)
From your kind hand I should receive a cure:
When, lo! instead of healing remedies,
You cherish, and encourage the disease:
Inhuman, you help the distemper on,
Which was before but too inveterate grown:
As a kind looker on, who interest shares,
Though not in's stake, yet in his hopes and fears,
Would to his friend a pushing gamester do,
Recall his elbow when he hastes to throw;
Such a wise course you should have took with me,
A rash and venturing fool in poetry.
Poets are cullies, whom rook fame draws in,*
And wheedles with deluding hopes to win:
But, when they hit, and most successful are,
They scarce come off with a bare saving share.

    Oft, I remember, did wise friends dissuade,
And bid me quit the trifling barren trade;
Oft have I tried, Heaven knows! to mortify
This vile and wicked lust of poetry;
But still unconquered it remains within,
Fixed as a habit, or some darling sin.
In vain I better studies there would sow,
Often I've tried, but none will thrive or grow:
All my best thoughts, when I'd most serious be,
Are never from its foul infection free:
Nay, God forgive me! when I say my prayers,
I scarce can help polluting them with verse:
That fabulous wretch of old reversed I seem,
Who turn whate'er I touch to dross and rhyme.

---

    * The verb to cully—to cuddle or wheedle—is still in use in some
of the provincial dialects. Rook, to designate a cheat or sharper, is
frequently employed by Wycherley and the comedy writers of the
seventeenth century.

Oft to divert the wild caprice, I try
If sovereign wisdom and philosophy
Rightly applied, will give a remedy:
Straight the great Stagyrite I take in hand,
Seek nature, and myself to understand:
Much I reflect on his vast worth and fame,
And much my low and grovelling aims condemn,
And quarrel, that my ill-packed fate should be
This vain, this worthless thing called poetry:
But when I find this unregarded toy
Could his important thoughts and pains employ,
By reading there, I am but more undone,
And meet that danger which I went to shun.
Oft when ill humour, chagrin, discontent,
Give leisure my wild follies to resent,
I thus against myself my passion vent:
' Enough, mad rhyming sot, enough for shame,
Give o'er, and all thy quills to tooth-picks damn;
Didst ever thou the altar rob, or worse,
Kill the priest there, and maids receiving, force?
What else could merit this so heavy curse?
The greatest curse, I can, I wish on him,
(If there be any greater than to rhyme)
Who first did of the lewd invention think,
First made two lines with sounds resembling clink,
And, swerving from the easy paths of prose,
Fetters and chains did on free sense impose:
Cursed too be all the fools, who since have went
Misled in steps of that ill precedent:
Want be entailed their lot:'——and on I go,
Wreaking my spite on all the jingling crew:
Scarce the belovèd Cowley 'scapes, though I
Might sooner my own curses fear, than he:
And thus resolved against the scribbling vein,
I deeply swear never to write again.
But when bad company and wine conspire
To kindle and renew the foolish fire,

Straightways relapsed, I feel the raving fit
Return, and straight I all my oaths forget:
The spirit, which I thought cast out before,
Enters again with stronger force and power,
Worse than at first, and tyrannizes more.
No sober good advice will then prevail,
Nor from the raging frenzy me recall:
Cool reason's dictates me no more can move
Than men in drink, in Bedlam, or in love:
Deaf to all means which might most proper seem
Towards my cure, I run stark mad in rhyme:
A sad poor haunted wretch, whom nothing less
Than prayers of the Church can dispossess.
   Sometimes, after a tedious day half spent,
When fancy long has hunted on cold scent,
Tired in the dull and fruitless chase of thought,
Despairing I grow weary, and give out:
As a dry lecher pumped of all my store,
I loathe the thing, 'cause I can do't no more:
But, when I once begin to find again
Recruits of matter in my pregnant brain,
Again, more eager, I the hunt pursue,
And with fresh vigour the loved sport renew:
Tickled with some strange pleasure, which I find,
And think a secrecy to all mankind,
I please myself with the vain, false delight,
And count none happy, but the fops that write.
   'Tis endless, sir, to tell the many ways
Wherein my poor deluded self I please:
How, when the fancy labouring for a birth,
With unfelt throes brings its rude issue forth:
How after, when imperfect shapeless thought
Is by the judgment into fashion wrought;
When at first search I traverse o'er my mind,
Nought but a dark and empty void I find:
Some little hints at length, like sparks, break thence,
And glimmering thoughts just dawning into sense:

Confused a while the mixed ideas lie,
With nought of mark to be discovered by,
Like colours undistinguished in the night,
Till the dusk images, moved to the light,
Teach the discerning faculty to choose,
Which it had best adopt, and which refuse.*
Here, rougher strokes, touched with a careless dash,
Resemble the first setting of a face:
There, finished draughts in form more full appear,
And to their justness ask no further care.
Meanwhile with inward joy I proud am grown,
To see the work successfully go on:
And prize myself in a creating power,
That could make something, what was nought before.
Sometimes a stiff, unwieldy thought I meet,
Which to my laws will scarce be made submit:
But when, after expense of pains and time,
'Tis managed well, and taught to yoke in rhyme,
I triumph more than joyful warriors would,
Had they some stout and hardy foe subdued,
And idly think, less goes to their command,
That make armed troops in well-placed order stand,

---

* Mr. Cornish, in a communication to *Notes and Queries*, refers to
two passages in the writings of Dryden and Lord Byron in which the
idea thrown out in these excellent lines is to be found. The passage
in Dryden occurs in the dedication of the *Rival Ladies*, and is as follows: ' When it was only a *confused mass of thoughts* tumbling over one
another in the dark; when the fancy was as yet in its first work,
moving the sleeping images of things towards the light, there to be *distinguished*, and there to be *chosen* or rejected by the *judgment*.' ' Had
Oldham or Dryden the prior claim to the thought?' asks Mr. Cornish.
The question is easily answered. The *Rival Ladies* was acted at the
King's House in 1664, and printed in the same year. Oldham's poem
was written in 1678. Byron's appropriation of the idea is in the
Marino Faliero, and it is clear from the verbal evidence that he took
it from the original source:

'— as yet 'tis but a chaos
Of darkly brooding thoughts; my *fancy is
In her first work*, more nearly to the light
Holding *the sleeping images of things*
For the *selection* of the pausing *judgment*.'—Act. i. sc. 2.

Than to the conduct of my words, when they
March in due ranks, are set in just array.
    Sometimes on wings of thought I seem on high,
As men in sleep, though motionless they lie,
Fledged by a dream, believe they mount and fly:
So witches some enchanted wand bestride,
And think they through the airy regions ride,
Where fancy is both traveller, way, and guide:
Then straight I grow a strange exalted thing,
And equal in conceit at least a king:
As the poor drunkard, when wine stums* his brains,
Anointed with that liquor, thinks he reigns.
Bewitched by these delusions 'tis I write,
(The tricks some pleasant devil plays in spite)
And when I'm in the freakish trance, which I,
Fond silly wretch, mistake for ecstasy,
I find all former resolutions vain,
And thus recant them, and make new again:
    ' What was't I rashly vowed? shall ever I
Quit my belovèd mistress, poetry?
Thou sweet beguiler of my lonely hours,
Which thus glide unperceived with silent course ;
Thou gentle spell, which undisturbed dost keep
My breast, and charm intruding care asleep;
They say, thou'rt poor and unendowed; what though?
For thee, I this vain, worthless world forego:
Let wealth and honour be for fortune's slaves,
The alms of fools, and prize of crafty knaves:
To me thou art whate'er the ambitious crave,
And all that greedy misers want, or have:
In youth or age, in travel or at home,
Here or in town, at London or at Rome,
Rich or a beggar, free or in the Fleet,
Whate'er my fate is, 'tis my fate to write.'

* Stum—the unfermented juice of the grape; or new wine, sometimes used to raise a fermentation in wines that have lost their strength.

Thus I have made my shrifted muse confess,
Her secret feebleness, and weaknesses:
All her hid faults she sets exposed to view,
And hopes a gentle confessor in you:
She hopes an easy pardon for her sin,
Since 'tis but what she is not wilful in,
Nor yet has scandalous nor open been.
Try if your ghostly counsel can reclaim
The heedless wanton from her guilt and shame:
At least be not ungenerous to reproach
That wretched frailty which you've helped debauch.
   'Tis now high time to end, for fear I grow
More tedious than old doters, when they woo,
Than travelled fops, when far-fetched lies they prate,
Or flattering poets, when they dedicate.
No dull forgiveness I presume to crave,
Nor vainly for my tiresome length ask leave:
Lest I, as often formal coxcombs use,
Prolong that very fault I would excuse:
May this the same kind welcome find with you,
As yours did here, and ever shall; adieu.

SATIRES UPON THE JESUITS.

PROLOGUE.*

FOR who can longer hold? when every press,
  The bar and pulpit too, has broke the peace?
When every scribbling fool at the alarms
Has drawn his pen, and rises up in arms?
And not a dull pretender of the town,
But vents his gall in pamphlet up and down?
When all with licence rail, and who will not,
Must be almost suspected of the plot,†
And bring his zeal or else his parts in doubt?
  In vain our preaching tribe attack the foes,
In vain their weak artillery oppose;

---

* Oldham tells us that he designed this prologue ‘ in imitation of
Persius, who has prefixed somewhat by that name before his book of
Satires ;’ and that he drew the first Satire from that of Sylla's ghost in
Ben Jonson's tragedy of *Catiline.* It will be admitted that he kept
close to his original in the accumulation of horrors.

† The popish plot was disclosed to the King in August, 1678, and
from that time till the dissolution of parliament in the following
January it kept the country in a state of consternation. The agitation was renewed by the elections, and so great was the terror of
popery inspired by the revelations of Tonge, Oates, and the rest, that
the candidates who were supported by the influence of the court were
everywhere defeated. At this election, it is said, the practice of
splitting freeholders for the purpose of multiplying votes was adopted
for the first time. When parliament met again in March 1679, articles
of impeachment were exhibited by the Commons against the Roman
Catholic peers ; and the King, in the hope of pacifying the hostility of
the opposition, dismissed his chief adviser, Danby, and formed a new
council with a strong infusion of protestant zeal in it. This device
was regarded in most quarters as a juggle, and detestation of the
Roman Catholics, especially of the Jesuits, broke out with greater fury
than ever. It was at this moment Oldham published his Satires.
Their appearance was opportune, and they were read with avidity.
The pamphleteers alluded to in the prologue, who deluged the town
with violent and ribald tracts, merely addressed themselves to the
temporary passions of the occasion ; while Oldham assailed the whole
system of the Jesuits with a fearlessness of invective scarcely paralleled
in the language. He had the field to himself. Dryden had not yet
come to the rescue of the King, and two years elapsed before the publication of *Absalom and Achitophel.* In the meanwhile the Satires still
continued to sell, and a third edition was called for in 1685.

Mistaken honest men, who gravely blame,
And hope that gentle doctrine should reclaim.
Are texts, and such exploded trifles, fit
To impose, and sham upon a Jesuit?
Would they the dull old fishermen compare
With mighty Suarez, and great Escobar?*
Such threadbare proofs, and stale authorities
May us, poor simple heretics, suffice;
But to a seared Ignatian's conscience,
Hardened, as his own face, with impudence,
Whose faith in contradiction bore, whom lies,
Nor nonsense, nor impossibilities,
Nor shame, nor death, nor damning can assail,
Not these mild fruitless methods will avail.

'Tis pointed satire, and the shafts of wit
For such a prize are the only weapons fit;
Nor needs there art, or genius here to use,
Where indignation can create a muse:
Should parts, and nature fail, yet very spite
Would make the arrantest Wild,† or Wither‡ write.

---

* Suarez and Escobar were Spanish Jesuits who flourished in the
sixteenth century. The former, a voluminous author, held in high
esteem by his own order for his learning, rendered himself particularly
obnoxious in England by a book he wrote against the errors of the
English church, which James I. caused to be burned at St. Paul's.
Escobar was distinguished as a casuist, and published numerous works
on divinity, the most remarkable of which was his *Moral Theology*,
turned into ridicule by Pascal.

† Robert Wild, commonly called Dr. Wild, a nonconformist divine
and poet, who held the rectory of Aynho, in Northamptonshire, and
was ejected at the Restoration. He died at Oundle, at the age of 70,
in the year when this poem was published. He wrote some sermons,
but was better known by sundry indifferent poems, of which the *Iter
Boreale*, written on Monk's journey out of Scotland, was the most prominent. This piece obtained extraordinary popularity. Dryden
called Wild the Wither of the City, and said that they bought more
editions of his works than would lie under all the pies at the Lord
Mayor's Christmas. ' When his famous poem first came out in 1660,
I have seen them reading it in the midst of 'Change time; nay, so
vehemently were they at it, that they lost their bargain by the candles'
ends.' He adds that it was equally well received amongst great
people. Wood says that Wild was a ' fat, jolly, and boon presbyterian.'

‡ George Wither, the author of *Abuses Stript and Whipt*, for which

It is resolved: henceforth an endless war,
I and my muse with them, and theirs declare;
Whom neither open malice of the foes,
Nor private daggers, nor St. Omer's dose,
Nor all that Godfrey* felt, or monarchs fear,
Shall from my vowed and sworn revenge deter.

---

he was committed to the Marshalsea ; and of a charming collection of
eclogues called the *Shepherd's Hunting*. Wither's satires were distinguished by their severity, and in his eclogues he displayed unquestion-
able taste and genius. But he possessed a fatal facility for rhyming,
which tempted him to write a multitude of things of so inferior a
character that he fairly buried his reputation under a heap of rubbish,
and at last came to be regarded as a mere scribbler. Oldham is
nevertheless unjust to him ; for Wither, notwithstanding the mass of
worthless verse he produced, was undoubtedly a true poet. Wither
was a violent parliamentarian, and upon the Restoration was committed to Newgate, where he was denied the use of pen, ink, and
paper, and confined for three years. He died in 1667, and was interred
in the Savoy.

* Sir Edmundbury Godfrey, the magistrate who took the depo-
sitions of Tonge and Oates, and immediately afterwards disappeared.
At the end of five days his body was found in a ditch near Primrose-
hill, with his sword run through it, and a dark mark round his neck,
as if he had been strangled. This mysterious murder was at once
ascribed to the Roman Catholics, and the superstitions of the people
were appealed to by an anagram, extracted with a somewhat unscru-
pulous ingenuity from the murdered man's name—'I find murdered
by rogues.' The impression made on the public mind by this incident
was deepened by the disclosure that Godfrey had been unwilling to
take Oates' deposition, and that he had no sooner done so than he expressed to his friends his apprehensions that he would be himself the
first martyr. His body was exhibited in the public streets for two
days to exasperate the multitude ; and his funeral, at which seventy-
two divines preceded the coffin, was one of those terrible spectacles
which are so well calculated to inflame popular frenzy.

Godfrey was descended from a good family, of some ancient standing in Kent. His father represented New Romney in Parliament.
In his youth, Godfrey, after finishing his education at Westminster
School, travelled on the Continent, and afterwards became a member
of Gray's Inn, but returned to the country before he completed his
terms, and having obtained his younger son's portion, about 1000*l*.,
finally settled in London in partnership with Mr. Harrison, a near
relative, at Dowgate, where they established a wood-wharf. At the
end of a few years they dissolved partnership, and Godfrey removed
to a house at the bottom of Hartshorn-lane, or Alley, close on the
Thames, in the immediate neighbourhood of the Palace at Whitehall.
About 1760 or 1761, the old houses in Hartshorn-lane were pulled
down, and Northumberland-street, then considered 'a handsome

Sooner shall false court favourites prove just,
And faithful to their king's and country's trust;
Sooner shall they detect the tricks of state,
And knavery, suits, and bribes, and flattery hate;

---

street,' was built in their place. But Godfrey's house at the end of this street, overlooking the river, is still standing, and is now occupied by the Metropolitan Police. Here the wood-merchant acquired wealth and importance, and became a justice of the peace. He distinguished himself by his activity on several occasions, and was presented with a silver goblet by the King for his zeal in checking the ravages of the plague, and knighted for his services at the time of the Great Fire. He was a man of excellent character, and indefatigable in his station. Dr. Lloyd, who preached his funeral sermon, says that he was the best justice of the peace in the kingdom; that he dedicated himself wholly to it, and spared no labour to sustain law and justice, safety and liberty.

It appears from the particulars relating to the murder which came out upon confession and examination of witnesses, that the persons who actually committed it, Hill, an ale-house keeper, Girald, an Irish priest, Green, cushion-man to the Queen's Chapel, and Berry, the porter of Somerset House, were instigated by the priests, who urged it as an act of devotion to religion, and promised the murderers that they should get rewards from the Lord Bellasis. The conspirators beset Godfrey as he was passing Somerset House at night. Hill, affecting great haste and alarm, stepped up to him, and entreated his interference between two men who were quarrelling. Godfrey at first refused, but at last yielded to Hill's importunities, and followed him down a lane. Girald and Green went after, and as Sir Edmundbury was going down the stairs, Green threw a twisted handkerchief round his neck from behind, and flung him to the ground. Having succeeded in strangling him, they carried him to a room in an upper court, where they were joined by Prance, a silversmith in Prince's-street, Drury-lane. They afterwards conveyed the body to Primrose Hill, and flung it into a ditch, with his sword run through it, and his scabbard and gloves laid on the bank, that it might be supposed he had destroyed himself. Green, Berry, and Hill were executed for the murder; and Coleman and others for being concerned in the conspiracy. There is a silver tankard in the possession of the Corporation of Sudbury, in Suffolk, which appears to have belonged to Godfrey, and which is apparently the same that was presented to him by the King. It is inscribed and engraved with memorials of the Plague and the Fire. Godfrey's Christian name is sometimes written Edmondsbury, but this is a mistake. It should properly be Edmund Berry, both of which names he was called after his two godfathers, his father's cousin, Captain John Berrie, and Mr. Edmund Harrison, the King's embroiderer. His signature to the affidavit made by Oates, in 1678, shows that the two names were distinct—it is Edm. B. Godfrey. By a curious coincidence one of his murderers bore one of his own names.

6—2

Bawds shall turn nuns, salt duchesses grow chaste,*
And paint, and pride, and lechery detest;
Popes shall for kings' supremacy decide,
And cardinals for Huguenots be tried;
Sooner (which is the greatest impossible)
Shall the vile brood of Loyola and hell
Give o'er to plot, be villains, and rebel;
Than I with utmost spite, and vengeance cease
To prosecute, and plague their cursèd race.

The rage of poets damned, of women's pride
Contemned and scorned, or proffered lust denied;   .
The malice of religious angry zeal,
And all cashiered resenting statesmen feel;†
What prompts dire hags in their own blood to write,
And sell their very souls to hell for spite;
All this urge on my rank envenomed spleen,
And with keen satire edge my stabbing pen,
That its each home-set thrust their blood may draw,
Each drop of ink like aquafortis gnaw.

Red hot with vengeance thus, I'll brand disgrace
So deep, no time shall e'er the marks deface;
Till my severe and exemplary doom
Spread wider than their guilt, till it become
More dreaded than the bar, and frighten worse
Than damning Pope's anathemas and curse.

---

* Of the many duchesses to whom this allusion might with
propriety apply, the Duchess of Portsmouth, Louise de Quérouaille,
is the one directly referred to. She had just supplanted the Duchess
of Cleveland at Whitehall, and was at this time Lady of the Bed-
chamber to the Queen!

† The Lord Treasurer Darnley, charged with being concerned in an
application from the Court of Whitehall to the Court of Versailles for
the loan of a sum of money, had just been removed from his office by
the King in the hope of saving him from the vengeance of the
Commons. Parliament, however, was not to be diverted from its prey.
A bill of attainder was brought in against him, and at last, chased
for his life, he surrendered, and appeared on his knees at the bar of
the House of Lords, from whence he was committed to the Tower.

SATIRE I.—GARNET'S GHOST* ADDRESSING TO THE JESUITS, MET IN PRIVATE CABAL JUST AFTER THE MURDER OF GODFREY.

BY hell 'twas bravely done! what less than this,
    What sacrifice of meaner worth, and price
Could we have offered up for our success?
So fare all they, who e'er provoke our hate,
Who by like ways presume to tempt their fate;
Fare each like this bold meddling fool, and be
As well secured, as well dispatched as he:
Would he were here, yet warm, that we might drain
His reeking gore, and drink up every vein!
That were a glorious sanction, much like thine,
Great Roman! made upon a like design:
Like thine; we scorn so mean a sacrament,
To seal and consecrate our high intent,
We scorn base blood should our great league cement:
Thou didst it with a slave, but we think good
To bind our treason with a bleeding god.
    Would it were his (why should I fear to name,
Or you to hear 't?) at which we nobly aim!
Lives yet that hated enemy of our cause?
Lives he our mighty projects to oppose?
Can his weak innocence, and heaven's care
Be thought security from what we dare?
Are you then Jesuits? are you so for nought,
In all the Catholic depths of treason taught,
In orthodox, and solid poisoning read?
In each profounder art of killing bred?
And can you fail, or bungle in your trade?
Shall one poor life your cowardice upbraid?†

* Henry Garnet, a provincial of the Jesuits, who was executed in 1606, for being concerned in the Gunpowder Plot.

† 'Three or four schemes had been formed for assassinating the King. He was to be stabbed. He was to be poisoned in his medicine. He was to be shot with silver bullets.'—MACAULAY'S *Hist. of England*, i. 233. These schemes were only a part of what Mr. Macaulay calls ' the hideous romance' of Titus Oates.

Tame dastard slaves! who your profession shame,
And fix disgrace on our great founder's name.
  Think what late sectaries (an ignoble crew,
Not worthy to be ranked in sin with you)
Inspired with lofty wickedness, durst do:
How from his throne they hurled a monarch down,
And doubly eased him of both life and crown:
They scorned in covert their bold act to hide,
In open face of heaven the work they did,
And braved its vengeance, and its powers defied.
This is his son, and mortal too like him;
Durst you usurp the glory of the crime,
And dare ye not? I know, you scorn to be
By such as they outdone in villany,
Your proper province; true, you urged them on,
Were engines in the fact, but they alone
Shared all the open credit and renown.   [need
  But hold! I wrong our church and cause, which
No foreign instance, nor what others did.
Think on that matchless assassin, whose name
We with just pride can make our happy claim;
He, who at killing of an emperor,
To give his poison stronger force and power
Mixed a god with 't, and made it work more sure:
Blessed memory! which shall through age to come
Stand sacred in the lists of hell and Rome.
  Let our great Clement* and Ravaillac's† name,
Your spirits to like heights of sin inflame;

---

* Jacques Clement, a Dominican monk, who assassinated Henry III.
at St. Cloud, in 1589, in the same chamber, it is said, where Henry, as
Duke of Anjou, assented to the massacre of the Huguenots. Having
obtained admission under the pretext of business of importance, Clement, whose fanaticism was stimulated by the Duchess de Montpensier,
put a letter in the King's hand, and stabbed him while he was reading
it. The regicide was killed on the spot by the attendants. Clement
was almost deified for this deed. His portrait was placed on the altars
of Paris beside the Eucharist; a statue was erected to him in Notre
Dame; the Sorbonne demanded his canonization; and Pope Sextus V.
pronounced a panegyric upon his memory.
  † François Ravaillac, executed in 1610 for the murder of Henry IV.

Those mighty souls, who bravely chose to die,
To have each a royal ghost their company.
Heroic act! and worth their tortures well,
Well worth the suffering of a double hell,
That, they felt here, and that below, they feel.
    And if these cannot move you as they should,
Let me and my example fire your blood:
Think on my vast attempt, a glorious deed,
Which durst the fates have suffered to succeed,
Had rivalled hell's most proud exploit and boast,
Even that, which would the king of fates deposed.
Cursed be the day, and ne'er in time enrolled,
And cursed the star, whose spiteful influence ruled
The luckless minute, which my project spoiled;
Curse on that power, who, of himself afraid,
My glory with my brave design betrayed;
Justly he feared, lest I, who strook so high
In guilt, should next blow up his realm and sky;
And so I had; at least I would have durst,
And failing, had got off with fame at worst.
    Had you but half my bravery in sin,
Your work had never thus unfinished been;
Had I been man, and the great act to do,
He had died by this, and been what I am now,
Or what his father is: I would leap hell
To reach his life, though in the midst I fell,
And deeper than before,——
Let rabble souls, of narrow aim and reach,
Stoop their vile necks, and dull obedience preach;
Let them with slavish awe (disdained by me)
Adore the purple rag of majesty,
And think 't a sacred relic of the sky:
Well may such fools a base subjection own,
Vassals to every ass that loads a throne;

It was effected in the streets of Paris, where the assassin, taking advantage of a temporary stoppage, mounted the step, and, leaning into the carriage which contained the King and several of his suite, stabbed his majesty twice.

Unlike the soul, with which proud I was born,
Who could that sneaking thing a monarch scorn,
Spurn off a crown, and set my foot in sport
Upon the head that wore it, trod in dirt.
     But say, what is't that binds your hands? does fear
From such a glorious action you deter?
Or is't religion? but you sure disclaim
That frivolous pretence, that empty name—
Mere bugbear word, devised by us to scare
The senseless rout to slavishness and fear,
Ne'er known to awe the brave, and those that dare.
Such weak and feeble things may serve for checks
To rein and curb base mettled heretics;
Dull creatures, whose nice boggling consciences
Startle, or strain at such slight crimes as these;
Such, whom fond inbred honesty befools,
Or that old musty piece the Bible gulls:
That hated book, the bulwark of our foes,
Whereby they still uphold their tottering cause.
Let no such toys mislead you from the road
Of glory, nor infect your souls with good;
Let never bold encroaching virtue dare
With her grim holy face to enter there,
No, not in very dream: have only will
Like fiends and me to covet, and act ill;
Let true substantial wickedness take place,
Usurp, and reign; let it the very trace
(If any yet be left) of good deface.
If ever qualms of inward cowardice
(The thing which some dull sots call conscience) rise,
Let them in streams of blood and slaughter drown,
Or with new weights of guilt still press them down.
Shame, faith, religion, honour, loyalty,
Nature itself, whatever checks there be
To loose and uncontrolled impiety,
Be all extinct in you; own no remorse
But that you've balked a sin, have been no worse,
Or too much pity shown,——

Be diligent in mischief's trade, be each
Performing as a devil; nor stick to reach
At crimes most dangerous; where bold despair,
Mad lust, and heedless blind revenge would ne'er
Even look, march you without a blush or fear,
Inflamed by all the hazards that oppose,
And firm, as burning martyrs to your cause.
   Then you're true Jesuits, then you're fit to be
Disciples of great Loyola and me;
Worthy to undertake, worthy a plot,
Like this, and fit to scourge a Huguenot.
   Plagues on that name! may swift confusion seize,
And utterly blot out the cursèd race;
Thrice damned be that apostate monk,* from whom
Sprung first these enemies of us and Rome;
Whose poisonous filth, dropt from engendering brain,
By monstrous birth did the vile insects spawn,
Which now infest each country, and defile
With their o'erspreading swarms this goodly isle.
Once it was ours, and subject to our yoke,
Till a late reigning witch† the enchantment broke:
It shall again: hell and I say it: have ye
But courage to make good the prophecy,
Not fate itself shall hinder.——
   Too sparing was the time, too mild the day,
When our great Mary bore the English sway!
Unqueenlike pity marred her royal power,
Nor was her purple dyed enough in gore.
   Four or five hundred, such like petty sum
Might fall perhaps a sacrifice to Rome,
Scarce worth the naming: had I had the power,
Or been thought fit to have been her counsellor,
She should have raised it to a nobler score.
Big bonfires should have blazed, and shone each day,
To tell our triumphs, and make bright our way;

---

* Luther.   † Queen Elizabeth.

And when 'twas dark, in every lane and street
Thick flaming heretics should serve to light,
And save the needless charge of links by night;
Smithfield should still have kept a constant fire,
Which never should be quenched, never expire,
But with the lives of all the miscreant rout,
Till the last gasping breath had blown it out.
　　So Nero did, such was the prudent course
Taken by all his mighty successors,
To tame like heretics of old by force:
They scorned dull reason, and pedantic rules
To conquer and reduce the hardened fools;
Racks, gibbets, halters were their arguments,
Which did most undeniably convince;
Grave bearded lions managed the dispute,
And reverend bears their doctrines did confute;
And all, who would stand out in stiff defence,
They gently clawed, and worried into sense;
Better than all our Sorbonne* dotards now,
Who would by dint of words our foes subdue.
This was the rigid discipline of old,
Which modern sots for persecution hold;
Of which dull annalists in story tell
Strange legends, and huge bulky volumes swell
With martyred fools that lost their way to hell.
　　From these, our church's glorious ancestors,
We've learned our arts, and made their methods ours;
Nor have we come behind, the least degree,
In acts of rough and manly cruelty;
Converting faggots, and the powerful stake,
And sword resistless our apostles make.
　　This heretofore Bohemia felt, and thus
Were all the numerous proselytes of Huss

---

* The Society of the Sorbonne (so called from the name of the
village near Paris, where it was established) was founded in 1264, by
St. Louis IX., and Ralph de Sorbonne, his confessor.

Crushed with their head: so Waldo's* cursèd rout,
And those of Wickliffe† here were rooted out,
Their names scarce left.—Sure were the means we chose,
And wrought prevailingly; fire purged the dross
Of those foul heresies, and sovereign steel
Lopped off the infected limbs the church to heal.
    Renowned was that French brave, renowned his deed,
A deed for which the day deserves its red
Far more than for a paltry saint that died:
How goodly was the sight! how fine the show
When Paris saw through all its channels flow
The blood of Huguenots; when the full Seine,
Swelled with the flood, its banks with joy o'erran!
He scorned like common murderers to deal
By parcels and piecemeal; he scorned retail   [great,‡
In the trade of death; whole myriads died by the
Soon as one single life; so quick their fate,
Their very prayers and wishes came too late.
    This a king§ did: and great and mighty 'twas,
Worthy his high degree, and power and place,
And worthy our religion and our cause.
Unmatched 't had been, had not Maguire arose,
The bold Maguire (who read in modern fame,
Can be a stranger to his worth and name?)
Born to outsin a monarch, born to reign
In guilt, and all competitors disdain:
Dread memory! whose each mention still can make
Pale heretics with trembling horror quake!

---

* Peter Waldo, a rich merchant of Lyons, and one of the earliest reformers, erroneously supposed by some writers to be the founder of the Waldenses. He was anathematized by Alexander III. for his opposition to the doctrine of transubstantiation; and, after living in concealment for three years, he retired into Dauphiny, and preached there with great success. He afterwards settled in Bohemia, where he died in 1179.

† Dr. John Wickliffe. He died in 1385, and his body was dug up forty years afterwards and burned.

‡ *En gros*—by wholesale.

§ Charles IX., who ordered the massacre at Paris in 1572.

To undo a kingdom, to achieve a crime
Like his, who would not fall and die like him?
Never had Rome a nobler service done,
Never had hell; each day came thronging down
Vast shoals of ghosts, and mine was pleased and
    glad,
And smiled, when it the brave revenge surveyed.
   Nor do I mention these great instances
For bounds, and limits to your wickedness:
Dare you beyond, something out of the road
Of all example, where none yet have trod,
Nor shall hereafter: what mad Catiline
Durst never think, nor 's madder poet feign;*
Make the poor baffled pagan fool confess,
How much a Christian crime can conquer his;
How far in gallant mischief overcome,
The old must yield to new and modern Rome.
Mix ills past, present, future, in one act;
One high, one brave, one great, one glorious fact.
Which hell, and very I may envy ——
Such as a god himself might wish to be
Accomplice in the mighty villany,
And barter his heaven, and vouchsafe to die.
   Nor let delay (the bane of enterprise)
Mar yours, or make the great importance miss.
This fact has waked your enemies, and their fear;
Let it your vigour too, your haste and care.
Be swift, and let your deeds forestall intent,
Forestall even wishes, ere they can take vent,
Nor give the fates the leisure to prevent.
Let the full clouds, which a long time did wrap
Your gathering thunder, now with sudden clap,
Break out upon your foes; dash, and confound,
And spread avoidless ruin all around.

---

  * Garnet is here made to refer to Ben Jonson's opening to *Catiline,*
upon the model of which this first Satire is founded.

Let the fired city to your plot give light ;*
You razed it half before,† now raze it quite.
Do 't more effectually; I'd see it glow
In flames unquenchable as those below;
I'd see the miscreants with their houses burn,
And all together into ashes turn.
Bend next your fury to the cursed divan ;
That damned committee, whom the fates ordain
Of all our well-laid plots to be the bane.
Unkennel those state foxes where they lie
Working your speedy fate and destiny.‡
Lug by the ears the doting prelates thence,
Dash heresy together with their brains
Out of their shattered heads.   Lop off the lords
And commons at one stroke, and let your swords
Adjourn them all to the other world. ———
Would I were blest with flesh and blood again,
But to be actor in that happy scene!
Yet thus I will be by, and glut my view,
Revenge shall take its fill, in state I'll go
With captive ghosts to attend me down below.
Let these the handsels of your vengeance be,
But stop not here, nor flag in cruelty.

---

* Having enumerated some of the past deeds of papal persecution, the heads of the plot, as communicated by Oates, are next disclosed. London was to be fired, the Council, Bishops, and Ministers of State, were to be assassinated, and Lords and Commons to be destroyed, or, as Oldham has it, to be adjourned to the other world.

† The great fire of London took place in 1666, 'begun,' says the inscription on the monument, 'and carried on by the treachery and malice of the Popish faction;' which inscription, says Ned Ward, ' is as ignorant of the matter as myself, for the monument was neither built then nor I born; so I believe we are equally as able to tell the truth of the story,' &c.—*London Spy.*

‡ The proceedings of Parliament against the Roman Catholics, during the excitement that ensued upon the murder of Godfrey, were of the most stringent character. The Roman Catholic lords were for the first time excluded from the Upper House; the Duke of York driven from the Privy Council ; strong resolutions were adopted against the Queen ; and, adds Macaulay, they even attempted to wrest the command of the militia out of the King's hands.

Kill like a plague or inquisition; spare
No age, degree, or sex; only to wear
A soul, only to own a life, be here
Thought crime enough to lose 't; no time nor place
Be sanctuary from your outrages;
Spare not in churches kneeling priests at prayer,
Though interceding for you, slay even there;
Spare not young infants smiling at the breast,
Who from relenting fools their mercy wrest;
Rip teeming wombs, tear out the hated brood
From thence, and drown them in their mother's blood;
Pity not virgins, nor their tender cries,
Though prostrate at your feet with melting eyes
All drowned in tears; strike home, as 'twere in lust,
And force their begging hands to guide the thrust;
Ravish at the altar, kill when you have done,
Make them your rapes, and victims too in one;
Nor let grey hoary hairs protection give
To age, just crawling on the verge of life;
Snatch from its leaning hands the weak support,
And with it knock 't into the grave with sport;
Brain the poor cripple with his crutch, then cry,
You've kindly rid him of his misery.
  Seal up your ears to mercy, lest their words
Should tempt a pity, ram them with your swords
(Their tongues too) down their throats; let them not
To mutter for their souls a gasping prayer,   [dare
But in the utterance chok't, and stab it there.
'Twere witty handsome malice (could you do 't)
To make 'em die, and make 'em damned to boot.
  Make children by one fate with parent die,
Kill even revenge in next posterity;
So you'll be pestered with no orphans' cries,
No childless mothers curse your memories.
Make death and desolation swim in blood
Throughout the land, with nought to stop the flood
But slaughtered carcasses; till the whole isle
Become one tomb, become one funeral pile;

Till such vast numbers swell the countless sum,
That the wide grave, and wider hell want room.
　　Great was that tyrant's wish, which should be mine,
Did I not scorn the leavings of a sin;
Freely I would bestow 't on England now,
That the whole nation with one neck might grow,
To be sliced off, and you to give the blow.
What neither Saxon rage could here inflict,
Nor Danes more savage, nor the barbarous Pict;
What Spain or Eighty-eight could e'er devise,
With all its fleet, and freight of cruelties;
What ne'er Medina* wished, much less could dare,
And bloodier Alva† would with trembling hear;
What may strike out dire prodigies of old,
And make their mild and gentler acts untold;
What heaven's judgments, nor the angry stars,
Foreign invasions, nor domestic wars,
Plague, fire, nor famine could effect or do;
All this, and more be dared, and done by you.
　　But why do I with idle talk delay
Your hands, and while they should be acting, stay?
Farewell——
If I may waste a prayer for your success,
Hell be your aid, and your high projects bless!
May that vile wretch, if any here there be,
That meanly shrinks from brave iniquity;
If any here feel pity or remorse,
May he feel all I've bid you act, and worse!
May he by rage of foes unpitied fall,
And they tread out his hated soul to hell.
May his name and carcass rot, exposed alike to be
The everlasting mark of grinning infamy.

　　* The Duke of Medina-Sidonia, who commanded the Spanish Armada in 1588.
　　† The Duke of Alva, employed by Philip of Spain in the Netherlands, and distinguished in history by his merciless wholesale massacres. He boasted that he had himself consigned 18,000 persons to the executioner. Amongst these were the two popular leaders, Counts Egmont and Horn.

SATIRE II.

NAY, if our sins are grown so high of late,
　That heaven no longer can adjourn our fate,
May 't please some milder vengeance to devise,
Plague, fire, sword, dearth, or anything but this,
Let it rain scalding showers of brimstone down,
To burn us, as of old the lustful town;
Let a new deluge overwhelm again,
And drown at once our land, our lives, our sin.
Thus gladly we'll compound, all this we'll pay,
To have this worst of ills removed away.
Judgments of other kinds are often sent
In mercy only, not for punishment;
But where these light, they show a nation's fate
Is given up, and past for reprobate.
　When God his stock of wrath on Egypt spent
To make a stubborn land and king repent,
Sparing the rest, had he this one plague sent,
For this alone his people had been quit,
And Pharaoh circumcised a proselyte.
　Wonder no longer why no curse, like these,
Was known, or suffered in the primitive days;
They never sinned enough to merit it,
'Twas therefore what Heaven's just power thought fit,
To scourge this latter, and more sinful age
With all the dregs and squeezings of his rage.
　Too dearly is proud Spain with England quit
For all her loss sustained in Eighty-eight;
For all the ills our warlike virgin wrought,
Or Drake, or Raleigh, her great scourges, brought.
Amply she was revenged in that one birth,
When hell for her the Biscain plague brought forth;*
Great counter plague! in which unhappy we
Pay back her sufferings with full usury:

---

* Ignatius Loyola, who was born in 1491 in Guipuzcoa, one of the Basque provinces. In this Satire, Oldham is speaking in his own person.

Than whom alone none ever was designed
To entail a wider curse on human kind,
But he, who first begot us, and first sinned.
Happy the world had been, and happy thou,
(Less damned at least, and less accursed than now)
If early with less guilt in war th' hadst died,
And from ensuing mischiefs mankind freed;
Or when thou view'dst the Holy Land, and tomb,
Th' hadst suffered there thy brother traitor's doom.*
Cursed be the womb that with the firebrand teemed,
Which ever since has the whole globe inflamed;
More cursed that ill-aimed shot, which basely missed,
Which maimed a limb, but spared thy hated breast,
And made thee at once a cripple and a priest.†

But why this wish? The church if so might lack
Champions, good works, and saints for the almanac.
These are the Janissaries of the cause,
The life-guard of the Roman Sultan, chose
To break the force of Huguenots and foes;
The church's hawkers in divinity,
Who 'stead of lace and ribbons, doctrine cry;
Rome's strollers, who survey each continent,
Its trinkets and commodities to vent;
Export the Gospel, like mere ware, for sale,
And truck 't for indigo, and cochineal,
As the known factors here, the brethren, once
Swopped Christ about for bodkins, rings, and spoons.

And shall these great Apostles be contemned,
And thus by scoffing heretics defamed?
They, by whose means both Indies now enjoy
The two choice blessings, lust and popery?
Which buried else in ignorance had been,
Nor known the worth of beads and Bellarmine?‡

---

* Loyola's original profession was that of a soldier, in which he is said to have displayed courage and ability. Having renounced arms for a religious life, he determined to make a pilgrimage to Jerusalem, for which he made elaborate preparations in the way of prayer and penance.   † See note p. 123.

‡ An Italian Jesuit, created a cardinal by Sextus V., and after-

It pitied holy mother church to see
A world so drowned in gross idolatry:
It grieved to see such goodly nations hold
Bad errors and unpardonable gold.
Strange! what a fervent zeal can coin infuse!
What charity pieces of eight produce!
So were you chosen the fittest to reclaim
The pagan world, and give it a Christian name.
And great was the success; whole myriads stood
At font, and were baptized in their own blood;
Millions of souls were hurled from hence to burn
Before their time, be damned before their turn.

    Yet these were in compassion sent to hell,
The rest reserved in spite, and worse to feel,
Compelled instead of fiends to worship you,
The more inhuman devils of the two.
Rare way and method of conversion this,
To make your votaries your sacrifice!
If to destroy be Reformation thought,
A plague as well might the good work have wrought.

    Now see we why your founder, weary grown
Would lay his former trade of killing down;
He found 'twas dull, he found a crown would be
A fitter case, and badge of cruelty.
Each snivelling hero seas of blood can spill,
When wrongs provoke, and honour bids him kill;
Each tiny bully lives can freely bleed,
When pressed by wine, or punk to knock on the head;
Give me your thorough-paced rogue, who scorns to be
Prompted by poor revenge, or injury,
But does it of true inbred cruelty;
Your cool and sober murderer, who prays
And stabs at the same time, who one hand has
Stretched up to heaven, the other to make the pass.

    So the late saints of blessèd memory,
Cut-throats in godly pure sincerity,

---

wards made Archbishop of Capua; one of the most temperate and
learned controversialists of his time. His writings are distinguished
by perspicuity of statement and integrity of reasoning.

So they with lifted hands, and eyes devout,
Said grace, and carved a slaughtered monarch out.
   When the first traitor Cain (too good to be
Thought patron of this black fraternity)
His bloody tragedy of old designed,
One death alone quenched his revengeful mind,
Content with but a quarter of mankind:
Had he been Jesuit, and but put on
Their savage cruelty, the rest had gone;
His hand had sent old Adam after too,
And forced the godhead to create anew.
   And yet 'twere well, were their foul guilt but
      thought
Bare sin : 'tis something even to own a fault.
But here the boldest flights of wickedness
Are stamped religion, and for current pass.
The blackest, ugliest, horridest, damnedst deed,
For which hell-flames, the schools a title need,
If done for holy church is sanctified.
This consecrates the blessèd work and tool,
Nor must we ever after think 'em foul.
To undo realms, kill parents, murder kings, ·
Are thus but petty trifles, venial things,
Not worth a confessor; nay, heaven shall be
Itself invoked to abet the impiety.
   ' Grant, gracious Lord,' some reverend villain prays,
' That this the bold assertor of our cause
May with success accomplish that great end,
For which he was by thee and us designed.
Thou to his arm and sword thy strength impart,
And guide 'em steady to the tyrant's heart;
Grant him for every meritorious thrust
Degrees of bliss above, among the just;
Where holy Garnet, and St. Guy are placed,
Whom works, like this, before have thither raised;
Where they are interceding for us now—
For sure they're there.' Yes, questionless; and so
Good Nero is, and Dioclesian too,

And that great ancient saint Herostratus,
And the late godly martyr at Toulouse.
     Dare something worthy Newgate and the Tower,
If you'll be canonized, and heaven insure.
Dull primitive fools of old! who would be good,
Who would by virtue reach the blessed abode!
Far other are the ways found out of late,
Which mortals to that happy place translate:
Rebellion, treason, murder, massacre,
The chief ingredients now of saintship are,
And Tyburn only stocks the calendar.
     Unhappy Judas, whose ill fate, or chance,
Threw him upon gross times of ignorance;
Who knew not how to value, or esteem
The worth and merit of a glorious crime!
Should his kind stars have let him acted now,
He had died absolved, and died a martyr too.
     Hear'st thou, great God, such daring blasphemy,
And let'st thy patient thunder still lay by?
Strike, and avenge, lest impious atheists say,
Chance guides the world, and has usurped thy sway;
Lest these proud prosperous villains too confess,
Thou'rt senseless, as they make thy images.
Thou just and sacred Power! wilt thou admit
Such guests should in thy glorious presence sit?
If Heaven can with such company dispense,
Well did the Indian pray, might he keep thence!
     But this we only feign, all vain and false
As their own legends, miracles, and tales;
Either the groundless calumnies of spite,
Or idle rants of poetry and wit.
     We wish they were: but you hear Garnet cry,
'I did it, and would do 't again; had I
As much of blood, as many lives as Rome
Has spilt in what the fools call martyrdom,
As many souls as sins, I'd freely stake
All them, and more for mother church's sake.
For that I'll stride o'er crowns, swim through a flood,
Made up of slaughtered monarchs' brains and blood.

For that no lives of heretics I'll spare,
But reap 'em down with less remorse and care
Than Tarquin did the poppy-heads of old,
Or we drop beads, by which our prayers are told.'
    Bravely resolved! and 'twas as bravely dared:
But, lo! the recompense, and great reward
The wight is to the almanac preferred.
Rare motives to be damned for holy cause,
A few red letters, and some painted straws!
Fools! who thus truck with hell by Mohatra,
And play their souls against no stakes away.
    'Tis strange with what an holy impudence
The villain caught, his innocence maintains;
Denies with oaths the fact, until it be
Less guilt to own it than the perjury;
By the mass and blessed sacraments he swears,
This Mary's milk, and the other Mary's tears,
And the whole muster-roll in calendars.
Not yet swallow the falsehood? if all this
Wont gain a resty faith, he will on his knees
The evangelists, and lady's psalter kiss,
To vouch the lie; nay, more, to make it good,
Mortgage his soul upon't, his heaven, and God.
Damned faithless heretics! hard to convince,
Who trust no verdict but dull obvious sense.
Unconscionable courts! who priests deny
Their benefit of the clergy, perjury.
    Room for the martyred saints! behold they come!
With what a noble scorn they meet their doom!
Not knights o' the post,* nor often carted whores
Show more of impudence, or less remorse.

---

* Persons who were ready to take false oaths for a consideration.
Thus, in one of the Roxburghe ballads:—

        ' I'll be no knight of the post,
          To sell my soul for a bribe.'

They were called knights of the post, because they waited at the posts
which it was the custom of the sheriffs to have at their doors for fixing
proclamations upon. The custom is alluded to by Ben Jonson in
Cynthia's Revels, A. i. Sc. 4.

O glorious and heroic constancy!
That can forswear upon the cart, and die
With gasping souls expiring in a lie.
None but tame sheepish criminals repent,
Who fear the idle bugbear, punishment:
Your gallant sinner scorns that cowardice,
The poor regret of having done amiss;
Brave he, to his first principles still true,
Can face damnation, sin with hell in view,
And bid it take the soul he does bequeath,
And blow it thither with his dying breath.
  Dare such as these profess religion's name?
Who, should they own 't, and be believed, would shame
It's practice out of the world, would atheists make
Firm in their creed, and vouch it at the stake?
Is heaven for such, whose deeds make hell too good,
Too mild a penance for their cursèd brood?
For whose unheard of crimes, and damnèd sake,
Fate must below new sorts of torture make,
Since, when of old it framed that place of doom,
'Twas thought no guilt, like this, could thither come.
  Base recreant souls! would you have kings trust you,
Who never yet kept your allegiance true
To any but hell's prince? who with more ease
Can swallow down most solemn perjuries,
Than a town-bully common oaths and lies?
Are the French Harry's fates so soon forgot?
Our last best Tudor? or the powder-plot?
And those fine streamers that adorned so long
The bridge, and Westminster, and yet had hung,
Were they not stolen, and now for relics gone?
  Think Tories loyal, or Scotch Covenanters;
Robbed tigers gentle; courteous, fasting bears;
Atheists devout, and thrice wracked mariners;
Take goats for chaste and cloistered marmosites;
For plain and open, two-edged parasites;
Believe bawds modest, and the shameless stews;
And binding drunkards' oaths, and strumpets' vows;

And when in time these contradictions meet,
Then hope to find 'em in a Loyolite:
To whom, though gasping, should I credit give,
I'd think 'twere sin, and damned like unbelief.
   Oh for the Swedish law enacted here!
No scarecrow frightens like a priest-gelder,
Hunt them, as beavers are, force them to buy
Their lives with ransom of their lechery.
Or let that wholesome statute be revived,
Which England heretofore from wolves relieved;
Tax every shire instead of them to bring
Each year a certain tale of Jesuits in;
And let their mangled quarters hang the isle
To scare all future vermin from the soil.
Monsters avaunt! may some kind whirlwind sweep
Our land, and drown these locusts in the deep;
Hence ye loathed objects of our scorn and hate,
With all the curses of an injured state;
Go, foul impostors, to some duller soil,
Some easier nation with your cheats beguile;
Where your gross common gulleries may pass,
To slur and top on bubbled consciences;
Where ignorance, and the inquisition rules,
Where the vile herd of poor implicit fools
Are damned contentedly, where they are led
Blindfold to hell, and thank, and pay their guide!
   Go, where all your black tribe before are gone,
Follow Chastel, Ravaillac, Clement down,
Your Catesby, Faux, and Garnet, thousands more,
And those who hence have lately raised the score;
Where the grand traitor now, and all the crew
Of his disciples must receive their due;
Where flames, and tortures of eternal date
Must punish you, yet ne'er can expiate:
Learn duller fiends your unknown cruelties,
Such as no wit, but yours, could e'er devise,
No guilt, but yours, deserve; make hell confess
Itself outdone, it's devils damned for less.

SATIRE III.—LOYOLA'S WILL.*

LONG had the famed impostor found success,
　Long seen his damned fraternity's increase.
In wealth, and power, mischief, guile improved,
By popes, and pope-rid kings upheld, and loved;
Laden with tears, and sins, and numerous scars,
Got some i' the field, but most in other wars,
Now finding life decay, and fate draw near,
Grown ripe for hell, and Roman calendar,
He thinks it worth his holy thoughts, and care,
Some hidden rules, and secrets to impart,
The proofs of long experience and deep art,
Which to his successors may useful be
In conduct of their future villany.
Summoned together, all the officious band
The orders of their bedrid chief attend;
Doubtful, what legacy he will bequeath,
And wait with greedy ears his dying breath:
With such quick duty vassal fiends below
To meet commands of their dread monarch go.
　On pillow raised, he does their entrance greet,
And joys to see the wished assembly meet:
They in glad murmurs tell their joy aloud,
Then a deep silence stills the expecting crowd.
Like Delphic hag of old, by fiend possessed,
He swells; wild frenzy heaves his panting breast;
His bristling hairs stick up, his eyeballs glow,
And from his mouth long streaks of drivel flow:
Thrice with due reverence he himself doth cross,
Then thus his hellish oracles disclose.
　'Ye firm associates of my great design,
Whom the same vows, and oaths, and order join,

---

* The institution and mission of the Jesuits were never more
fiercely assailed than in this and the following Satire, which produced, on their first publication, as powerful a temporary effect in
England as the *Provincial Letters* upon public opinion in the Roman
Catholic states of Europe.

The faithful band, whom I and Rome have chose,
The last support of our declining cause;
Whose conquering troops I with success have led
'Gainst all opposers of our Church and Head;
Who e'er to the mad German owe their rise,
Geneva's rebels, or the hot-brained Swiss;
Revolted heretics, who late have broke
And durst throw off the long-worn sacred yoke;
You, by whose happy influence Rome can boast
A greater empire than by Luther lost:
By whom wide nature's far-fetched limits now,
And utmost Indies to its crosier bow.
  'Go on, ye mighty champions of our cause,
Maintain our party, and subdue our foes;
Kill heresy, that rank and poisonous weed,
Which threatens now the church to overspread;
Fire Calvin, and his nest of upstarts out,
Who tread our sacred mitre under foot;
Strayed Germany reduce; let it no more
The incestuous monk of Wittemberg adore;
Make stubborn England once more stoop its crown,
And fealty to our priestly sovereign own;
Regain our church's rights, the island clear
From all remaining dregs of Wickliffe there.
Plot, enterprize, contrive, endeavour; spare
No toil nor pains; no death, nor danger fear;
Restless your aims pursue; let no defeat
Your sprightly courage, and attempts rebate,
But urge to fresh, and bolder, ne'er to end
Till the whole world to our great Caliph bend;
Till he through every nation everywhere
Bear sway, and reign as absolute as here;
Till Rome without control or contest be
The universal ghostly monarchy.
  'Oh! that kind Heaven a longer thread would give,
And let me to that happy juncture live:
But 'tis decreed!'——at this he paused and wept,
The rest alike time with his sorrow kept:

Then thus continued he——'Since unjust fate
Envies my race of glory longer date,
Yet, as a wounded general, e'er he dies,
To his sad troops, sighs out his last advice,
(Who, though they must his fatal absence moan,
By those great lessons conquer, when he's gone)
So I to you my last instructions give,
And breathe out counsel with my parting life:
Let each to my important words give ear,
Worth your attention, and my dying care.
 ' First, and the chiefest thing by me enjoined,
The solemnest tie, that must your order bind,
Let each without demur, or scruple pay
A strict obedience to the Roman sway :*
To the unerring chair all homage swear,
Although a punk, a witch, a fiend sit there.
Whoe'er is to the sacred mitre reared,
Believe all virtues with the place conferred;
Think him established there by Heaven, though he
Has altars robbed for bribes the choice to buy,
Or pawned his soul to hell for simony;
Though he be atheist, heathen, Turk, or Jew,
Blasphemer, sacrilegious, perjured too:
Though he be bawd, pimp, pathick, panderer,
Whate'er old Sodom's nest of lechers were;
Though tyrant, traitor, poisoner, parricide,
Magician, monster, all that's bad beside;
Fouler than infamy; the very lees,
The sink, the jakes, the common-sewer of vice;
Strait count him holy, virtuous, good, devout,
Chaste, gentle, meek, a saint, a god, who not?
 ' Make fate hang on his lips, nor Heaven have
Power to predestinate without his leave;

---

 * The three vows of the Jesuits laid down by Loyola were poverty,
chastity, and strict obedience to the chief of the order. It was the
last which made Paul III. withhold his sanction from the institution;
but his scruples were removed by the addition of a fourth vow, of implicit submission to himself.

SATIRES UPON THE JESUITS.

None be admitted there, but whom he please,
Who buys from him the patent for the place.
Hold those amongst the highest rank of saints,
Whome'er he to that honour shall advance,
Though here the refuse of the jail, and stews,
Which hell itself would scarce for lumber choose.
But count all reprobate, and damned, and worse,
Whom he, when gout, or phthisic rage, shall curse;
Whom he in anger excommunicates,
For Friday meals, and abrogating sprats;
Or in just indignation spurns to hell
For jeering holy toe, and pantofle.
  'Whate'er he says, esteem for holy writ,
And text apocryphal, if he think fit;
Let arrant legends, worst of tales and lies,
Falser than Capgraves, and Voragines,
Than Quixote, Rabelais, Amadis de Gaul,
If signed with sacred lead, and fisher's seal,
Be thought authentic and canonical.
Again, if he ordain 't in his decrees,
Let every gospel for mere fable pass;
Let right be wrong, black white, and virtue vice,
No sun, no moon, nor no antipodes;
Forswear your reason, conscience, and your creed,
Your very sense, and Euclid, if he bid.
  'Let it be held less heinous, less amiss,
To break all God's commands, than one of his.
When his great missions call, without delay,
Without reluctance readily obey,
Nor let your inmost wishes dare gainsay.
Should he to Bantam, or Japan command,
Or farthest bounds of southern unknown land,
Farther than avarice its vassals drives,
Through rocks, and dangers, loss of blood, and lives,
Like great Xavier's* be your obedience shown;
Outstrip his courage, glory, and renown,

---

* St. Francis Xavier, generally called the Apostle of the Indies.
He was one of the disciples of Loyola, and the most indefatigable and

Whom neither yawning gulfs of deep despair,
Nor scorching heats of burning line could scare;
Whom seas, nor storms, nor wrecks could make
    refrain
From propagating holy faith, and gain.
  'If he but nod commissions out to kill,
But beckon lives of heretics to spill,
Let the inquisition rage, fresh cruelties
Make the dire engines groan with tortured cries:
Let Campo Flori every day be strowed
With the warm ashes of the Lutheran brood;
Repeat again Bohemian slaughters o'er,
And Piedmont valleys drown with floating gore
Swifter than murdering angels, when they fly
On errands of avenging destiny,
Fiercer than storms let loose, with eager haste
Lay cities, countries, realms, whole nature waste,
Sack, ravish, burn, destroy, slay, massacre,
Till the same grave their lives and names inter.
  'These are the rights to our great Mufti due,
The sworn allegiance of your sacred vow.
What else we in our votaries require,
What other gift, next follows to enquire.
  'And first it will our great advice befit,
What soldiers to your lists you ought admit.
To natives of the church, and faith, like you,
The foremost rank of choice is justly due:
'Mongst whom the chiefest place assign to those,
Whose zeal has mostly signalized the cause.
But let not entrance be to them denied,
Whoever shall desert the adverse side;
Omit no promises of wealth, or power,
That may inveigled heretics allure;

---

successful of all the Roman Catholic missionaries. The great scene of
his labours was the East Indies and Japan. His zeal led him to con-
template the conversion of the Chinese; but he died on the voyage.
He was the patron saint of the Queen of James II., and his aid was
invoked when her majesty desired a son. In reference to this august
occasion, his life by Bouhours was translated into English by Dryden.

Those, whom great learning, parts, or wit renowns.
Cajole with hopes of honours, scarlet gowns,
Provincialships, and palls, and triple crowns.
This must a rector, that a provost be,
A third succeed to the next abbacy;
Some, princes' tutors, others, confessors
To dukes, and kings, and queens, and emperors:
These are strong arguments, which seldom fail,
Which more than all your weak disputes prevail.
    ' Exclude not those of less desert; decree
To all revolters your foundation free;
To all, whom gaming, drunkenness, or lust,
To need, and popery shall have reduced:
To all, whom slighted love, ambition crossed,
Hopes often bilked, and sought preferment lost,
Whom pride, or discontent, revenge, or spite,
Fear, frenzy, or despair shall proselyte:
Those powerful motives, which the most bring in,
Most converts to our church, and order win.
Reject not those, whom guilt, and crimes at home
Have made to us for sanctuary come;
Let sinners of each hue, and size, and kind,
Here quick admittance, and safe refuge find;
Be they from justice of their country fled,
With blood of murders, rapes, and treasons dyed,
No varlet, rogue, or miscreant refuse,
From galleys, jails, or hell itself broke loose.
By this you shall in strength, and numbers grow,
And shoals each day to your thronged cloisters flow:
So Rome's and Mecca's first great founders did,
By such wise methods, make their churches spread.
    ' When shaven crown and hallowed girdle's power
Has dubbed him saint, that villain was before,
Entered, let it his first endeavour be
To shake off all remains of modesty,
Dull sneaking modesty, not more unfit
For needy flattering poets, when they write,
Or trading punks, than for a Jesuit.
If any novice feel at first a blush,

Let wine, and frequent converse with the stews,
Reform the fop, and shame it out of use,
Unteach the puling folly by degrees,
And train him to a well-bred shamelessness.
Get that great gift, and talent, impudence,
Accomplished mankind's highest excellence:
'Tis that alone prefers, alone makes great,
Confers alone wealth, titles, and estate,
Gains place at court, can make a fool a peer,
An ass a bishop, vilest blockheads rear
To wear red hats, and sit in porphyry chair.
'Tis learning, parts, and skill, and wit, and sense,
Worth, merit, honour, virtue, innocence.
  'Next for religion, learn what's fit to take,
How small a dram does the just compound make,
As much as is by crafty statesmen worn
For fashion only, or to serve a turn.
To bigot fools its idle practice leave,
Think it enough the empty form to have.
The outward show is seemly, cheap, and light,
The substance cumbersome, of cost, and weight;
The rabble judge by what appears to the eye,
None, or but few, the thoughts within descry.
Make it an engine to ambitious power
To stalk behind, and hit your mark more sure;
A cloak to cover well-hid knavery,
Like it, when used, to be with ease thrown by;
A shifting card, by which your course to steer,
And taught with every changing wind to veer.
Let no nice, holy, conscientious ass
Amongst your better company find place,
Me, and your foundation to disgrace.
Let truth be banished, ragged virtue fly,
And poor unprofitable honesty;
Weak idols, who their wretched slaves betray,
To every rook, and every knave a prey:
These lie remote, and wide from interest,
Farther than heaven from hell, or east from west,
Far, as they e'er were distant from the breast.

'Think not yourselves to austerities confined,
Or those strict rules which other orders bind;
To Capuchins, Carthusians, Cordeliers
Leave penance, meagre abstinence, and prayers;
In lousy rags let begging friars lie,
Content on straw or boards to mortify;
Let them with sackcloth discipline their skins,
And scourge them for their madness and their sins;
Let pining anchorets in grottos starve,
Who from the liberties of nature swerve,
Who make 't their chief religion not to eat,
And place 't in nastiness, and want of meat.
Live you in luxury and pampered ease,
As if whole nature were your cateress;
Soft be your beds, as those which monarchs' whores
Lie on, or gouts of bedrid emperors;
Your wardrobes stored with choice of suits more dear
Than cardinals on high processions wear;
With dainties load your boards, whose every dish
May tempt cloyed gluttons, or Vitellius' wish,
Each fit a longing queen; let richest wines
With mirth your heads inflame, with lust your veins,
Such as the friends of dying popes would give
For cordials to prolong their gasping life.
    'Ne'er let the Nazarene, whose badge and name
You wear,* upbraid you with a conscious shame;
Leave him his slighted homilies and rules,
To stuff the squabbles of the wrangling schools;
Disdain, that He, and the poor angling tribe,
Should laws and government to you prescribe;
Let none of those good fools your patterns make,
Instead of them, the mighty Judas take:
Renowned Iscariot! fit alone to be
The example of our great society,
Whose darling guilt despised the common road,
And scorned to stop at sin beneath a god.

---

* The Jesuits were established by a bull in 1540, under the name
of the Society of Jesus. The term Jesuits was originally applied to
them in ridicule of their institution.

'And now 'tis time I should instructions give,
What wiles and cheats the rabble best deceive.
Each age and sex their different passions wear,
To suit with which requires a prudent care:
Youth is capricious, headstrong, fickle, vain,
Given to lawless pleasure, age to gain;
Old wives, in superstition overgrown,
With chimney-tales and stories best are won;
'Tis no mean talent rightly to descry,
What several baits to each you ought apply.
The credulous and easy of belief
With miracles and well-framed lies deceive;
Empty whole Surius and the Talmud; drain
Saint Francis, and Saint Mahomet's Alcoran;
Sooner shall popes and cardinals want pride,
Than you a stock of lies and legends need.
'Tell how blessed Virgin to come down was seen,
Like playhouse punk descending in machine;
How she writ billet-doux, and love-discourse,
Made assignations, visits, and amours;
How hosts, distressed, her smock for banner bore,
Which vanquished foes, and murdered at twelve score.
Relate how fish in conventicles met,
And mackerel were with bait of doctrine caught;
How cattle have judicious hearers been,
And stones pathetically cried Amen!
How consecrated hive with bells was hung,
And bees kept mass, and holy anthems sung;
How pigs to the rosary kneeled, and sheep were taught
To bleat Te Deum and Magnificat;
How flyflap of church-censure houses rid
Of insects, which at curse of friar died;
How travelling saints, well mounted on a switch,
Ride journeys through the air, like Lapland witch;
And ferrying cowls religious pilgrims bore,
O'er waves without the help of sail or oar.
Nor let Xavier's great wonders pass concealed,
How storms were by the almighty wafer quelled;

How zealous crab the sacred image bore,
And swam a catholic to the distant shore:
With shams like these the giddy rout mislead,
Their folly and their superstition feed.
   "'Twas found a good and gainful art of old
(And much it did our church's power uphold)
To feign hobgoblins, elves, and walking sprites,
And fairies dancing salenger* o' nights;
White sheets for ghosts, and will-a-wisps have passed
For souls in purgatory unreleased,
And crabs in churchyard crawled in masquerade,
To cheat the parish, and have masses said.
By this our ancestors in happier days,
Did store of credit and advantage raise:
But now the trade is fallen, decayed, and dead.
E'er since contagious knowledge has o'erspread,
With scorn the grinning rabble now hear tell
Of Hecla, Patrick's Hole, and Mongibel,
Believed no more than tales of Troy, unless
In countries drowned in ignorance, like this.
Henceforth be wary how such things you feign,
Except it be beyond the Cape or Line,
Except at Mexico, Brazil, Peru,
At the Moluccos, Goa, or Pegu,
Or any distant and remoter place,
Where they may current and unquestioned pass,
Where never poaching heretics resort,
To spring the lie, and make 't their game and sport.
   'But I forget (what should be mentioned most)
Confession, our chief privilege and boast,
That staple ware, which ne'er returns in vain,
Ne'er balks the trader of expected gain.
'Tis this that spies through court intrigues, and brings
Admission to the cabinets of kings;
By this we keep proud monarchs at our becks,
And make our footstools of their thrones and necks,

---

* One of the oldest dances in England was called Sellinger's Round.

OLDHAM.						8

Give 'em command, and if they disobey,
Betray them to the ambitious heir a prey;
Hound the officious curs on heretics,
The vermin which the church infest, and vex;
And when our turn is served, and business done,
Dispatch them for reward, as useless grown.
　'Nor are these half the benefits and gains,
Which by wise managery accrue from thence.
By this we unlock the miser's hoarded chests
And treasure, though kept close as statesmen's breasts;
This does rich widows to our nets decoy,
Let us their jointures and themselves enjoy;
To us the merchant does his customs bring,
And pays our duty, though he cheats his king;
To us court-ministers refund, made great
By robbery, and bankrupt of the state;
Ours is the soldier's plunder, padder's prize,
Gabels* on lechery, and the stew's excise;
By this our colleges in riches shine,
And vie with Becket's and Loretto's shrine.
　'And here I must not grudge a word or two,
My younger votaries, of advice to you,
To you, whom beauty's charms, and generous fire
Of boiling youth to sports of love inspire.
This is your harvest; here, secure and cheap,
You may the fruits of unbought pleasure reap;
Riot in free and uncontrolled delight,
Where no dull marriage clogs the appetite;
Taste every dish of lust's variety,
Which popes and scarlet lechers dearly buy
With bribes, and bishoprics, and simony.
But this I ever to your care commend,—
Be wary how you openly offend,
Lest scoffing lewd buffoons descry our shame,
And fix disgrace on the great order's fame.

---

* A tax or duty. The term is Anglo-Norman, and there is a
little inconsistency in putting it into the mouth of Ignatius Loyola.

'When the unguarded maid alone repairs
To ease the burthens of her sins and cares;
When youth in each, and privacy conspire
To kindle wishes, and befriend desire;
If she has practised in the trade before,
(Few else of proselytes to us brought o'er)
Little of force, or artifice will need,
To make you in the victory succeed:
But if some untaught innocent she be,
Rude, and unknowing in the mystery,
She'll cost more labour to be made comply.
Make her by pumping understand the sport,
And undermine with secret trains the fort,
Sometimes, as if you'd blame her gaudy dress,
Her naked pride, her jewels, point, and lace,
Find opportunity her breasts to press;
Oft feel her hand, and whisper in her ear,
You find the secret marks of lewdness there;
Sometimes with naughty sense her blushes raise,
And make 'em guilt, she never knew, confess;
'Thus,' may you say, 'with such a leering smile,
So languishing a look you hearts beguile;
Thus with your foot, hand, eye, you tokens speak,
These signs deny, these assignations make;
Thus 'tis you clip, with such a fierce embrace
You clasp your lover to your breast and face;
Thus are your hungry lips with kisses cloyed,
Thus is your hand, and thus your tongue employed.'
    'Ply her with talk like this; and, if she incline
To help devotion, give her Aretine*
Instead of the rosary.   Never despair;
She, that to such discourse will lend an ear,
Though chaster than cold cloistered nuns she were,

---

* Peter Aretino, born in Tuscany 1492, died 1557; a writer of inde-
cent lampoons.   He stood so high in favour with the leading sovereigns
of Europe, and three of the Popes, that he obtained an employment in
the Vatican, expected to be made a cardinal, and took the title of
Il Divino.

Will soon prove soft, and pliant to your use,
As strumpets on the carnival let loose.
Credit experience; I have tried them all,
And never found the unerring methods fail.
Not Ovid, though 'twere his chief mastery,
Had greater skill in these intrigues than I;
Nor Nero's learnèd pimp, to whom we owe
What choice records of lust are extant now.
This heretofore, when youth and sprightly blood
Ran in my veins, I tasted, and enjoyed:
Ah those blest days!'—(here the old lecher smiled,
With sweet remembrance of past pleasures filled)
'But they are gone!   Wishes alone remain,
And dreams of joy, ne'er to be felt again:
To abler youth I now the practice leave,
To whom this counsel and advice I give.
  'But the dear mention of my gayer days
Has made me farther, than I would, digress.
'Tis time we now should in due place expound,
How guilt is after shrift to be atoned:
Enjoin no sour repentance, tear, and grief;
Eyes weep no cash, and you no profit give:
Sins, though of the first rate, must punished be,
Not by their own, but the actor's quality:
The poor, whose purse cannot the penance bear,
Let whipping serve, bare feet, and shirts of hair:
The richer fools to Compostella send,*
To Rome, Montserrat, or the Holy Land;
Let pardons, and the indulgence office drain
Their coffers, and enrich the Pope's with gain,
Make 'em build churches, monasteries found,
And dear-bought masses for their crimes compound.
  'Let law and gospel rigid precepts set,
And make the paths to bliss rugged and strait;

* Ships used to be fitted out from the different ports with cargoes of pilgrims to the shrine of St. James of Compostella, as a regular article of exportation.   See Ellis's *Original Letters:* Second Series.   A MS. ballad of the time of Henry VI., in the Trinity Library, Cambridge, describes one of these voyages.

Teach you a smooth, an easier way to gain
Heaven's joys, yet sweet and useful sin retain.
With every frailty, every lust comply,
To advance your spiritual realm and monarchy;
Pull up weak virtue's fence, give scope and space
And purlieus to out-lying consciences;
Show that the needle's eye may stretch, and how
The largest camel-vices may go through.
  ' Teach how the priest pluralities may buy,
Yet fear no odious sin of simony,
While thoughts, and ducats well directed be:
Let whores adorn his exemplary life,
But no lewd heinous wife a scandal give.*
Sooth up the gaudy atheist, who maintains
No law but sense, and owns no god but chance;
Bid thieves rob on, the boisterous ruffian tell
He may for hire, revenge, or honour kill;
Bid strumpets persevere, absolve them too,
And take their dues in kind for what you do;
Exhort the painful and industrious bawd
To diligence and labour in her trade,
Nor think her innocent vocation ill,
Whose incomes does the sacred treasure fill;
Let griping usurers extortion use,
No rapine, falsehood, perjury refuse,
Stick at no crime, which covetous popes would scarce
Act to enrich themselves and bastard-heirs:
A small bequest to the church can all atone,
Wipes off all scores, and heaven and all's their own.
Be these your doctrines, these the truths you preach,
But no forbidden Bible come in reach
Your cheats and artifices to impeach,
Lest thence lay-fools pernicious knowledge get,
Throw off obedience, and your laws forget:

---

* A remarkable instance of Oldham's negligence. With a perfect
rhyme in the middle of the line, easily transferable to the close by an
inversion, he prefers the direct construction that seems first to have
presented itself.

Make them believe 't a spell, more dreadful far
Than Bacon,* Halley,† or Albumazar. ‡
Happy the time, when the unpretending crowd
No more than I its language understood!
When the worm-eaten book, linked to a chain,
In dust lay mouldering in the Vatican,
Despised, neglected, and forgot; to none
But poring rabbies, or the Sorbonne known :
Then in full power our sovereign prelate swayed,
By kings, and all the rabble world obeyed;
Here, humble monarchs at his feet kneeled down,
And begged the alms and charity of a crown;
There, when in solemn state he pleased to ride,
Poor sceptred slaves ran henchboys by his side;
None, though in thought, his grandeur durst blaspheme,
Nor in their very sleep a treason dream.
　'But since the broaching that mischievous piece,
Each alderman a Father Lombard is,
And every cit dares impudently know
More than a council, pope, and conclave too.
Hence the late damnèd friar, and all the crew
Of former crawling sects their poison drew;
Hence all the troubles, plagues, rebellion's breed,
We've felt, or feel, or may hereafter dread.
Wherefore enjoin, that no lay coxcomb dare
About him that unlawful weapon wear;
But charge him chiefly not to touch at all
The dangerous works of that old Lollard, Paul;
That arrant Wickliffist, from whom our foes
Take all their batteries to attack our cause.
Would he in his first years had martyred been,
Never Damascus, nor the Vision seen;

---

* Friar Bacon, a learned English Franciscan of the thirteenth
century, whose discoveries were so much in advance of his age, that he
was denounced and imprisoned many years on a charge of necromancy.
　† Haly in all the editions; a misprint for Halley, the astronomer,
who had recently (1679) returned to England after completing
his observations at St. Helena, and publishing his famous *Catalogus
Stellarum Australium.*
　‡ An Arabian astronomer of the ninth century, celebrated amongst
Eastern writers by his treatise on astrology, entitled *Thousands of Years.*

Then he our party was, stout, vigorous,
And fierce in chase of heretics, like us;
Till he at length, by the enemy seduced,
Forsook us, and the hostile side espoused.
   'Had not the mighty Julian* missed his aims,
These holy shreds had all consumed in flames;
But since the immortal lumber still endures,
In spite of all his industry and ours,
Take care at least it may not come abroad,
To taint with catching heresy the crowd.
Let them be still kept low in sense,—they'll pay
The more respect, more readily obey;
Pray that kind Heaven would on their hearts dispense
A bounteous and abundant ignorance,
That they may never swerve, nor turn awry
From sound and orthodox stupidity.
   ' But these are obvious things, easy to know,
Common to every monk, as well as you.
Greater affairs, and more important, wait
To be discussed, and call for our debate;
Matters that depth require, and well befit
The address and conduct of a Jesuit;
How kingdoms are embroiled, what shakes a throne,
How the first seeds of discontent are sown
To spring up in rebellion; how are set
The secret snares that circumvent a state;
How bubbled monarchs are at first beguiled,
Trepanned, and gulled, at last deposed, and killed.
   'When some proud prince, a rebel to our head,
For disbelieving holy church's creed,
And Peter-pence,† is heretic decreed,
And by a solemn and unquestioned power
To death, and hell, and you delivered o'er:
Choose first some dexterous rogue, well tried, and known,
(Such by confession your familiars grown)

---

* Julian, the Apostate Emperor of Rome.
  † A tribute, or tax, formerly paid by the English to the Pope. It was levied at Lammas-day, and was called Peter-pence, the rate being a penny for every house. It was called also by the no less significant name of Romescot.

Let him by art and nature fitted be
For any great, and gallant villany,
Practised in every sin, each kind of vice,
Which deepest casuists in their searches miss,
Watchful as jealousy, wary as fear,
Fiercer than lust, and bolder than despair,
But close, as plotting fiends in council are.
To him, in firmest oaths of silence bound,
The worth and merit of the deed propound:
Tell of whole reams of pardon, new come o'er,
Indies of gold, and blessings, endless store,
Choice of preferments, if he overcome;
And if he fail, undoubted martyrdom,
And bills for sums in heaven, to be drawn
On factors there, and at first sight paid down.
With arts and promises like these allure,
And make him to your great design secure.
  'And here to know the sundry ways to kill,
Is worth the genius of a Machiavel.
Dull northern brains, in these deep arts unbred,
Know nought but to cut throats, or knock o' th' head;
No sleight of murder of the subtlest shape,
Your busy search and observation 'scape;
Legerdemain of killing, that dives in,
And juggling steals away a life unseen;
How gaudy fate may be in presents sent,
And creep insensibly by touch, or scent;
How ribands, gloves, or saddle-pommel may
An unperceived, but certain death convey,
Above the reach of antidotes, above the power
Of the famed Pontick Mountebank to cure;
Whate'er is known to quaint Italian spite,
In studied poisoning skilled, and exquisite,
Whate'er great Borgia, or his sire could boast,
Which the expense of half the conclave cost.
  'Thus may the business be in secret done,
Nor authors, nor the accessories known,
And the slurred guilt with ease on others thrown.

But if ill fortune should your plot betray,
And leave you to the rage of foes a prey;
Let none his crime by weak confession own,
Nor shame the church, while he'd himself atone.
Let varnished guile, and feigned hypocrisies,
Pretended holiness, and useful lies,
Your well dissembled villanies disguise.
A thousand wily turns, and doubles try,
To foil the scent, and to divert the cry;
Cog, sham, out-face, deny, equivocate,
Into a thousand shapes yourselves translate.
Remember what the crafty Spartan taught,
Children with rattles, men with oaths are caught;
Forswear upon the rack, and if you fall,
Let this great comfort make amends for all,—
Those whom they damn for rogues, next age shall see
Made advocates i' th' church's Litany.
Whoever with bold tongue, or pen shall dare
Against your arts and practices declare;
What fool shall e'er presumptuously oppose,
Your holy cheats and godly frauds disclose;
Pronounce him heretic, firebrand of hell,
Turk, Jew, fiend, miscreant, pagan, infidel;
A thousand blacker names, worse calumnies,
All wit can think, and pregnant spite devise;
Strike home, gash deep, no lies, nor slanders spare;
A wound, though cured, yet leaves behind a scar.
'Those whom your wit and reason can't decry,
Make scandalous with loads of infamy;
Make Luther monster, by a fiend begot,
Brought forth with wings and tail, and cloven foot;
Make whoredom, incest, worst of vice, and shame,
Pollute and foul his manners, life and name;
Tell how strange storms ushered his fatal end,
And hell's black troops did for his soul contend.
'Much more I had to say; but now grow faint,
And strength and spirits for the subject want.

Be these great mysteries, I here unfold,
Amongst your order's institutes enrolled;
Preserve them sacred, close and unrevealed,
As ancient Rome her Sybil's books concealed.
Let no bold heretic with saucy eye
Into the hidden unseen archives pry,
Lest the malicious flouting rascals turn
Our church to laughter, raillery, and scorn.
Let never rack, or torture, pain, or fear,
From your firm breasts the important secrets tear.
If any treacherous brother of your own
Shall to the world divulge, and make them known,
Let him by worst of deaths his guilt atone.
Should but his thoughts, or dreams suspected be,
Let him for safety, and prevention die,
And learn in the grave the art of secrecy.
  'But one thing more, and then with joy I go,
Nor urge a longer stay of fate below.
Give me again once more your plighted faith,
And let each seal it with his dying breath.
As the great Carthagenian* heretofore
The bloody reeking altar touched, and swore
Eternal enmity to the Roman power,
Swear you (and let the Fates confirm the same)
An endless hatred to the Lutheran name!
Vow never to admit, or league, or peace,
Or truce, or commerce with the cursèd race;
Now, through all age, when time or place soe'er
Shall give you power, wage an immortal war;
Like Theban feuds, let yours yourselves survive,
And in your very dust and ashes live;
Like mine, be your last gasp their curse.'——At this
They kneel, and all the sacred volume kiss;
Vowing to send each year an hecatomb
Of Huguenots, an offering to his tomb.
  In vain he would continue;—abrupt death
A period puts, and stops his impious breath;

---

* Hannibal.

In broken accents he is scarce allowed
To falter out his blessing on the crowd.
Amen is echoed by infernal howl,
And scrambling spirits seize his parting soul.

SATIRE IV.—ST. IGNATIUS'S IMAGE BROUGHT IN, DISCOVER-
ING THE ROGUERIES OF THE JESUITS, AND RIDI-
CULOUS SUPERSTITION OF THE CHURCH OF ROME.

ONCE I was common wood, a shapeless log,
    Thrown out a kennel post for every dog;
The workman, yet in doubt what course to take,
Whether I'd best a saint, or hog-trough make,
After debate resolved me for a saint,
And thus famed Loyola I represent:
And well I may resemble him, for he
As stupid was, as much a block as me.
My right leg maimed, at halt I seem to stand,
To tell the wounds at Pampelune sustained.*
My sword, and soldier's armour here had been,
But they may in Montserrat's church be seen:
Those to the blessèd Virgin I laid down
For cassock, sursingle, and shaven crown,
The spiritual garb, in which I now am shown.†
    With due accoutrements, and fit disguise
I might for sentinel of corn suffice;
As once the lusty god of old stood guard,
And the invading crows from forage scared.
Now on my head the birds their relics leave,
And spiders in my mouth their arras weave;

* In the early part of his life Loyola served in the Spanish army
against the French, and at the siege of Pampeluna received a severe
wound in his left leg, and had his right thigh shattered by a cannon
ball. The perusal of the *Lives of the Saints* during the progress of a
lingering cure heated his imagination with religious enthusiasm, and
is said to have given that direction to the rest of his life which finally
led to the establishment of the order of Jesuits.

† Before he went to Jerusalem, Loyola hung up his arms in the
Church of Montserrat, and dedicated himself to the Virgin.

And persecuted rats oft find in me
A refuge, and religious sanctuary.
But you profaner heretics, whoe'er
The Inquisition and its vengeance fear,
I charge, stand off, at peril come not near;
Let none at twelve score impiously untruss,
He enters Fox's lists that dare transgress;
For I'm by holy church in reverence had,
And all good catholic folk implore my aid.
   These pictures, which you see, my story give,
The acts and monuments of me alive;
That frame, wherein with pilgrim weeds I stand,
Contains my travels to the Holy Land;
This, me and my Decemvirate at Rome,
When I for grant of my great order come.
There, with devotion wrapt, I hang in air,
With dove, like Mahomet's, whispering in my ear;
Here, Virgin in calash of clouds descends,
To be my safeguard from assaulting fiends.
   Those tables by, and crutches of the lame,
My great achievements since my death proclaim:
Plague, ague, dropsy, palsy, stone, and gout,
Legions of maladies by me cast out,
More than the college knows, or ever fill
Quack's wiping-paper, and the weekly bill.
What Peter's shadow did of old, the same
Is fancied done by my all-powerful name;
For which some wear't about their necks and arms,
To guard from dangers, sicknesses, and harms;
And some on wombs the barren to relieve,
A miracle I better did alive.
   Oft I by crafty Jesuit am taught
Wonders to do, and many a juggling feat.
Sometimes with chafing-dish behind me put,
I sweat like debauchee in hothouse shut,
And drip like any spitchcocked Huguenot;
Sometimes by secret springs I learn to stir,
As pasteboard saints dance by miraculous wire;

Then I Tradescant's rarities outdo,*
Sand's water-works, and German clock-work too,†
Or any choice device at Bartholomew.
Sometimes I utter oracles, by priest
Instead of a familiar possessed.
The church I vindicate, Luther confute,
And cause amazement in the gaping rout.
    Such holy cheats, such hocus tricks, as these,
For miracles amongst the rabble pass.
By this, in their esteem I daily grow,
In wealth enriched, increased in votaries too;
This draws each year vast numbers to my tomb,
More than in pilgrimage to Mecca come;
This brings each week new presents to my shrine,
And makes it those of India gods outshine;
This gives a chalice, that a golden cross,
Another massy candlesticks bestows,
Some, altar-cloths of costly work and price,
Plush, tissue, ermine, silks of noblest dies,
The Birth and Passion in embroideries;
Some jewels, rich as those the Ægyptian punk
In jellies to her Roman lover drunk;
Some offer gorgeous robes, which serve to wear
When I on holy days in state appear;
When I'm in pomp on high processions shown,
Like pageants of Lord Mayor, or Skimmington.
Lucullus could not such a wardrobe boast;
Less those of popes at their election cost;

---

* John Tradescant, usually called Tradeskin by his contemporaries,
a celebrated collector of curiosities, originally gardener to the Duke of
Buckingham, and subsequently to Charles I. He lived in South Lambeth, where he had his museum and botanic garden. His house, since
known as Turret House, contained so vast a variety of rarities that it
was commonly called Tradescant's Ark. Evelyn records a visit to him
in 1657. After his death his son gave the whole collection to Elias
Ashmole, who presented it to the University of Oxford, where it
formed the foundation of the Ashmolean Museum.

† German clock-work was much in vogue in this reign. Pepys
speaks of a 'brave clock,' belonging to the King, that went with
bullets; and describes another which, by its mechanism, displayed the
various stages of man's life. This latter was made by an Englishman.

Less those, which Sicily's tyrant heretofore
From plundered gods, and Jove's own shoulders tore.
　　Hither, as to some fair, the rabble come,
To barter for the merchandize of Rome;
Where priests, like mountebanks, on stage appear,
To expose the frippery of their hallowed ware;
This is the laboratory of their trade,
The shop where all their staple drugs are made;
Prescriptions and receipts to bring in gain,
All from the church dispensatories ta'en.
　　The pope's elixir, holy water's here,
Which they with chemic art distilled prepare;
Choice above Goddard's drops,* and all the trash
Of modern quacks; this is that sovereign wash
For fetching spots and morphew† from the face,
And scouring dirty clothes, and consciences.
One drop of this, if used, had power to fray
The legion from the hogs of Gadara;
This would have silenced quite the Wiltshire Drum,
And made the prating fiend of Mascon dumb.
　　That vessel consecrated oil contains,
Kept sacred, as the famed ampoule‡ of France,
Which some profaner heretics would use
For liquoring wheels of jacks, of boots, and shoes;
This makes the chrism,§ which, mixed by cunning priests,
Anoints young catholics for the church's lists;
And when they're crossed, confessed, and die, by this
Their launching souls slide off to endless bliss;
As Lapland saints, when they on broomsticks fly,
By help of magic unctions mount the sky.
　　Yon altar-pix ‖ of gold is the abode
And safe repository of their god.
A cross is fixed upon 't the fiends to scare,
And flies which would the deity besmear;

---

* Dr. Jonathan Goddard, who had been physician to Cromwell,
and Member of Parliament for Oxfordshire in 1653.
† A rash or scurf on the skin.　The word is obsolete.
‡ The phial in which holy oil is kept.
§ The unguent used in the sacraments of the Roman Catholic Church.
‖ The vessel in which the consecrated Host is kept.

And mice, which oft might unprepared receive,
And to lewd scoffers cause of scandal give.
    Here are performed the conjurings and spells,
For christening saints, and hawks, and carriers' bells;
For hallowing shreds, and grains, and salts, and
    balms,*
Shrines, crosses, medals, shells, and waxen lambs:
Of wondrous virtue all (you must believe)
And from all sorts of ill preservative;
From plague, infection, thunder, storm, and hail,
Love, grief, want, debt, sin, and the devil and all.
Here beads are blest, and pater nosters framed,
(By some the tallies of devotion named)
Which of their prayers, and orisons keep tale,
Lest they and Heaven should in the reckoning fail.
Here sacred lights, the altar's graceful pride,
Are by priests' breath perfumed and sanctified;
Made some of wax, of heretics' tallow some,
A gift, which Irish Emma sent to Rome;
For which great merit worthily (we're told)
She's now amongst her country-saints enrolled.
Here holy banners are reserved in store,
And flags, such as the famed Armada bore;
And hallowed swords, and daggers kept for use,
When restive kings the papal yoke refuse;
And consecrated ratsbane, to be laid
For heretic vermin, which the church invade.
    But that which brings in most of wealth and gain,
Does best the priests' swollen tripes and purses strain,
Here they each week their constant auctions hold
Of reliques, which by candle's inch are sold:
Saints by the dozen here are set to sale,
Like mortals wrought in gingerbread on stall.
Hither are loads from emptied channels brought,
And voiders of the worms from sextons bought,
Which serve for retail through the world to vent,
Such as of late were to the Savoy sent;

---

* Balsams used in embalming.

Hair from the skulls of dying strumpets shorn,
And felons' bones, from rifled gibbets torn,
Like those, which some old hag at midnight steals,
For witchcrafts, amulets, and charms, and spells,
Are passed for sacred to the cheapening rout,
And worn on fingers, breasts, and ears about.
This boasts a scrap of me, and that a bit
Of good St. George, St. Patrick, or St. Kit;
These locks St. Bridget's were, and those St. Clare's;
Some for St. Catharine's go, and some for her's
That wiped her Saviour's feet, washed with her tears.
    Here you may see my wounded leg, and here
Those which to China bore the great Xavier.
Here may you the grand traitor's halter see,
Some call 't the arms of the society;
Here is his lantern too, but Faux's not,
That was embezzled by the Huguenot.
Here Garnet's straws, and Becket's bones and hair,
For murdering whom, some tails are said to wear,
As learnèd Capgrave does record their fate,
And faithful British histories relate.
Those are St. Lawrence' coals exposed to view,
Strangely preserved, and kept alive till now;
That's the famed Wildefortis' wondrous beard,
For which her maidenshame the tyrant spared;
Yon is the Baptist's coat, and one of 's heads,
The rest are shown in many a place besides;
And of his teeth as many sets there are,
As on their belts six operators wear.
Here blessed Mary's milk, not yet turned sour,
Renowned (like asses') for its healing power,
Ten Holland kine scarce in a year give more.
Here is her manteau, and a smock of hers,
Fellow to that, which once relieved Poictiers;*
Besides her husband's utensils of trade,
Wherewith some prove that images were made.

---

* The *Maid of Orleans.*

Here is the soldier's spear, and passion-nails
Whose quantity would serve for building Paul's;
Chips, some from Holy Cross, from Tyburn some,
Honoured by many a Jesuit's martyrdom;
All held of special and miraculous power,
Not Tabor more approved for ague's cure.
Here shoes, which once perhaps at Newgate hung,
Angling their charity that passed along,*
Now for St. Peter's go, and the office bear
For priests, they did for lesser villains there.

    These are the Fathers' implements and tools,
Their gaudy trangums† for inveigling fools;
These serve for baits the simple to ensnare,
Like children spirited with toys at fair.
Nor are they half the artifices yet,
By which the vulgar they delude and cheat;
Which should I undertake, much easier I,
Much sooner, might compute what sins there be
Wiped off, and pardoned at a jubilee;
What bribes enrich the datary‡ each year,
Or vices treated on by Escobar;
How many punks in Rome profess the trade,
Or greater numbers by confession made.

    One undertakes by scale of miles to tell
The bounds, dimensions, and extent of hell;
How far and wide the infernal monarch reigns,
How many German leagues his realm contains;
Who are his ministers, pretends to know,
And all their several offices below;
How many chaldrons he each year expends
In coals for roasting Huguenots and fiends;

---

* Alluding to the old custom by which prisoners solicited charity
from the passers-by. A shoe, into which alms were dropped, was
suspended by a string to the level of the street.
  † Sometimes trinkum-trankums—trinkets, toys. There was an old
engine, called a trink, which was used for catching fish.
  ‡ The officer in the Chancery of Rome, who affixes the *datum Romæ*
to the Pope's bulls.

And with as much exactness states the case,
As if he had been surveyor of the place.
  Another frights the rout with rueful stories,
Of wild chimeras, limbos, purgatories,
And bloated souls in smoky durance hung,
Like a Westphalia gammon, or neat's tongue,
To be redeemed with masses and a song.
A good round sum must the deliverance buy,
For none may there swear out on poverty.
Your rich, and bounteous shades are only eased;
No Fleet, or King's-bench ghosts are thence released.
  A third, the wicked and debauched to please,
Cries up the virtue of indulgences,
And all the rates of vices does assess;
What price they in the holy chamber bear,
And customs for each sin imported there;
How you at best advantages may buy
Patents for sacrilege and simony;
What tax is in the lechery-office laid
On panders, bawds, and punks, that ply the trade;
What costs a rape, or incest, and how cheap
You may an harlot, or an ingle keep;
How easy murder may afforded be
For one, two, three, or a whole family—
But not of heretics; there no pardon lacks,
'Tis one of the church's meritorious acts.
  For venial trifles, less and slighter faults,
They ne'er deserve the trouble of your thoughts,
Ten Ave Maries mumbled to the cross,
Clear scores of twice ten thousand such as those.
Some are at sound of christened bell forgiven,
And some by squirt of holy water driven;
Others by anthems played are charmed away,
As men cure bites of the tarantula.
  But nothing with the crowd does more enhance
The value of these holy charlatans,
Than when the wonders of the mass they view,
Where spiritual jugglers their chief mastery shew.

'Hey jingo, sirs! What's this?' 'Tis bread you see;
' Presto begone!' 'Tis now a deity.
Two grains of dough, with cross, and stamp of priest,
And five small words pronounced, make up their Christ.
To this they all fall down, this all adore,
And straight devour, what they adored before.—
   'Tis this that does the astonished rout amuse,
And reverence to shaven crown infuse,
To see a silly, sinful, mortal wight
His Maker make, create the infinite.
None boggles at the impossibility;
Alas, 'tis wondrous heavenly mystery!—
   And here I might (if I but durst) reveal
What pranks are played in the confessional:
How haunted virgins have been dispossessed,
And devils were cast out, to let in priest:
What fathers act with novices alone,
And what to punks in shrieving seats is done,
Who thither flock to ghostly confessor,
To clear old debts, and tick with Heaven for more.
Oft have I seen these hallowed altars stained
With rapes, those pews which infamies profaned;
Not great Cellier,* nor any greater bawd,
Of note, and long experience in the trade,
Has more, and fouler scenes of lust surveyed.
But I these dangerous truths forbear to tell,
For fear I should the Inquisition feel.
Should I tell all their countless knaveries,
Their cheats, and shams, and forgeries, and lies,
Their cringings, crossings, censings, sprinklings, chrisms,
Their conjurings, and spells, and exorcisms,
Their motley habits, maniples, and stoles,
Albs, ammits, rochets, chimers, hoods, and cowls;†

---

* This notorious person narrowly escaped the gibbet in 1680, when she was tried for high treason. She was condemned in a fine of 1000l. and sentenced three times to the pillory for a libel.

† The *alb* is the vestment of white linen reaching to the feet—*ammit* (more correctly *ammis*, and sometimes spelt variously as *amyse, ammys,*

Should I tell all their several services,
Their trentals,* masses, dirges, rosaries;
Their solemn pomps, their pageants, and parades,
Their holy masks, and spiritual cavalcades,
With thousand antic tricks, and gambols more;
'Twould swell the sum to such a mighty score,
That I at length should more voluminous grow,
Than Crabb, or Surius,† lying Fox, or Stow.
    Believe whate'er I have related here,
As true, as if 'twere spoke from porphyry chair.
If I have feigned in aught, or broached a lie,
Let worst of fates attend me, let me be
Made the next bonfire for the powder-plot,
The sport of every sneering Huguenot;
There like a martyred pope in flames expire,
And no kind catholic dare quench the fire.

---

amice),the vestment lined with fur that covered the head and shoulders
—*rochet*, the surplice—*chimer*, a vestment worn by bishops, both of
the Anglican and Roman church, between their gown and rochet.

    * Thirty masses for the dead. According to Burnet, they were
distributed over a whole year, three being said at each of the principal
festivals of the Church, under the impression that they possessed additional efficacy on those occasions.

    † Laurentius Surius, a Carthusian friar, born at Lubeck in 1522,
died at Cologne in 1578. He obtained celebrity by the quantity of
his works, rather than by the extent or accuracy of his learning, and
is one of the most voluminous compilers of history, biography, and
ecclesiastical records in the annals of the Church. His principal works
are a *History of his own Times*, from 1500 to 1566; a *Collection of
Councils*; and *The Lives of the Saints*.

THE CARELESS GOOD FELLOW.*

SONG.

I

A PLAGUE of this fooling and plotting of late,
  What a pother and stir has it kept in the State;
Let the rabble run mad with suspicions and fears,
Let them scuffle and jar, till they go by the ears;
  Their grievances never shall trouble my pate,
  So I can enjoy my dear bottle at quiet.

2

What coxcombs were those who would barter their ease
And their necks for a toy, a thin wafer and mass;
At old Tyburn thay never had needed to swing,
Had they been but true subjects to drink and their king;
  A friend and a bottle is all my design;
  He has no room for treason, that's top-full of wine.

3

I mind not the members and makers of laws,
Let them sit or prorogue, as his majesty please;
Let them damn us to woollen,† I'll never repine
At my lodging when dead, so alive I have wine;
  Yet oft in my drink I can hardly forbear
  To curse them for making my claret so dear.

4

I mind not grave asses who idly debate
About right and succession, the trifles of state;
We've a good king already; and he deserves laughter
That will trouble his head with who shall come after;
  Come, here's to his health, and I wish he may be
  As free from all care and all trouble as we.

5

What care I how leagues with the Hollander go?
Or intrigues betwixt Sidney and Monsieur D'Avaux?

---

* Written in March, 1680.
† The Woollen Act came into operation on the 1st August, 1678.

What concerns it my drinking, if Cassel be sold,
If the conqueror take it by storming, or gold?
 Good Bordeaux alone is the place that I mind,
 And when the fleet's coming, I pray for a wind.

6

The bully of France, that aspires to renown
By dull cutting of throats, and venturing his own,
Let him fight and be damned, and make matches and
   treat,
To afford the newsmongers and coffee-house chat;
 He's but a brave wretch, while I am more free,
 More safe, and a thousand times happier than he.

7

Come he, or the pope, or the devil to boot,
Or come faggot and stake, I care not a groat;
Never think that in Smithfield I porters will heat:
No. I swear, Mr. Fox, pray excuse me for that.
 I'll drink in defiance of gibbet and halter,
 This is the profession that never will alter.

AN IMITATION OF HORACE.

BOOK I.—SATIRE IX.*

Ibam forte via sacra, &c.

AS I was walking in the Mall of late,
 Alone, and musing on I know not what;
Comes a familiar fop, whom hardly I
Knew by his name, and rudely seizes me:
'Dear sir, I'm mighty glad to meet with you:
And pray, how have you done this age, or two?'
'Well, I thank God,' said I, 'as times are now:
I wish the same to you.' And so passed on,
Hoping with this, the coxcomb would be gone.

---

 * This is one of the pieces selected for particular approbation by
Pope. It was written in June, 1681.

But when I saw I could not thus get free,
I asked, what business else he had for me?
'Sir,' answered he, 'if learning, parts, or sense
Merit your friendship, I have just pretence.'
'I honour you,' said I, 'upon that score,
And shall be glad to serve you to my power.'
Meantime, wild to get loose, I try all ways
To shake him off; sometimes I walk apace,
Sometimes stand still; I frown, I chafe, I fret,
Shrug, turn my back, as in the Bagnio, sweat;
And show all kinds of signs to make him guess
At my impatience and uneasiness.
'Happy the folk in Newgate!' whispered I,
'Who, though in chains, are from this torment free;
Would I were like rough Manly* in the play,
To send impertinents with kicks away!'
 He all the while baits me with tedious chat,
Speaks much about the drought, and how the rate
Of hay is raised, and what it now goes at;
Tells me of a new comet at the Hague,
Portending God knows what, a dearth, or plague;
Names every wench that passes through the park,
How much she is allowed, and who the spark;
Who had ill hap at the groom-porter's board,
Three nights ago, in play with such a lord;
When he observed I minded not a word,
And did no answer to his trash afford,
'Sir, I perceive you stand on thorns,' said he,
'And fain would part; but, faith, it must not be;
Come, let us take a bottle.' I cried, 'No;
Sir, I'm an invalid, and dare not now.'
'Then tell me whither you desire to go:
I'll wait upon you.' 'Oh! sir, 'tis too far:
I visit cross the water; therefore spare
Your needless trouble.' 'Trouble! sir, 'tis none:
'Tis more by half to leave you here alone.

---

* A character in the *Plain-Dealer*.

I have no present business to attend,
At least, which I'll not quit for such a friend.
Tell me not of the distance; for, I vow,
I'll cut the Line, double the Cape for you;
Good faith, I will not leave you; make no words;
Go you to Lambeth? Is it to my lord's?
His steward I most intimately know,
Have often drunk with his comptroller too.'
By this I found my wheedle would not pass,
But rather served my sufferings to increase;
And seeing 'twas in vain to vex, or fret,
I patiently submitted to my fate.
　　Straight he begins again: 'Sir, if you knew
My worth but half so thoroughly as I do;
I'm sure you would not value any friend
You have, like me; but that I wont commend
Myself, and my own talents, I might tell
How many ways to wonder I excel.
None has a greater gift in poetry,
Or writes more verses with more ease than I;
I'm grown the envy of the men of wit,
I killed even Rochester with grief and spite;
Next for the dancing part I all surpass,
St. André* never moved with such a grace;
And 'tis well known, whene'er I sing or set,
Humphreys, nor Blow,† could ever match me yet.'
　　Here I got room to interrupt: 'Have you
A mother, sir, or kindred living now?'
'Not one: they are all dead.' 'Troth, so I guessed:
'The happier they,' said I, 'who are at rest!
Poor I am only left unmurdered yet;
Haste, I beseech you, and despatch me quite;
For I am well convinced, my time is come:
When I was young, a gipsy told my doom:

---

* The famous dancing-master.
† The composer. Humphreys was a singer.

This lad (said she, and looked upon my hand,)
Shall not by sword, or poison come to's end,
Nor by the fever, dropsy, gout, or stone,
But he shall die by an eternal tongue;
Therefore, when he's grown up, if he be wise,
Let him avoid great talkers, I advise.'
By this time we were got to Westminster,
Where he by chance a trial had to hear,
And, if he were not there, his cause must fall:
'Sir, if you love me, step into the Hall
For one half-hour.' 'The devil take me now,'
Said I, 'if I know anything of law:
Besides, I told you whither I'm to go.'
Hereat he made a stand, pulled down his hat
Over his eyes, and mused in deep debate:
'I'm in a strait,' says he, 'what I shall do:
Whether forsake my business, sir, or you.'
'Me by all means,' say I. 'No,' says my sot,
'I fear you'll take it ill, if I should do't;
I'm sure you will.' 'Not I, by all that's good,
But I've more breeding, than to be so rude.
Pray, don't neglect your own concerns for me;
Your cause, good sir!' 'My cause be damned,' says he,
'I value't less than your dear company.'
With this he came up to me, and would lead
The way; I, sneaking after, hung my head.
Next he begins to plague me with the plot,
Asks, whether I were known to Oates or not?
'Not I, thank Heaven! I no priest have been;
Have never Douay, nor St. Omer seen.'
'What think you, sir; will they the Joiner try?*
Will he die, think you?' 'Yes, most certainly.'
'I mean, be hanged.' 'Would thou wert so,' wished I!

---

* College, the 'Protestant joiner,' who wrote a satirical ballad on
the removal of the Parliament, and was tried and executed on the
31st August, 1681, two months after the date of this humorous para-
phrase of Horace.

Religion came in next, though he'd no more
Than the noble peer, his punk, or confessor.
'Oh! the sad times, if once the king should die!
Sir, are you not afraid of popery?'
'No more than my superiors: why should I?
Come popery, come anything,' thought I,
'So heaven would bless me to get rid of thee!
But 'tis some comfort, that my hell is here;
I need no punishment hereafter fear.'
   Scarce had I thought, but he falls on anew:
'How stands it, sir, betwixt his grace and you?'
'Sir, he's a man of sense above the crowd,
And shuns the converse of a multitude.'
'Ay, sir,' says he, 'you're happy who are near
His grace, and have the favour of his ear;
But let me tell you, if you'll recommend
This person here, your point will soon be gained.
Gad, sir, I'll die, if my own single wit
Don't fob his minions, and displace 'em quite,
And make yourself his only favourite.'
'No, you are out abundantly,' said I,
'We live not, as you think; no family
Throughout the whole three kingdoms is more free
From those ill customs, which are used to swarm
In great men's houses; none e'er does me harm,
Because more learnèd, or more rich than I;
But each man keeps his place, and his degree.'
''Tis mighty strange,' says he, 'what you relate.'
'But nothing truer, take my word for that.'
'You make me long to be admitted too
Amongst his creatures; sir, I beg, that you
Will stand my friend; your interest is such,
You may prevail; I'm sure you can do much;
He's one that may be won upon, I've heard,
Though at the first approach access be hard.
I'll spare no trouble of my own, or friends,
No cost in fees, and bribes to gain my ends;

I'll seek all opportunities to meet
With him; accost him in the very street;
Hang on his coach, and wait upon him home,
Fawn, scrape and cringe to him, nay, to his groom.
Faith, sir, this must be done, if we'll be great;
Preferment comes not at a cheaper rate.'
　　While at this savage rate he worried me,
By chance a doctor, my dear friend, came by,
That knew the fellow's humour passing well;
Glad of the sight I join him; we stand still:
' Whence came you, sir? and whither go you now?'
And such like questions passed betwixt us two.
Straight I begin to pull him by the sleeve,
Nod, wink upon him, touch my nose, and give
A thousand hints, to let him know that I
Needed his help for my delivery;
He, naughty wag, with an arch fleering smile,
Seems ignorant of what I mean the while;
I grow stark wild with rage.　' Sir, said not you,
You'd somewhat to discourse, not long ago,
With me in private?'　' I remember 't well.
Some other time be sure, I will not fail;
Now I am in great haste upon my word;
A messenger came for me from a lord
That's in a bad condition, like to die.'
' Oh! sir, he can't be in a worse than I;
Therefore for God's sake do not stir from hence.'
' Sweet sir! your pardon; 'tis of consequence;
I hope you're kinder than to press my stay,
Which may be heaven knows what out of my way.'
This said, he left me to my murderer.
Seeing no hopes of my relief appear,
' Confounded be the stars,' said I, ' that swayed
This fatal day! would I had kept my bed
With sickness, rather than be visited
With this worse plague! what ill have I e'er done,
To pull this curse, this heavy judgment down?'

While I was thus lamenting my ill hap,
Comes aid at length; a brace of bailiffs clap
The rascal on the back: 'Here take your fees,
Kind gentlemen,' said I, 'for my release.'
He would have had me bail. 'Excuse me, sir,
I've made a vow ne'er to be surety more;
My father was undone by 't heretofore.'
Thus I got off, and blessed the fates that he
Was prisoner made, I set at liberty.

PARAPHRASE UPON HORACE.

BOOK I.—ODE XXXI.

Quid dedicatum poscit Apollinem
Vates? &c.

I

WHAT does the poet's modest wish require?
    What boon does he of gracious heaven desire?
Not the large crops of Esham's goodly soil,
Which tire the mower's and the reaper's toil;
Not the soft flocks on hilly Cotswold fed,
Nor Lempster fields with living fleeces clad;
He does not ask the grounds, where gentle Thames,
Or swifter Severn, spread their fattening streams,
    Where they with wanton windings play,
And eat their widened banks insensibly away;
    He does not ask the wealth of Lombard-street,
    Which consciences and souls are pawned to get;
    Nor those exhaustless mines of gold,
Which Guinea and Peru in their rich bosoms hold.

2

Let those that live in the Canary Isles,
On which indulgent nature ever smiles,

Take pleasure in their plenteous vintages,
And from the juicy grape its racy liquor press;
　　Let wealthy merchants, when they dine,
　　Run o'er their costly names of wine,
Their chests of Florence, and their Mont-Alchine,
Their Mants, Champagnes, Chablis, Frontiniacs tell.
　　Their aumes* of Hock, of Backrach, and Moselle;
　　He envies not their luxury,
Which they with so much pains and danger buy;
For which so many storms and wrecks they bear,
For which they pass the Straits so oft each year,
And 'scape so narrowly the bondage of Algier.

3

　　He wants no Cyprus birds, nor ortolans,
　　Nor dainties fetched from far to please his sense;
Cheap wholesome herbs content his frugal board,
　　The food of unfallen innocence,
Which the meanest village garden does afford;
Grant him, kind heaven, the sum of his desires,
What nature, not what luxury requires;
He only does a competency claim,
And, when he has it, wit to use the same.
Grant him sound health, impaired by no disease,
　　　Nor by his own excess;
Let him in strength of mind and body live,
But not his reason, nor his sense survive;
His age (if age he e'er must live to see)
Let it from want, contempt, and care be free,
But not from mirth, and the delights of poetry.
　　Grant him but this, he's amply satisfied,
And scorns whatever fate can give beside.

---

* A Dutch measure for Rhenish wine, containing forty gallons.

PARAPHRASE UPON HORACE.

BOOK II.—ODE XIV.

Eheu fugaces Posthume, Posthume,
Labuntur anni, &c.

I

ALAS! dear friend, alas! time hastes away,
  Nor is it in our power to bribe its stay;
The rolling years with constant motion run,
Lo! while I speak, the present minute's gone,
And following hours still urge the foregoing on.
    'Tis not thy wealth, 'tis not thy power,
'Tis not thy piety can thee secure;
    They're all too feeble to withstand
Grey hairs, approaching age, and thy avoidless end.
    When once thy glass is run,
    When once thy utmost thread is spun,
'Twill then be fruitless to expect reprieve;
    Couldst thou ten thousand kingdoms give
In purchase for each hour of longer life,
    They would not buy one gasp of breath,
Not move one jot inexorable death.

2

All the vast stock of human progeny,
    Which now, like swarms of insects, crawl
Upon the surface of earth's spacious ball,
Must quit this hillock of mortality,
    And in its bowels buried lie.
The mightiest king, and proudest potentate
In spite of all his pomp, and all his state,
Must pay this necessary tribute unto fate.
The busy, restless monarch of the world, which now
   Keeps such a pother, and so much ado
        To fill gazettes alive,
And after in some lying annal to survive,

Even he, even that great mortal man must die,
And stink, and rot, as well as thou and I,
As well as the poor tattered wretch that begs his
    bread,
And is with scraps out of the common basket fed.

3

In vain from dangers of the bloody field we keep,
        In vain do we escape
        The sultry Line, and stormy Cape,
        And all the treacheries of the faithless deep;
In vain for health to foreign countries we repair,
    And change our English for Montpellier air,   .
    In hope to leave our fears of dying there;
    In vain with costly far-fetched drugs we strive
    To keep the wasting vital lamp alive;
    In vain on doctor's feeble art rely;
Against resistless death there is no remedy.
    Both we and they, for all their skill, must die,
And fill alike the bead-rolls of mortality.

4   .

Thou must, thou must resign to fate, my friend,
And leave thy house, thy wife, and family behind;
    Thou must thy fair and goodly manors leave,
    Of these thy trees thou shalt not with thee take,
    Save just as much as will thy coffin make;
Nor wilt thou be allowed of all thy land, to have
    But the small pittance of a six-foot grave.
        Then shall thy prodigal young heir
    Lavish the wealth, which thou for many a year
    Hast hoarded up with so much pains and care;
    Then shall he drain thy cellars of their stores,
Kept sacred now as vaults of buried ancestors;
    Shall set the enlargèd butts at liberty,
    Which there close prisoners under durance lie,
    And wash these stately floors with better wine
Than that of consecrated prelates when they dine.

HORACE'S ART OF POETRY, IMITATED IN ENGLISH.*

ADDRESSED BY WAY OF LETTER TO A FRIEND.

SHOULD some ill painter, in a wild design,
To a man's head a horse's shoulders join,
Or fish's tail to a fair woman's waist,
Or draw the limbs of many a different beast,
Ill matched, and with as motley feathers dressed;
If you by chance were to pass by his shop,
Could you forbear from laughing at the fop,
And not believe him whimsical or mad?
Credit me, sir, that book is quite as bad,
As worthy laughter, which throughout is filled
With monstrous inconsistencies, more vain, and wild
Than sick men's dreams, whose neither head, nor tail,
Nor any parts in due proportion fall.
But 'twill be said, 'None ever did deny
Painters and poets their free liberty

---

* Oldham, in his introduction to this translation, or rather, adaptation of the *Art of Poetry*, explains the object he kept in view throughout. He says that he thought of turning the work to an advantage which had not occurred to those who went before him in the translation, by making Horace speak as if he were then living. ' I therefore,' he adds, 'resolved to alter the scene from Rome to London, and to make use of English names of men, places, and customs, where the parallel would decently permit, which I conceived would give a kind of new air to the poem, and render it more agreeable to the relish of the present age.' And it may be added, that this is the feature which constitutes its chief attraction for the modern reader. Of his plan of translation, and the liberties he took with his original, he says, ' I have not, I acknowledge, been over nice in keeping to the words of the original, for that were to transgress a rule therein contained. Nevertheless I have been religiously strict to its sense, and expressed it in as plain and intelligible a manner as the subject would bear. Where I may be thought to have varied from it (which is not above once or twice, and in passages not much material), the skilful reader will perceive 'twas necessary for carrying on my proposed design, and the author himself, were he again alive, would (I believe) forgive me. I have been careful to avoid stiffness, and made it my endeavour to hit (as near as I could) the easy and familiar way of writing, which is peculiar to Horace in his *Epistles*, and was his proper talent above any of mankind.'

Of feigning anything.' We grant it true,
And the same privilege crave and allow;
But to mix natures clearly opposite,
To make the serpent and the dove unite,
Or lambs from savage tigers seek defence,
Shocks reason, and the rules of common sense.
    Some, who would have us think they meant to treat
At first on arguments of greatest weight,
Are proud, when here and there a glittering line
Does through the mass of their coarse rubbish shine. .
In gay digressions they delight to rove,
Describing here a temple, there a grove,
A vale enamelled o'er with pleasant streams,
A painted rainbow, or the gliding Thames.
But how does this relate to their design?
Though good elsewhere, 'tis here but foisted in.
A common dauber may perhaps have skill
To paint a tavern sign, or landscape well;
But what is this to drawing of a fight,
A wreck, a storm, or the last judgment right?
When the fair model and foundation shews,
That you some great Escurial would produce,
How comes it dwindled to a cottage thus?
In fine, whatever work you mean to frame,
Be uniform, and everywhere the same.
    Most poets, sir, ('tis easy to observe)
Into the worst of faults are apt to swerve;
Through a false hope of reaching excellence,
Avoiding length, we often cramp our sense,
And make 't obscure; oft, when we'd have our style
Easy and flowing, lose its force the while;
Some, striving to surmount the common flight,
Soar up in airy bombast out of sight;
Others, who fear to a bold pitch to trust
Themselves, flag low, and humbly sweep the dust;
And many fond of seeming marvellous,
While they too carelessly transgress the laws

OLDHAM.   10

Of likelihood, most odd chimeras feign,
Dolphins in woods, and boars upon the main.
Thus they who would take aim, but want the skill,
Miss always, and shoot wide, or narrow still.
One of the meanest workmen in the town
Can imitate the nails, or hair in stone,
And to the life enough perhaps, who yet
Wants mastery to make the work complete.
Troth, sir, if 'twere my fancy to compose,
Rather than be this bungling wretch, I'd choose
To wear a crooked and unsightly nose,
'Mongst other handsome features of a face,
Which only would set off my ugliness.
    Be sure all you that undertake to write,
To choose a subject for your genius fit;
Try long and often what your talents are;
What is the burthen which your parts will bear,
And where they'll fail; he that discerns with skill
To cull his argument and matter well,
Will never be to seek for eloquence
To dress, or method to dispose his sense.
They the chief art and grace in order show
(If I may claim any pretence to know)
Who time discreetly what's to be discoursed,
What should be said at last, and what at first;
Some passages at present may be heard,
Others till afterward are best deferred;
Verse, which disdains the laws of history,
Speaks things not as they are, but ought to be;
Whoever will in poetry excel,
Must learn, and use his hidden secret well.
    'Tis next to be observed, that care is due,
And sparingness in framing words anew.
You show your mastery, if you have the knack
So to make use of what known word you take,
To give 't a newer sense; if there be need
For some uncommon matter to be said,

Power of inventing terms may be allowed,
Which Chaucer and his age ne'er understood;
Provided always, as 'twas said before,
We seldom, and discreetly use that power.
Words new and foreign may be best brought in,
If borrowed from a language near akin.
Why should the peevish critics now forbid
To Lee and Dryden, what was not denied
To Shakespeare, Ben, and Fletcher heretofore,
For which they praise, and commendation bore?
If Spenser's Muse be justly so adored
For that rich copiousness wherewith he stored
Our native tongue, for God's sake why should I
Straight be thought arrogant, if modestly
I claim and use the self-same liberty?
This the just right of poets ever was,
And will be still, to coin what words they please,
Well fitted to the present age and place.

   Words with the leaves of trees a semblance hold
In this respect, where every year the old
Fall off, and new ones in their places grow;
Death is the fate of all things here below:
Nature herself by art has changes felt,
The Tangier mole (by our great monarch built)
Like a vast bulwark in the ocean set,
From pirates and from storms defends our fleet;
Fens every day are drained, and men now plough,
And sow, and reap, where they before might row;
And rivers have been taught by Middleton*
From their old course within new banks to run,
And pay their useful tribute to the town.

----

* Sir Hugh Middleton, goldsmith, and citizen of London. He procured an Act of Parliament, in 1608, to bring a supply of water to the
City from the streams of Middlesex and Hertfordshire. He nearly
ruined himself by the undertaking, the Corporation refusing to assist
him; but prevailing at last upon the King to take a share in the concern, he completed his work in 1613, when the reservoir at Islington
was opened with great ceremony. The value of a share in the New

If man's and nature's works submit to fate,
Much less must words expect a lasting date;
Many, which we approve for current now,
In the next age out of request shall grow;
And others, which are now thrown out of doors,
Shall be revived, and come again in force,
If custom please, from whence their vogue they draw,
Which of our speech is the sole judge and law.

    Homer first showed us in heroic strains,
To write of wars, of battles, and campaigns,
Kings and great leaders, mighty in renown,
And him we still for our chief pattern own.

    Soft elegy, designed for grief and tears,
Was first devised to grace some mournful hearse;
Since to a brisker note 'tis taught to move,
And clothes our gayest passions, joy and love.
But who was first inventor of the kind,
Critics have sought, but never yet could find.
Gods, heroes, warriors, and the lofty praise
Of peaceful conquerors in Pisa's race,
The mirth and joys which love and wine produce,
With other wanton sallies of a muse,
The stately ode does for its subjects choose.

    · Archilochus to vent his gall and spite,
In keen iambics first was known to write;
Dramatic authors used this sort of verse
On all the Greek and Roman theatres,
As for discourse and conversation fit,
And aptest to drown the noises of the pit.

    If I discern not the true style and air,
Nor how to give the proper character
To every kind of work, how dare I claim
And challenge to myself a poet's name?
And why had I, with awkward modesty,
Rather than learn, always unskilful be? ,

River, originally worth 100*l*., has since risen to 10,000*l*. Middleton
was knighted for his labours, and created a baronet in 1622.

Volpone and Morose will not admit
Of Catiline's high strains; nor is it fit
To make Sejanus on the stage appear
In the low dress which comic persons wear.
Whate'er the subject be on which you write,
Give each thing its due place and time aright.
　　Yet comedy sometimes may raise her style,
And angry Chremes is allowed to swell;
And tragedy alike sometimes has leave
To throw off majesty, when 'tis to grieve:
Peleus and Telephus in misery,
Lay their big words and blustering language by,
If they expect to make their audience cry.
'Tis not enough to have your plays succeed,
That they be elegant; they must not need
Those warm and moving touches which impart
A kind concernment to each hearer's heart,
And ravish it which way they please with art.
Where joy and sorrow put on good disguise,
Ours with the person's looks straight sympathize.
Would'st have me weep? thyself must first begin;
Then, Telephus, to pity I incline,
And think thy case and all thy sufferings mine;
But if thou'rt made to act thy part amiss,
I can't forbear to sleep, or laugh, or hiss.
Let words express the looks which speakers wear;
Sad, fit a mournful and dejected air;
The passionate must huff, and storm, and rave;
The gay be pleasant, and the serious grave.
For nature works, and moulds our frame within,
To take all manner of impressions in;
Now makes us hot, and ready to take fire,
Now hope, now joy, now sorrow does inspire,
And all these passions in our face appear,
Of which the tongue is sole interpreter;
But he whose words and fortunes do not suit,
By pit and gallery both is hooted out.

Observe what characters your persons fit,
Whether the master speak, or Todelet;
Whether a man, that's elderly in growth,
Or a brisk Hotspur in his boiling youth;
A roaring bully, or a shirking cheat,
A court-bred lady, or a tawdry cit;
A prating gossip, or a jilting whore,
A travelled merchant, or a homespun boor;
Spaniard or French, Italian, Dutch, or Dane,
Native of Turkey, India, or Japan.
    Either from history your persons take,
Or let them nothing inconsistent speak;
If you bring great Achilles on the stage,
Let him be fierce and brave, all heat and rage,
Inflexible, and headstrong to all laws,
But those which arms and his own will impose.
Cruel Medea must no pity have,
Ixion must be treacherous, Juno grieve,
Io must wander, and Orestes rave;
But if you dare to tread in paths unknown,
And boldly start new persons of your own,
Be sure to make them in one strain agree,
And let the end like the beginning be.
    'Tis difficult for writers to succeed
On arguments which none before have tried;
The *Iliad*, or the *Odyssey*, with ease
Will better furnish subjects for your plays,
Than that you should your own invention trust,
And broach unheard of things yourself the first.
In copying other works, to make them pass,
And seem your own, let these few rules take place:
When you some of their story represent,
Take care that you new episodes invent;
Be not too nice the author's words to trace,
But vary all with a fresh air and grace;
Nor such strict rules of imitation choose,
Which you must still be tied to follow close,

Or, forced to a retreat for want of room,
Give over, and ridiculous become.
    Do not, like that affected fool, begin,
'King Priam's fate, and Troy's famed war, I sing!'
What will this mighty promiser produce?
You look for mountains, and out creeps a mouse.
How short is this of Homer's fine address
And art, who ne'er says anything amiss?
'Muse, speak the man, who, since Troy's laying waste,
Into such numerous dangers has been cast,
So many towns and various people passed.'
He does not lavish at a blaze his fire,
To glare awhile, and in a snuff expire;
But modestly at first conceals his light;
In dazzling wonders then breaks forth to sight,
Surprises you with miracles all o'er,
Makes dreadful Scylla and Charybdis roar,
Cyclops, and bloody Lestrygons devour;
Nor does he time in long preambles spend,
Describing Meleager's rueful end,
When he's of Diomed's return to treat;
Nor when he would the Trojan war relate,
The tale of brooding Leda's eggs repeat;
But still to the designed event hastes on,
And at first dash, as if before 'twere known,
Embarks you in the middle of the plot,
And what is unimprovable leaves out,
And mixes truth and fiction skilfully,
That nothing in the whole may disagree.
    Whoe'er you are, that set yourselves to write,
If you expect to have your audience sit
Till the fifth act be done, and curtain fall,
Mind what instructions I shall further tell,
Our guise and manners alter with our age,
And such they must be brought upon the stage.
    A child, who newly has to speech attained,
And now can go without the nurse's hand,

To play with those of his own growth is pleased,
Suddenly angry, and as soon appeased,
Fond of new trifles, and as quickly cloyed,
And loathes next hour what he the last enjoyed.

The beardless youth from pedagogue got loose,
Does dogs and horses for his pleasure choose;
Yielding, and soft to every print of vice,
Resty to those who would his faults chastise,
Careless of profit, of expenses vain,
Haughty, and eager his desires to obtain,
And swift to quit the same desires again.

Those, who to manly years and sense are grown,
Seek wealth and friendship, honour and renown;
And are discreet, and fearful how to act
What after they must alter and correct.

Diseases, ills, and troubles numberless
Attend old men, and with their age increase;
In painful toil they spend their wretched years,
Still heaping wealth, and with that wealth new cares;
Fond to possess, and fearful to enjoy;
Slow, and suspicious in their managery;
Full of delays and hopes, lovers of ease,
Greedy of life, morose, and hard to please;
Envious at pleasures of the young and gay,
Where they themselves now want a stock to play;
Ill-natured censors of the present age,
And what has passed since they have quit the stage;
But loud admirers of Queen Bess's time,
And what was done when they were in their prime.

Thus, what our tide of flowing years brings in,
Still with our ebb of life goes out again;
The humours of fourscore will never hit
One of fifteen, nor a boy's part befit
A full-grown man; it shows no mean address,
If you the tempers of each age express.

Some things are best to act, others to tell;
Those by the ear conveyed do not so well,

Nor half so movingly affect the mind,
As what we to our eyes presented find.
Yet there are many things which should not come
In view, nor pass beyond the tiring-room;
Which, after in expressive language told,
Shall please the audience more than to behold;
Let not Medea show her fatal rage,
And cut her children's throats upon the stage;
Nor Œdipus tear out his eyeballs there,
Nor bloody Atreus his dire feast prepare;
Cadmus, nor Progne their odd changes take,
This to a bird, the other to a snake;
Whatever so incredible you show,
Shocks my belief, and straight does nauseous grow.

    Five acts, no more nor less, your play must have, .
If you'll a handsome third day's share receive.*
Let not a god be summoned to attend
On a slight errand, nor on wire descend,
Unless the importance of the plot engage;
And let but three at once speak on the stage.

    Be sure to make the chorus still promote
The chief intrigue and business of the plot;
Betwixt the acts there must be nothing sung
Which does not to the main design belong;
The praises of the good must here be told,
The passions curbed, and foes of vice extolled;
Here thrift and temperance, and wholesome laws,
Strict justice, and the gentle calms of peace,
Must have their commendations and applause;
And prayers must be sent up to heaven to guide
Blind fortune's blessing to the juster side,
To raise the poor, and lower prosperous pride.

---

  * The custom of paying writers for the stage by the profits of the third night prevailed generally at this period, and not many years have elapsed since it was finally abandoned. But the rule was not arbitrary. At an earlier date, the second night's profits were assigned to the author, and, in Henslowe's time, plays were frequently purchased, and paid for in advance.

At first the music of our stage was rude,
Whilst in the cockpit and Blackfriars it stood ;
And this might please enough in former reigns,
A thrifty, thin, and bashful audience,
When *Bussy d'Ambois** and his fustian took,
And men were ravished with *Queen Gordobuc.*†
But since our monarch, by kind heaven sent,
Brought back the arts with him from banishment,
And by his gentle influence gave increase
To all the harmless luxuries of peace ;
Favoured by him, our stage has flourished too,
And every day in outward splendour grew ;
In music, song, and dance of every kind,
And all the grace of action 'tis refined ;
And since that opera 's at length come in,
Our players have so well improved the scene
With gallantry of habit, and machine,
As makes our theatre in glory vie
With the best ages of antiquity ;‡
And mighty Roscius were he living now,
Would envy both our stage and acting too. §
    Those who did first in tragedy essay,
(When the vile groat was all the poet's pay)

---

* By Chapman.

† By Sackville, Lord Buckhurst. The same mistake was made in the sex of *Gordubuc* by Dryden, from whom it was copied, probably, by Oldham.

‡ The improvements in scenery and machinery (of which the first magnificent example was the *Aglaura* of Suckling), and the introduction of foreign operas, noticed with such applause by Oldham, were reprobated by Dryden as one of the causes of the degeneracy of the drama.

§ While Oldham was thus recording the prosperity of the stage, the dramatists were bitterly deploring its decline. At this very time the theatres were on the verge of bankruptcy in consequence of the political agitation, and the actors were migrating from the metropolis to the provinces in the hope of bettering their fortunes. Thus Dryden, in an epilogue spoken towards the close of 1681, describes the state of the players :

' We act by fits and starts, like drowning men,
    But just peep up, and then pop down again.
    Let those who call us wicked change their sense,
    For never men lived more on Providence.
    Not lottery cavaliers are half so poor,' &c.
                    DRYDEN, Ann. Ed. iii. p. 257.

Used to allay their subjects' gravity
With interludes of mirth and raillery;
Here they brought rough and naked satyrs in,
Whose farce-like gesture, motion, speech and mien,
Resemble those of modern harlequin;
Because such antic tricks, and odd grimace,
After their drunken feasts on holidays,
The giddy and hot-headed rout would please:
As the wild feats of merry-andrews now,
Divert the senseless crowd at Bartholomew.

But he that would in this mock-way excel,
And exercise the art of railing well,
Had need with diligence observe this rule,
In turning serious things to ridicule:
If he a hero, or a god bring in,
With kingly robes and sceptre lately seen,
Let them not speak, like burlesque characters,
The wit of Billingsgate and Temple-stairs;
Nor, while they of those meannesses beware,
In tearing lines of Bajazet appear.
Majestic tragedy as much disdains
To condescend to low and trivial strains,
As a court-lady thinks herself disgraced
To dance with dowdies at a May-pole feast.

If in this kind you will attempt to write,
You must no broad and clownish words admit;
Nor must you so confound your characters,
As not to mind what person 'tis appears.
Take a known subject, and invent it well,
And let your style be smooth and natural;
Though others think it easy to attain,
They'll find it hard, and imitate in vain:
So much does method and connexion grace
The commonest things, the plainest matters raise.

In my opinion, 'tis absurd and odd
To make wild satyrs, coming from the wood,
Speak the fine language of the Park and Mall,
As if they had their training at Whitehall.

Yet, though I would not have their words too quaint,
Much less can I allow them impudent;
For men of breeding and of quality
Must needs be shocked with fulsome ribaldry,
Which, though it pass the footboy and the cit,
Is always nauseous to the box and pit.
    There are but few, who have such skilful ears,
To judge of artless and ill-measured verse.
This till of late was hardly understood,
And still there's too much liberty allowed.
But will you therefore be so much a fool
To write at random, and neglect a rule?
Or, while your faults are set to general view,
Hope all men should be blind, or pardon you?
Who would not such foolhardiness condemn,
Where, though perchance you may escape from blame,
Yet praise you never can expect, or claim?
Therefore be sure you study to apply
To the great patterns of antiquity;
Ne'er lay the Greeks and Romans out of sight,
Ply them by day, and think on them by night.
Rough hobbling numbers were allowed for rhyme,
And clench for deep conceit in former time;
With too much patience (not to call it worse)
Both were applauded in our ancestors;
If you or I have sense to judge aright,
Betwixt a quibble and true sterling wit;
Or ear enough to give the difference
Of sweet well sounding verse from doggrel strains.
    Thespis, 'tis said, did tragedy devise,
Unknown before, and rude at its first rise;
In carts the gypsy actors strolled about,
With faces smeared with lees of wine and soot,
And through the towns amused the wondering rout;
Till Æschylus appearing to the age,
Contrived a playhouse, and convenient stage,
Found out the use of vizards, and a dress,
(A handsomer, and more genteel disguise)

And taught the actors with a stately air
And mien to speak, and tread, and whatsoe'er
Gave port and grandeur to the theatre.
　　Next this, succeeded ancient comedy,
With good applause, till too much liberty,
Usurped by writers, had debauched the stage,
And made it grow the grievance of the age;
No merit was secure, no person free
From its licentious buffoonery;
Till for redress the magistrate was fain
By law those insolencies to restrain.
　　Our authors in each kind their praise may claim,
Who leave no paths untrod that lead to fame;
And well they merit it, who scorned to be
So much the vassals of antiquity,
As those who know no better than to cloy
With the old musty tales of Thebes and Troy,
But boldly the dull beaten track forsook,
And subjects from our country-story took.
Nor would our nation less in wit appear,
Than in its great performances of war,
Were there encouragements to bribe our care,
Would we to file and finish spare the pains,
And add but justness to our manly sense.
But, sir, let nothing tempt you to belie
Your skill and judgment, by mean flattery;
Never pretend to like a piece of wit,
But what you're certain is correctly writ;
But what has stood all tests, and is allowed
By all to be unquestionably good.
　　Because some wild enthusiasts there be,
Who bar the rules of art in poetry,
Would have it rapture all, and scarce admit
A man of sober sense to be a wit;
Others by this conceit have been misled
So much, that they're grown statutably mad;
The sots affect to be retired alone,
Court solitude, and conversation shun,

In dirty clothes and a wild garb appear,
And scarce are brought to cut their nails and hair,
And hope to purchase credit and esteem,
When they, like Cromwell's porter,* frantic seem;
Strange! that the very height of lunacy,
Beyond the cure of Allen,† e'er should be
A mark of the elect in poetry.
How much an ass am I that used to bleed,
And take a purge each spring to clear my head!
None otherwise would be so good as I,
At lofty strains, and rants of poetry;
But, faith, I am not yet so fond of fame,
To lose my reason for a poet's name.
Though I myself am not disposed to write,
In others I may serve to sharpen wit;
Acquaint them what a poet's duty is,
And how he shall perform it with success;
Whence the materials for his work are sought,
And how with skilful art they must be wrought;
And show what is, and is not, decency,
And where his faults and excellencies lie.

  Good sense must be the certain standard still,
To all that will pretend to writing well;
If you'll arrive at that, you needs must be
Well versed and grounded in philosophy;
Then choose a subject which you thoroughly know,
And words unsought thereon will easy flow.
Whoe'er will write, must diligently mind
The several sorts and ranks of human kind;
He that has learned what to his country's due,
What we to parents, friends, and kindred owe,
What charge a statesman or a judge does bear,
And what the parts of a commander are,
Will ne'er be at a loss (he may be sure)
To give each person their due portraiture.

------

* A poor fellow, so called, who died in Bedlam.
† Dr. Thomas Allen, to whom some allusions will be found in
Pepys.

Take human life for your original,
Keep but your draughts to that, you'll never fail.
Sometimes in plays, though else but badly writ,
With nought of force or grace of art or wit,
Some one well-humoured character we meet,
That takes us more than all the empty scenes,
And jingling toys of more elaborate pens.
　　Greece had command of language, wit, and sense,
For cultivating which she spared no pains;
Glory her sole design, and all her aim
Was how to gain herself immortal fame.
Our English youth another way are bred,
They're fitted for apprenticeship and trade,
And Wingate's all the authors which they've read.
'The boy has been a year at writing-school,
Has learned division and the golden rule;
Scholar enough!' cries the old doting fool,
'I'll hold a piece, he'll prove an Alderman,
And come to sit at church with 's furs and chain.'
This is the top design, the only praise,
And sole ambition of the booby race.
While this base spirit in the age does reign,
And men mind nought but wealth and sordid gain,
Can we expect or hope it should bring forth
A work in poetry of any worth,
Fit for the learnèd Bodley to admit
Among its sacred monuments of wit?
　　A poet should inform us, or divert,
But joining both he shows his chiefest art.
Whatever precepts you pretend to give,
Be sure to lay them down both clear and brief;
By that, they're easier far to apprehend,
By this, more faithfully preserved in mind;
All things superfluous are apt to cloy
The judgment, and surcharge the memory.
　　Let whatsoe'er of fiction you bring in,
Be so like truth, to seem at least akin;

Do not improbabilities conceive,
And hope to ram them into my belief;
Ne'er make a witch upon the stage appear,
Riding enchanted broomstick through the air;
Nor cannibal a living infant spew,
Which he had murdered, and devoured but now.
The graver sort dislike all poetry
Which does not (as they call it) edify;
And youthful sparks as much that wit despise,
Which is not strewed with pleasant gaieties;
But he that has the knack of mingling well
What is of use with what's agreeable,
That knows at once how to instruct and please,
Is justly crowned by all men's suffrages:
These are the works, which, valued everywhere,
Enrich Paul's Churchyard, and the stationer;
These, admiration through all nations claim,
And through all ages spread their author's fame.
    Yet there are faults wherewith we ought to bear:
An instrument may sometimes chance to jar
In the best hand, in spite of all its care;
Nor have I known that skilful marksman yet
So fortunate, who never missed the white.
But where I many excellencies find,
I'm not so nicely critical to mind
Each slight mistake an author may produce,
Which human frailty justly may excuse.
Yet he, who having oft been taught to mend
A fault, will still pursue it to the end,
Is like that scraping fool, who the same note
Is ever playing, and is ever out;
And silly as that bubble every whit,
Who at the self-same blot is always hit.
When such a lewd incorrigible sot
Lights by mere chance upon some happy thought,
Among such filthy trash I vex to see't,
And wonder how the devil he came by't.

In works of bulk and length we now and then
May grant an author to be overseen;
Homer himself, how sacred e'er he is,
Yet claims not a pretence to faultlessness.

   Poems with pictures a resemblance bear;
Some, best at distance, shun a view too near;
Others are bolder, and stand off to sight;
These love the shade, those choose the clearest light,
And dare the survey of the skilfullest eyes;
Some once, and some ten thousand times will please.

   Sir, though yourself so much of knowledge own
In these affairs, that you can learn of none,
Yet mind this certain truth which I lay down:
Most callings else do deference allow,
Where ordinary parts, and skill may do;
I've known physicians who respect might claim,
Though they ne'er rose to Willis's* great fame;
And there are preachers who have great renown,
Yet ne'er come up to Sprat, or Tillotson;
And counsellors, or pleaders in the Hall,
May have esteem and practice, though they fall
Far short of smooth-tongued Finch in eloquence,
Though they want Selden's learning, Vaughan's sense;
But verse alone does of no mean admit;
Whoe'er will please, must please us to the height;
He must a Cowley or a Flecknoe† be,
For there's no second-rate in poetry.
A dull insipid writer none can bear,
In every place he is the public jeer,
And lumber of the shops and stationer.

   No man that understands to make a feast,
With a coarse dessert will offend his guest,

---

* Dr. Willis was the most celebrated physician of his day. Lower, with whom Oldham was intimate, was his pupil and friend, and succeeded him in his practice.

† The Irish priest immortalized by Dryden's satire. A curious sketch of him appears in Marvel's poems.

OLDHAM.   **11**

Or bring ill music in to grate the ear,
Because 'tis what the entertained might spare:
'Tis the same case with those that deal in wit,
Whose main design and end should be delight;
They must by this same sentence stand, or fall,
Be highly excellent, or not at all.
    In all things else, save only poetry,
Men show some signs of common modesty.
You'll hardly find a fencer so unwise,
Who at Bear-garden e'er will fight a prize,
Not having learnt before; nor at a wake
One, that wants skill and strength, the girdle take,
Or be so vain the ponderous weight to sling,
For fear they should be hissed out of the ring.*
Yet every coxcomb will pretend to verse,
And write in spite of nature and his stars;
All sorts of subjects challenge at this time
The liberty and property of rhyme.†
The sot of honour, fond of being great
By something else than title and estate,
As if a patent gave him claim to sense,
Or 'twere entailed with an inheritance,
Believes a cast of footboys, and a set
Of Flanders ‡ must advance him to a wit.
But you who have the judgment to descry
Where you excel, which way your talents lie,

---

* Throwing for the hammer, leaping for slippers, and dancing for the ring were amongst the sports practised at wakes. See Brand's *Antiquities*, by Ellis: Herriot's *Hesperides*.

† Dryden had brought rhyme into universal fashion by his use and defence of it in his heroic plays. But he had renounced the heresy three years before this poem of Oldham's was published. His recantation dates from the production of *All for Love* (the only play, according to Dr. Johnson, he wrote to please himself), in 1678. It was not so easy, however, to check the impulse he had given to the use of rhyme, and we here learn from Oldham that it was the common vice of every coxcomb about town.

‡ Flemish barbs were in general request amongst people of quality, and are frequently mentioned in the comedies of the Restoration. Some of the nobility used to drive six Flemish horses in the time of Elizabeth. The custom is alluded to by Massinger.

I'm sure will never be induced to strain
Your genius, or attempt against your vein.
Yet (this let me advise) if e'er you write,
Let none of your composures see the light
Till they've been thoroughly weighed, and passed the test
Of all those judges who are thought the best;
While in your desk they're locked up from the press,
You've power to correct them as you please;
But when they once come forth to view of all,
Your faults are chronicled, and past recall.
    Orpheus, the first of the inspired train,
By force of powerful numbers did restrain
Mankind from rage and bloody cruelty,
And taught the barbarous world civility;
Hence rose the fiction, which the poets framed,
That lions were by's tuneful magic tamed,
And tigers, charmed by his harmonious lays,
Grew gentle, and laid by their savageness.
Hence that which of Amphion too they tell,
The power of whose miraculous lute could call
The well-placed stones into the Theban wall.
Wondrous were the effects of primitive verse,
Which settled and reformed the universe;
This did all things to their due ends reduce,
To public, private, sacred, civil use;
Marriage for weighty causes was ordained.
That bridled lust, and lawless love restrained;
Cities with walls, and rampiers were enclosed,
And property with wholesome laws disposed;
And bounds were fixed of equity and right,
To guard weak innocence from wrongful might.
Hence poets have been held a sacred name,
And placed them with first-rates in the lists of fame.
Next these, great Homer to the world appeared,
Around the globe his loud alarms were heard,
Which all the brave to warlike action fired;
And Hesiod after him with useful skill
Gave lessons to instruct the ploughman's toil.

Verse was the language of the gods of old,
In which their sacred oracles were told;
In verse were the first rules of virtue taught,
And doctrine thence, as now from pulpits sought;
By verse some have the love of princes gained,
Who oft vouchsafe so to be entertained,
And with a muse their weighty cares unbend.
Then think it no disparagement, dear sir,
To own yourself a member of that choir
Whom kings esteem, and Heaven does inspire.

    Concerning poets there has been contest,
Whether they're made by art or nature best;
But if I may presume in this affair,
Amongst the rest my judgment to declare,
No art without a genius will avail,
And parts without the help of art will fail:
But both ingredients jointly must unite
To make the happy character complete.

    None at Newmarket ever won the prize,
But used his airings and his exercise,
His courses and his diets long before,
And wine and women for a time forbore;
Nor is there any singing-man, we know,
Of good repute in a cathedral now,
But was a learner once, he'll freely own,
And by long practice to that skill has grown.
But each conceited dunce, without pretence
To the least grain of learning, parts, or sense,
Or anything but hardened impudence,
Sets up for poetry, and dares engage
With all the topping writers of the age:
'Why should not he put in among the rest?
Damn him! he scorns to come behind the best;
Declares himself a wit, and vows to draw
On the next man, whoe'er disowns him so.'

    Scribblers of quality who have estate,
To gain applauding fools at any rate,

Practise as many tricks as shopkeepers
To force a trade, and put off naughty wares.
Some hire the house their follies to expose,
And are at charge to be ridiculous;
Others, with wine and ordinaries treat
A needy rabble to cry up their wit:
'Tis strange, that such should the true difference find
Betwixt a spunging knave and faithful friend.
Take heed how you e'er prostitute your sense
To such a fawning crew of sycophants;
All signs of being pleased the rogues will feign,
Wonder, and bless themselves at every line;
Swearing, 'Tis soft! 'tis charming! 'tis divine!'
Here they'll look pale, as if surprised,—and there,
In a disguise of grief, squeeze out a tear;
Oft seem transported with a sudden joy,
Stamp and lift up their hands in ecstasy;
But if by chance your back once turned appear,
You'll have 'em straight put out their tongues in jeer,
Or point, or gibe you with a scornful sneer.
As they who truly grieve at funerals, show
Less outward sorrow than hired mourners do,
So true admirers less concernment wear
Before your face than the sham flatterer.
    They tell of kings, who never would admit
A confidant, or bosom favourite,
Till store of wine had made his secrets float,
And by that means they'd found his temper out.
'Twere well if poets knew some way like this,
How to discern their friends from enemies.
    Had you consulted learnèd Ben of old,
He would your faults impartially have told:
' This verse correction wants,' he would have said,
' And so does this.' If you replied, you had
To little purpose several trials made—
He presently would bid you strike a dash
On all, and put in better in the place;

But if he found you once a stubborn sot,
That would not be corrected in a fault,
He would no more his pains and counsel spend
On an abandoned fool that scorned to mend;
But bid you in the devil's name go on,
And hug your dear impertinence alone.
   A trusty knowing friend will boldly dare
To give his sense and judgment, wheresoe'er
He sees a fault: ' Here, sir, good faith, you're low,
And must some heightning on the place bestow;
There, if you mind, the rhyme is harsh and rough,
And should be softened to go smoothlier off;
Your strokes are here of varnish left too bare,
Your colours there too thick laid on appear;
Your metaphor is coarse, that phrase not pure,
This word improper, and that sense obscure.'
In fine, you'll find him a strict censurer,
That will not your least negligences spare
Through a vain fear of disobliging you.
They are but slight and trivial things, 'tis true;
Yet these same trifles (take a poet's word)
Matter of high importance will afford,
Whene'er by means of them you come to be
Exposed to laughter, scorn, and infamy.
   Not those with ' Lord have mercy!' on their doors,
Venom of adders, or infected whores,
Are dreaded worse by men of sense and wit,
Than a mad scribbler in his raving fit;
Like dog, whose tail is pegged into a bone,
The hooting rabble all about the town
Pursue the cur, and pelt him up and down.
Should this poor frantic, as he passed along,
Intent on 's rhyming work amidst the throng,
Into Fleet-ditch, or some deep cellar fall,
And till he rent his throat for succour bawl,
No one would lend an helping hand at call;
For who, the plague! could guess at his design,
Whether he did not for the nonce drop in?

I'd tell you, sir, but questionless you've heard
Of the odd end of a Sicilian bard:
Fond to be deemed a god, this fool, it seems,
In 's fit leapt headlong into Etna's flames.
Troth, I could be content an act might pass,
Such poets should have leave, whene'er they please,
To die, and rid us of our grievances.
A God's name let 'em hang, or drown, or choose
What other way they will themselves dispose;
Why should we life against their wills impose?
Might that same fool I mentioned now revive,
He would not be reclaimed, I dare believe,
But soon be playing his odd freaks again,
And still the same capricious hopes retain.
    'Tis hard to guess, and harder to allege,
Whether for parricide, or sacrilege,
Or some more strange, unknown, and horrid crime,
Done in their own, or their forefathers' time,
These scribbling wretches have been damned to rhyme:
But certain 'tis, for such a cracked-brained race
Bedlam, or Hogsdon, is the fittest place.
Without their keepers you had better choose
To meet the lions of the Tower broke loose,
Than these wild savage rhymers in the street,
Who with their verses worry all they meet;
In vain you would release yourself; so close
The leeches cleave, that there's no getting loose.
Remorseless they to no entreaties yield,
Till you are with inhuman nonsense killed.

THE PRAISE OF HOMER.

ODE.

I

HAIL, God of Verse! pardon that thus I take in vain
        Thy sacred, everlasting name,
            And in unhallowed lines blaspheme:
Pardon, that with strange fire thy altars I profane.

Hail thou! to whom we mortal bards our faith submit,
Whom we acknowledge our sole text, and holy writ:
   None other judge infallible we own,
But thou, who art the canon of authentic wit alone.
   Thou art the unexhausted ocean, whence
Sprung first, and still do flow the eternal rills of sense.
   To none but thee our art divine we owe,
From whom it had its rise, and full perfection too.
Thou art the mighty bank, that ever dost supply
Throughout the world the whole poetic company;
   With thy vast stock alone they traffic for a name,
And send their glorious ventures out to all the coasts
      of fame.

2

How trulier blind was dull antiquity,
   Who fastened that unjust reproach on thee!
     Who can the senseless tale believe?
Who can to the false legend credit give,
Or think thou wantedst sight, by whom all others see?
   What land, or region, how remote soe'er,
Does not so well described in thy great draughts appear,
   That each thy native country seems to be,   [thee?
And each t' have been surveyed, and measured out by
Whatever earth does in her pregnant bowels bear,
     Or on her fruitful surface wear;
   Whate'er the spacious fields of air contain,
Or far extended territories of the main;
Is by thy skilful pencil so exactly shown,
We scarce discern where thou, or nature best has drawn.
     Nor is thy quick all-piercing eye
       Or checked, or bounded here;
But farther does surpass, and farther does descry,
   Beyond the travels of the sun, and year.
Beyond this glorious scene of starry tapestry,
     Where the vast purlieus of the sky,
      And boundless waste of nature lies,
Thy voyages thou makest, and bold discoveries.

What there the gods in parliament debate,
What votes, or acts i'th' heavenly houses pass,
By thee so well communicated was,
As if thou'dst been of that cabal of state,
As if thou hadst been sworn the privy counsellor of
    fate.

3

What chief who does thy warrior's great exploits
      survey,
  Will not aspire to deeds as great as they?
  What generous readers would he not inspire
With the same gallant heat, the same ambitious fire?
Methinks from Ida's top with noble joy I view
The warlike squadrons, by his daring conduct led;
I see the immortal host engaging on his side,
    And him the blushing gods outdo.
  Where'er he does his dreadful standards bear,
Horror stalks in the van, and slaughter in the rear;
  Whole swarms of enemies his sword does mow,
  And limbs of mangled chiefs his passage strew,
  And floods of reeking gore the field o'erflow;
  While Heaven's dread monarch from his throne of
      state,
  With high concern upon the fight looks down,
And wrinkles his majestic brow into a frown,
  To see bold man, like him, distribute fate.

4

While the great Macedonian youth in nonage grew,
  Nor yet by charter of his years set free
  From guardians, and their slavish tyranny,
No tutor, but the budge philosophers he knew;
  And well enough the grave and useful tools
  Might serve to read him lectures, and to please
With unintelligible jargon of the schools,
And airy terms and notions of the colleges;
They might the art of prating and of brawling teach,
And some insipid homilies of virtue preach;

But when the mighty pupil had outgrown
Their musty discipline, when manlier thoughts pos-
   His generous princely breast,   [sessed
Now ripe for empire and a crown,
And filled with lust of honour and renown,
   He then learnt to contemn
The despicable things, the men of phlegm;
Straight he to the dull pedants gave release,
And a more noble master straight took place:—
Thou, who the Grecian warrior so couldst praise,
   As might in him just envy raise,
Who, one would think, had been himself too high
To envy anything of all mortality,
   'Twas thou that taught'st him lessons loftier far,
   The art of reigning, and the art of war,
   And wondrous was the progress which he made,
   While he the acts of thy great pattern read.
The world too narrow for his boundless conquests
   grew,
   He conquered one, and wished, and wept for new;
   From thence he did those miracles produce,
And fought, and vanquished by the conduct of a muse.

5

No wonder rival nations quarrelled for thy birth,
   A prize of greater and of higher worth
   Than that which led whole Greece and Asia forth,
   Than that for which thy mighty hero fought,
And Troy with ten years' war, and its destruction
   bought.   .
Well did they think it noble to have borne that name,
Which the whole world would with ambition claim;
   Well did they temples raise
To thee, at whom nature herself stood in amaze,
   A work she never tried to amend, nor could,
In which mistaking man, by chance she formed a god.
How gladly would our willing isle resign
Her fabulous Arthur, and her boasted Constantine,

And half her worthies of the Norman line,   [thine!
And quit the honour of their births to be ensured to
 How justly might it the wise choice approve,
Prouder in this than Crete to have brought forth
 Almighty Jove!

6

Unhappy we, thy British offspring here,
Who strive by thy great model monuments to rear;
 In vain for worthless fame we toil,
Who're pent in the straight limits of a narrow isle;
 In vain our force and art we spend
With noble labours to enrich our land,   [stand.
Which none beyond our shores vouchsafe to under-
 Be the fair structure ne'er so well designed,
 The parts with ne'er so much proportion joined, .
Yet foreign bards (such is their pride or prejudice)
All the choice workmanship for the materials' sake
 despise.
 But happier thou thy genius didst dispense
 In language universal as thy sense;
All the rich bullion which thy sovereign stamp does
On every coast of wit does equal value bear,   [wear,
 Allowed by all, and current everywhere.
 No nation yet has been so barbarous found,
 Where thy transcendent worth was not renowned.
 Throughout the world thou art with wonder read,
 Wherever learning does its commerce spread,
 Wherever fame with all her tongues can speak,
Wherever the bright god of wit does his vast journeys
 take.

7

Happy above mankind that envied name,
Which fate ordained to be thy glorious theme:
 What greater gift could bounteous Heaven bestow
 On its chief favourite below?
 What nobler trophy could his high deserts befit,
Than these thy vast erected pyramids of wit?

Not statues cast in solid brass,
Nor those, which art in breathing marble does express,
  Can boast an equal life, or lastingness,
  With their well-polished images, which claim
A niche in thy majestic monuments of fame.
Here their embalmed, incorruptible memories
Can proudest Louvres and Escurials despise,
And all the needless helps of Egypt's costly vanities.
  No blasts of Heaven, or ruin of the spheres,
  Not all the washing tides of rolling years,
Nor the whole race of battering time shall e'er wear
      out
  The great inscriptions which thy hand has wrought;
Here thou and they shall live, and bear an endless
      date,
Firm as enrolled in the eternal register of fate.
  For ever cursed be that mad emperor,
    (And cursed enough he is, be sure)
  May future poets on his hated name
  Shed all their gall and foulest infamy,
And may it here stand branded with eternal shame,
  Who thought thy works could mortal be,
  And sought the glorious fabric to destroy.
  In this (could fate permit it to be done)
  His damned successor he had outgone,
Who Rome and all its palaces in ashes laid,
And the great ruins with a savage joy surveyed:
He burned but what might be rebuilt, and richer made;
  But had the impious wish succeeded here,
  'T had razed what age nor art could e'er repair.
    Not that vast universal flame,
      Which, at the final doom,
  This beauteous work of nature must consume,
And Heaven, and all its glories, in one urn entomb,
  Will burn a nobler or more lasting frame;
  As firm and strong as that, it shall endure,
  Through all the injuries of time secure,
Nor die, till the whole world its funeral pile become.

THE THIRTEENTH SATIRE OF JUVENAL, IMITATED.*

ARGUMENT.—The Poet comforts a friend that is overmuch concerned for the loss of a considerable sum of money, of which he has lately been cheated by a person to whom he intrusted the same. This he does by showing, that nothing comes to pass in the world without Divine Providence, and that wicked men (however they seem to escape its punishment here) yet suffer abundantly in the torments of an evil conscience. And, by the way, takes occasion to lash the degeneracy and villany of the present times.

THERE is not one base act which men commit,
But carries this ill sting along with it,
That to the author it creates regret;
And this is some revenge at least, that he
Can ne'er acquit himself of villany,
Though a bribed judge and jury set him free.

All people, sir, abhor (as 'tis but just)
Your faithless friend, who lately broke his trust,
And curse the treacherous deed; but, thanks to fate,
That has not blessed you with so small estate,
But that with patience you may bear the cross,
And need not sink under so mean a loss.
Besides, your case for less concern does call,
Because 'tis what does usually befall;
Ten thousand such might be alleged with ease,
Out of the common crowd of instances.

Then cease, for shame, immoderate regret,
And don't your manhood and your sense forget;
'Tis womanish and silly to lay forth
More cost in grief than a misfortune's worth.†

---

* Written in April, 1682.

† When remedies are past, the griefs are ended,
By knowing the worst, which late on hopes depended.
To mourn a mischief that is past and gone,
Is the next way to draw new mischief on.
What cannot be preserved when fortune takes,
Patience her injury a mockery makes.
The robbed that smiles steals something from the thief;
He robs himself that spends a bootless grief.
SHAKESPEARE.—*Othello.*

You scarce can bear a puny trifling ill,
It goes so deep, pray Heaven, it does not kill!
And all this trouble, and this vain ado,
Because a friend (forsooth) has proved untrue.
Shame o' your beard! can this so much amaze?
Were you not born in good King Jimmy's days?
And are not you at length yet wiser grown,
When threescore winters on your head have snown?
 Almighty Wisdom gives in Holy Writ
Wholesome advice to all that follow it;
And those that will not its great counsels hear,
May learn from mere experience how to bear
(Without vain struggling) fortune's yoke, and how
They ought her rudest shocks to undergo.
There's not a day so solemn through the year,
Not one red letter in the calendar,
But we of some new crime discovered hear:
Theft, murder, treason, perjury, what not?
Money by cheating, padding, poisoning got.
Nor is it strange; so few are now the good,
That fewer scarce were left at Noah's flood;
Should Sodom's angel here in fire descend,
Our nation wants ten men to save the land.
Fate has reserved us for the very lees
Of time, where ill admits of no degrees;
An age so bad old poets ne'er could frame,
Nor find a metal out to give 't a name.
This your experience knows, and yet for all
On faith of God, and man, aloud you call,
Louder than on Queen Bess's day the rout
For Antichrist burned in effigy shout.*

---

* 'The horrid designs and contrivances of the Papists,' says a pamphlet, entitled *An Account of the Burning of the Pope at Temple-bar* (1679), 'for many years past, for rooting out the Protestant religion from under heaven in this kingdom, as well as in all the Protestant countries in Europe, has raised such a just indignation in the breast of every good Christian and true Englishman, that the people of this nation have, upon all occasions, endeavoured to discover their generous detestation of those cursed invaders of their religious and civil liber-

But, tell me, sir, tell me, grey-headed boy,
Do you not know what lechery men enjoy
In stolen goods?   For God's sake don't you see
How they all laugh at your simplicity,
When gravely you forewarn of perjury?
Preach up a god, and hell, vain empty names,
Exploded now for idle threadbare shams,

---

ties.'   One of the occasions selected for the display of this ' generous detestation' was that alluded to by Oldham. The commemoration of the day when Queen Bess ascended to the throne, which was celebrated in 1679, 1680, and 1681, by a solemn procession beginning at Moorgate, and winding its way through Bishopsgate-street, down Houndsditch to Aldgate, and thence by Leadenhall-street, Cornhill, past the Royal Exchange, through Cheapside to Temple-bar, where the object of the ceremonial was communicated.   First came six whifflers (pipers or horn blowers, who, going in advance, cleared the way); then, a bell-man ringing a bell, and calling out dolefully, ' Remember Justice Godfrey !'   Next a figure representing the dead body of the justice, mounted on a white horse, with one of his murderers behind to prevent him from falling off, with spots of blood over his dress, &c. ; then a priest, with deadmen's skulls, giving out pardons to all who would undertake to murder Protestants, another priest with a cross, Carmelite and Grey Friars, Jesuits with bloody daggers, followed by bishops, and cardinals, and the Pope's physician carrying Jesuit's powder in one hand, and a urinal in the other ; and lastly the Pope in effigy, in a grand scarlet chair of state, with two boys at his feet, and banners emblazoned with consecrated daggers for murdering Protestant kings and princes.   Behind his holiness stood the devil, hugging and whispering him, and instructing him how to set fire to the city, to destroy his Majesty, and to render other diabolical services to the ' church.   The procession was closed by a hundred and fifty flambeaux, which, it being evening when the demonstration took place, played a conspicuous part in the pageant.   As the procession advanced, it was augmented by thousands of idlers, who manifested their Protestant zeal by vociferous uproar.   Arrived at Temple-bar, where the four statues of Queen Elizabeth, and James, and Charles I. and II. were appropriately adorned, and lighted up with torches, the Pope was brought up close to the gate, and after a song, written in wretched doggrel, was sung by the assembled thousands, a bonfire was made into which his holiness was tumbled ; the devil, who, up to this time, had attended him faithfully, laughing out at the joke and abandoning him to his fate.   ' This last act of his holiness's tragedy,' adds the pamphlet referred to, from which these particulars are derived, ' was attended with such a prodigious shout of the joyful spectators, that it might be heard far beyond Somerset-house, and we hope the sound thereof will reach all Europe.'   Some account will be found in North's *Examen* of a Club, called the Green Ribbon Club, which sat in conclave at a neighbouring tavern to arrange and direct their proceedings.

Devised by priests, and by none else believed,
E'er since great Hobbes the world has undeceived!*
   This might have passed with the plain simple race
Of our forefathers in King Arthur's days;
Ere mingling with corrupted foreign seed,
We learned their vice, and spoiled our native breed;
Ere yet blessed Albion, high in ancient fame,
With her first innocence resigned her name.
Fair dealing then, and downright honesty,
And plighted faith were good security;
No vast engrossments for estates were made,
Nor deeds, large as the lands which they conveyed;
To bind a trust there lacked no formal ties
Of paper, wax, and seals, and witnesses,
Nor ready coin, but sterling promises;
Each took the other's word, and that would go
For current then, and more than oaths do now;
None had recourse to Chancery for defence,
Where you forego your right with less expense;
Nor traps were yet set up for perjurers,
That catch men by the heads, and whip off ears.
Then knave, and villain, things unheard of were,
Scarce in a century did one appear,
And he more gazed at that a blazing star.
If a young stripling put not off his hat
In high respect to every beard he met,
Though a lord's son and heir, 'twas held a crime,
That scarce deserved its clergy in that time;
So venerable then was four years odds,
And grey old heads were reverenced as gods.
   Now if a friend once in an age prove just,
If he miraculously keep his trust,
And without force of law deliver all
That's due, both interest and principal,

---

* Hobbes of Malmesbury, whose *Leviathan* brought down the censure of parliament and the special displeasure of the King, on account of its atheistical principles. Hobbes died in 1679, three years before the date of this Satire.

Prodigious wonder! fit for Stow to tell,
And stand recorded in his Chronicle;*
A thing less memorable would require
As great a monument as London fire.
A man of faith and uprightness is grown
So strange a creature, both in court and town,
That he with elephants may well be shown;
A monster, more uncommon than a whale
At Bridge, the last great comet, or the hail,
Than Thames his double tide, or should he run
With streams of milk or blood to Gravesend down.
You're troubled that you've lost five hundred pound
By treacherous fraud; another may be found,
Has lost a thousand; and another yet,
Double to that; perhaps his whole estate.
    Little do folks the heavenly powers mind,
If they but 'scape the knowledge of mankind.
Observe, with how demure and grave a look
The rascal lays his hand upon the book;
Then, with a praying face and lifted eye,
Claps on his lips, and seals the perjury;
If you persist his innocence to doubt,
And boggle in belief, he'll straight rap out
Oaths by the volley, each of which would make
Pale atheists start, and trembling bullies quake;
And more than would a whole ship's crew maintain
To the East Indies hence, and back again.
'As God shall pardon me, sir, I am free
Of what you charge me with; let me ne'er see
His face in heaven else; may these hands rot,
These eyes drop out, if I e'er had a groat
Of yours, or if they ever touched, or saw't.'

---

* John Stow, the antiquary, like Speed, the contemporary of Spelman and Cotton, was the son of a tailor, and born in London about 1525. His principal works were the *Summary of the Chronicles of England*, and the *Survey of London*. Notwithstanding the high reputation he obtained by these valuable publications, he died in great poverty at the age of eighty, in 1605.

Thus he'll run on two hours in length, till he
Spin out a curse long as the Litany;
Till heaven has scarce a judgment left in store
For him to wish, deserve, or suffer more.
   There are, who disavow all Providence,
And think the world is only steered by chance;
Make God at best an idle looker on,
A lazy monarch lolling in his throne,
Who his affairs does neither mind, nor know,
But leaves them all at random here below;
And such at every foot themselves will damn,
And oaths no more than common breath esteem;
No shame, nor loss of ears, can frighten these,
Were every street a grove of pillories.
Others there be, that own a God, and fear
His vengeance to ensue, and yet forswear:
Thus to himself, says one, 'Let Heaven decree
What doom soe'er, its pleasure will, of me;
Strike me with blindness, palsies, leprosies,
Plague, pox, consumption, all the maladies
Of both the Spittles;* so I get my prize
And hold it sure; I'll suffer these, and more;
All plagues are light to that of being poor.
There's not a begging cripple in the streets,
(Unless he with his limbs has lost his wits,
And is grown fit for Bedlam) but no doubt
To have his wealth would have the rich man's gout.
Grant Heaven's vengeance heavy be; what though?
The heaviest things move slowest still we know;
And, if it punish all that guilty be,
'Twill be an age before it come to me.
God, too, is merciful, as well as just;
Therefore I'll rather his forgiveness trust,
Than live despised and poor, as thus I must;
I'll try and hope he's more a gentleman
Than for such trivial things as these, to damn.
_____
   * The hospitals of St. Thomas in Southwark, and St. Bartholomew
in West Smithfield.

Besides, for the same fact, we've often known
One mount the cart, another mount the throne;
And foulest deeds, attended with success,
No longer are reputed wickedness,
Disguised with virtue's livery and dress.'

With these weak arguments they fortify,
And harden up themselves in villany;
The rascal now dares call you to account,
And in what court you please, join issue on't;
Next term he'll bring the action to be tried,
And twenty witnesses to swear on 's side;
And if that justice to his cause be found,
Expects a verdict of five hundred pound.
Thus he, who boldly dares the guilt out-face,
For innocent shall with the rabble pass;
While you, with impudence and sham run down,
Are only thought the knave by all the town.

Meantime, poor you at heaven exclaim, and rail,
Louder than Jeffreys* at the bar does bawl:
' Is there a power above? and does he hear?
And can he tamely thunderbolts forbear?
To what vain end do we with prayers adore,
And on our bended knees his aid implore?
Where is his rule, if no respect be had,
Of innocence, or guilt, of good, or bad?
And who henceforth will any credit show
To what his lying priests teach here below?
If this be providence, for aught I see,
Blessed Saint Vaninus!† I shall follow thee:

* Judge Jeffreys.—See p. 214, *note.*

† Lucilio Vanini, born at Tourosano, in the kingdom of Naples, in 1585. He appears to have been a physician by profession, but to have devoted his life to the active diffusion of the doctrines of atheism. He was an indefatigable propagandist, and travelled into Germany and the Low Countries, Geneva, and France, for the purpose of disseminating his opinions. In 1614 he was in London, where he was imprisoned for forty-nine days, and he was banished from Genoa, where he set up as a teacher. After this he attempted to reconcile himself to the church, by pretending to undertake a refutation of the atheistical writers, contriving insidiously to make his arguments in defence of

Little's the odds betwixt such a God, and that
Which atheist Lewis wore upon his hat.'
    Thus you blaspheme, and rave; but pray, sir, try
What comforts my weak reason can apply,
Who never yet read Plutarch, hardly saw,
And am but meanly versed in Seneca.
In cases dangerous, and hard of cure,
We have recourse to Scarborough,* or Lower;†
But if they don't so desperate appear,
We trust to meaner doctors' skill and care.
    If there were never in the world before
So foul a deed, I'm dumb, not one word more;
In God's name, then, let both your sluices flow,
And all the extravagance of sorrow show;
And tear your hair, and thump your mournful breast,
As if your dearest firstborn were deceased.

Christianity so vulnerable as to give an easy victory to the other side. In France he carried the imposition so far as to become a monk in the convent of Guienne, from whence he was afterwards expelled. He obtained high patronage, however, elsewhere; became chaplain to the Mareschal de Bassompierre, with a pension of two hundred crowns, and published, with the King's privilege, a book of *Dialogues*, in which he took some pains to disguise his real convictions; but the Doctors of the Sorbonne detected the fraud, and condemned the book to the flames. Thus exposed, and held up to universal obloquy, he left Paris, and went to Toulouse, where he commenced a course of lectures, in which he openly resumed and defended his former doctrines. For this offence he was prosecuted, and sentenced to be burned to death. His execution took place on the 19th February, 1619. Gramond, the President of the Parliament of Toulouse, describing his character, says of him, that 'he laughed at everything sacred, abominated the incarnation of our Saviour, and denied the being of a God, ascribing all things to chance.'

  * Sir Charles Scarborough, a distinguished fellow of the College of Physicians, knighted for his great attainments by Charles II., who appointed him his principal physician. Dr. Scarborough acquired considerable reputation by his anatomical lectures delivered at Surgeons' Hall, which he continued annually for sixteen or seventeen years, and is stated to have been the first person who introduced geometrical and mechanical reasoning on the muscles. Having espoused the King's side during the civil wars, he was ejected from a fellowship he held at Caius College, Cambridge; but upon the Restoration ample amends were made to him. He died at eighty years of age in 1696.

             † See *ante*, p. 10, *note*.

'Tis granted that a greater grief attends
Departed moneys than departed friends;
None ever counterfeits upon this score,
Nor need he do't; the thought of being poor
Will serve alone to make the eyes run o'er.
Lost money's grieved with true unfeignèd tears,
More true than sorrow of expecting heirs
At their dead fathers' funerals, though here
The back and hands no pompous mourning wear.

But if the like complaints be daily found
At Westminster, and in all courts abound;
If bonds, and obligations can't prevail,
But men deny their very hand and seal,
Signed with the arms of the whole pedigree
Of their dead ancestors to vouch the lie,
If Temple Walks,* and Smithfield† never fail
Of plying rogues, that set their souls to sale
To the first passenger, that bids a price,
And make their livelihood of perjuries;
For God's sake why are you so delicate,
And think it hard to share the common fate?
And why must you alone be favourite thought
Of heaven, and we for reprobates cast out?

The wrong you bear, is hardly worth regard,
Much less your just resentment, if compared

---

* ' My companions, the worthy knights of the most noble order of
the Post, your peripatetic philosophers of the Temple Walks.'—
OTWAY'S *Soldier's Fortune.*

> Retain all sorts of witnesses
> That ply i' th' Temple under trees,
> Or walk the Round with knights of the Post.
>   BUTLER.—*Hudibras.*

The lawyers made appointments with their clients in the Round,
where they discussed their business, the posts being the points of
established rendezvous.—See Mr. Peter Cunningham's *Hand-book of
London.*

† The horse-market in Smithfield was notorious for the cheats practised on purchasers. Pepys, going thither to buy horses for his coach,
records his opinion of the place. ' Here I do see instances of a piece
of craft and cunning that I never dreamed of, concerning the buying
and choosing of horses.'

With greater outrages to others done,
Which daily happen, and alarm the town.
Compare the villains who cut throats for bread,
Or houses fire, of late a gainful trade,
By which our city was in ashes laid;
Compare the sacrilegious burglary,
From which no place can sanctuary be,
That rifles churches of communion-plate,
Which good King Edward's days did dedicate;
Think, who durst steal St. Alban's font of brass,
That christened half the royal Scottish race;
Who stole the chalices at Chichester,
In which themselves received the day before;
Or that bold daring hand, of fresh renown,
Who, scorning common booty, stole a crown;
Compare too, if you please, the horrid plot,
With all the perjuries to make it out,
Or make it nothing, for these last three years;
Add to it Thynne's* and Godfrey's murderers;
And if these seem but slight and trivial things,
Add those, that have, and would have murdered kings.

And yet how little's this of villany
To what our judges oft in one day try?
This to convince you, do but travel down,
When the next Circuit comes, with Pemberton,
Or any of the Twelve, and there but mind,
How many rogues there are of human kind,
And let me hear you, when you're back again,
Say you are wronged, and, if you dare, complain.

None wonder, who in Essex hundreds live,
Or Sheppy Island, to have agues rife;

---

* Thomas Thynne, of Longleat, in Wiltshire, murdered in his coach,
close to Pall Mall, at the bottom of the Haymarket, by assassins hired
by Count Koningsmark, on the night of the 12th February, 1681-2.
Thynne was engaged in marriage to the Lady Elizabeth Percy, and
Koningsmark was instigated to this atrocious act either by jealousy,
or his desire to possess himself of the lady's wealth. He was tried for
the murder, and acquitted; but the assassins he employed were executed on the spot where it took place.

Nor would you think it much in Africa,
If you great lips and short flat noses saw,
Because 'tis so by nature of each place,
And, therefore, there for no strange things they pass.
In lands where pigmies are, to see a crane
(As kites do chickens here) swoop up a man
In armour clad, with us would make a show,
And serve to entertain at Bartholomew;
Yet there it goes for no great prodigy,
Where the whole nation is but one foot high.
Then why, fond man, should you so much admire,
Since knave is of our growth, and common here?
　'But must such perjury escape,' say you,
'And shall it ever thus unpunished go?'
Grant he were dragged to jail this very hour,
To starve, and rot; suppose it in your power
To rack and torture him all kinds of ways,
To hang, or burn, or kill him, as you please;
(And what would your revenge itself have more?)
Yet this, all this would not your cash restore;
And where would be the comfort, where the good,
If you could wash your hands in's reeking blood?
'But, oh, revenge more sweet than life!'　'Tis true,
So the unthinking say, and the mad crew
Of hectoring blades, who for slight cause, or none,
At every turn are into passion blown,
Whom the least trifles with revenge inspire,
And at each spark, like gunpowder, take fire;
These unprovoked kill the next man they meet,
For being so saucy as to walk the street;
And at the summons of each tiny drab,
Cry, 'Damme! Satisfaction!' draw, and stab.
　Not so of old, the mild good Socrates,
(Who showed how high without the help of grace,
Well cultivated nature might be wrought)
He a more noble way of suffering taught,
And, though he guiltless drank the poisonous dose,
Ne'er wished a drop to his accusing foes.

Not so our great, good martyred king of late,
(Could we his blessed example imitate,)
Who, though the great'st of mortal sufferers,
Yet kind to his rebellious murderers,
Forgave, and blessed them with his dying prayers.
  Thus we, by sound divinity and sense,
May purge our minds, and weed all errors thence;
These lead us into right, nor shall we need
Other than them through life to be our guide.
Revenge is but a frailty, incident
To crazed and sickly minds, the poor content
Of little souls, unable to surmount
An injury, too weak to bear affront;
And this you may infer, because we find,
'Tis most in poor unthinking womankind,
Who wreak their feeble spite on all they can,
And are more kin to brute than braver man.
  But why should you imagine, sir, that those
Escape unpunished, who still feel the throes
And pangs of a racked soul, and (which is worse
Than all the pains which can the body curse)
The secret gnawings of unseen remorse?
Believe't, they suffer greater punishment
Than Rome's inquisitors could e'er invent;
Nor all the tortures, racks, and cruelties,
Which ancient persecutors could devise,
Nor all, that Fox's* bloody records tell,
Can match what Bradshaw, and Ravaillac feel,
Who in their breasts carry about their hell.

---

* John Fox, a divine of the English Church, and author of the
Book of Martyrs. He was brought up in the Roman Catholic religion,
and reduced to great distress in consequence of having embraced the
doctrines of the Reformation. In this extremity, while he was one
day sitting in St. Paul's Church, exhausted by long fasting, a person
unknown to him came up, and, putting a sum of money in his hands,
told him that new means of subsistence would shortly be disclosed to
him. The prediction was fulfilled within three days, when he was
taken into the family of the Duchess of Richmond, as tutor to the

I've read this story, but I know not where,
Whether in Hakewill,* or Beard's *Theatre :*†
'A certain Spartan, whom a friend, like you,
Had trusted with a hundred pound or two,
Went to the Oracle, to know if he
With safety might the sum in trust deny.
'Twas answered, ' No, that if he durst forswear,
He should ere long for's knavery pay dear;'
Hence fear, not honesty, made him refund;
Yet to his cost the sentence true he found:
Himself, his children, all his family,
Even the remotest of his whole pedigree,
Perished,' as there 'tis told, ' in misery.'
Now to apply: if such be the sad end
Of perjury, though but in thought designed,
Think, sir, what fate awaits your treacherous friend,
Who has not only thought, but done to you
All this, and more; think, what he suffers now,
And think, what every villain suffers else,
That dares, like him, be faithless, base, and false.

---

children of her nephew, the famous Earl of Surrey. He never was
able to discover the person to whom he was indebted for this season-
able assistance. During the latter part of the reign of Queen Mary,
he was obliged to fly the kingdom, to escape the persecutions of
Gardner, Bishop of Winchester ; and, settling at Basle, on the Rhine,
he supported himself and his family by correcting the press for
Oporinus, the printer. Here he planned his great work, *The History of
the Acts and Monuments of the Church*, better known as *The Book of
Martyrs*. It occupied him eleven years, and amongst those who contributed to his assistance in the collection of materials was Grindal,
afterwards Archbishop of Canterbury. On the death of Queen Mary
(which he is said to have predicted), Fox returned to England, where
he had many powerful friends. Cecil procured for him a prebend
in the Church of Salisbury ; but he refused to subscribe to the Articles
of Conformity. So great was the respect, however, entertained for his
character and his labours, that he was allowed to hold his prebend till
his death, which occurred in 1587, in his 70th year. Fox wrote other
works; but his reputation rests exclusively on *The Acts and Monuments*.
   * Dr. George Hakewill. His works are enumerated by Wood.
   † *The Theatre of God's Judgments* (1597) written, or compiled, by
Dr. Thomas Beard, a puritan minister at Huntingdon, assisted by Dr.
Thomas Taylor. Beard was Oliver Cromwell's schoolmaster.

Pale horror, ghastly fear, and black despair
Pursue his steps, and dog him wheresoe'er
He goes, and if from his loathed self he fly,
To herd, like wounded deer, in company,
These straight creep in and pall his mirth and joy.
The choicest dainties, even by Lumly dressed,
Afford no relish to his sickly taste,
Insipid all as Damocles' feast.
Even wine, the greatest blessing of mankind,
The best support of the dejected mind,
Applied to his dull spirits, warms no more
Than to his corpse it could past life restore.
Darkness he fears, nor dares he trust his bed
Without a candle watching by his side;
And, if the wakeful troubles of his breast
To his tossed limbs allow one moment's rest,
Straightways the groans of ghosts, and hideous screams
Of tortured spirits, haunt his frightful dreams;
Straight then returns to his tormented mind
His perjured act, his injured God, and friend;
Straight he imagines you before his eyes,
Ghastly of shape, and of prodigious size,
With glaring eyes, cleft foot, and monstrous tail,
And bigger than the giants at Guildhall,
Stalking with horrid strides across the room,
And guards of fiends to drag him to his doom;
Hereat he falls in dreadful agonies,
And dead cold sweats his trembling members seize;
Then starting wakes, and with a dismal cry,
Calls to his aid his frighted family;
There owns the crime, and vows upon his knees
The sacred pledge next morning to release.
These are the men whom the least terrors daunt,
Who at the sight of their own shadows faint; -
These, if it chance to lighten, are aghast,
And quake for fear, lest every flash should blast;
These swoon away at the first thunderclap,
As if 'twere not what usually does hap,

The casual cracking of a cloud, but sent
By angry Heaven for their punishment;
And if unhurt they 'scape the tempest now,
Still dread the greater vengeance to ensue.
These the least symptoms of a fever fright,
Water high-coloured, want of rest at night,
Or a disordered pulse straight makes them shrink,
And presently for fear they're ready to sink
Into their graves; their time, they think, is come,
And Heaven in judgment now has sent their doom.
Nor dare they, though in whisper, waft a prayer,
Lest it by chance should reach the Almighty's ear,
And wake his sleeping vengeance, which before
So long has their impieties forbore.
　　These are the thoughts which guilty wretches haunt,
Yet entered, they still grow more impudent;
After a crime, perhaps, they now and then
Feel pangs and strugglings of remorse within,
But straight return to their old course again;
They who have once thrown shame and conscience by,
Ne'er after make a stop in villany;
Hurried along, down the vast steep they go,
And find 'tis all a precipice below.
　　Even this perfidious friend of yours, no doubt,
Will not with single wickedness give out;
Have patience but a while, you'll shortly see
His hand held up at bar for felony;
You'll see the sentenced wretch for punishment
To Scilly Isles, or the Caribbees sent;
Or, if I may his surer fate divine,
Hung like Boroski,* for a gibbet-sign;
Then may you glut revenge, and feast your eyes
With the dear object of his miseries;
And then, at length convinced, with joy you'll find
That the just God is neither deaf nor blind.

---

* Executed for the murder of Mr. Thynne.

A SATIRE, IN IMITATION OF THE THIRD
OF JUVENAL.*

The Poet brings in a friend of his, giving him an account why he removes from London to live in the country.

THOUGH much concerned to lose my dear old
   I must however his design commend   [friend,†
Of fixing in the country; for were I
As free to chose my residence as he,
The Peak, the Fens, the Hundreds, or Land's-end,
I would prefer to Fleet-street, or the Strand.‡
What place so desert, and so wild is there,
Whose inconveniences one would not bear,
Rather than the alarms of midnight fire,
The fall of houses,§ knavery of cits,
The plots of factions, and the noise of wits,
And thousand other plagues, which up and down
Each day and hour infest the cursèd town?
   As fate would have it, on the appointed day
Of parting hence, I met him on the way,

---

* Written in May, 1682.

† In the original this line stands
   ' Though much concerned to *leave* my dear old friend.'
This was evidently a blunder (for which no doubt the printer was solely responsible), as it was plain that Oldham was not going to leave his friend, but that his friend was going to leave him. Boswell supplies the emendation adopted in the text, which was suggested to him by a lady. The third satire of Juvenal, here imitated and applied to London by Oldham, had been previously applied to Paris by Boileau, and was afterwards adopted by Dr. Johnson as the groundwork of his poem of *London*.

‡ Or change the rocks of Scotland for the Strand.
               JOHNSON'S *London*.

' Whether Johnson,' says Boswell, ' had previously read Oldham's imitation I do not know; but it is not a little remarkable that there is scarcely any coincidence found between the two performances though upon the very same subject.' This judgment is hasty. The parallel passages are numerous, and generally there is more strength, though less finish, in Oldham.

§ Here falling houses thunder on your head.—*London*.

Hard by Mile-end, the place so famed of late,
In prose and verse, for the great faction's treat;
Here we stood still, and after compliments
Of course, and wishing his good journey hence,
I asked what sudden causes made him fly
The once loved town, and his dear company;
When, on the hated prospect looking back,
Thus with just rage the good old Timon spake.
  'Since virtue here in no repute is had,
Since worth is scorned, learning and sense unpaid,
And knavery the only thriving trade;
Finding my slender fortune every day
Dwindle, and waste insensibly away,
I, like a losing gamester, thus retreat,
To manage wiselier my last stake of fate;
While I have strength, and want no staff to prop
My tottering limbs, ere age has made me stoop
Beneath its weight, ere all my thread be spun,
And life has yet in store some sands to run,
'Tis my resolve to quit the nauseous town.
  'Let thriving Morecraft* choose his dwelling there,
Rich with the spoils of some young spendthrift heir;
Let the plot-mongers stay behind, whose art
Can truth to sham, and sham to truth convert;
Whoever has a house to build, or set,
His wife, his conscience, or his oath to let;
Whoever has, or hopes for offices,
A navy, guard, or custom-house's place;
Let sharping courtiers stay, who there are great
By putting the false dice on king and state;
Where they, who once were grooms and footboys known,
Are now to fair estates and honours grown;
Nor need we envy them, or wonder much
At their fantastic greatness, since they're such,
Whom fortune oft in her capricious freaks
Is pleased to raise from kennels, and the jakes,

---

* A fashionable head-dresser.

To wealth, and dignity above the rest,
When she is frolic, and disposed to jest.
   'I live in London! What should I do there?
I cannot lie, nor flatter, nor forswear;
I can't commend a book, or piece of wit,
Though a lord were the author, dully writ;
I'm no Sir Sidrophel* to read the stars,
And cast nativities for longing heirs,
When fathers shall drop off; no Gadbury†
To tell the minute when the king shall die,
And you know what—come in; nor can I steer,
And tack about my conscience, whensoe'er,
To a new point, I see religion veer.
Let others pimp to courtier's lechery,
I'll draw no city cuckold's curse on me;
Nor would I do it, though to be made great,
And raised to be chief minister of state.
Therefore I think it fit to rid the town
Of one, that is an useless member grown.
   'Besides, who has pretence to favour now,
But he, who hidden villany does know,
Whose breast does with some burning secret glow?
By none thou shalt preferred or valued be,
That trusts thee with an honest secrecy;
He only may to great men's friendship reach,
Who great men, when he pleases, can impeach.
Let others thus aspire to dignity;
For me, I'd not their envied grandeur buy
For all the Exchange is worth, that Paul's will cost,
Or was of late in the Scotch voyage lost.‡

---

  * *Hudibras*, P. ii. Can. 3. The character of Sidrophel is supposed by some to have been intended for Sir Paul Neal, but by others, with greater probability, for William Lilly.

  † John Gadbury, originally apprenticed to a tailor at Oxford, was a pupil of Lilly's, and afterwards set up in opposition to him as almanac-maker and astrologer.

  ‡ The Duke of York, making a voyage to Edinburgh for the purpose of accompanying the Duchess back to London, was nearly shipwrecked. An account of the disaster is given in a letter from Pepys to Mr. Hewer, 8th May, 1682.—*Diary*, v. 314.

What would it boot, if I, to gain my end,
Forego my quiet, and my ease of mind,
Still feared, at last betrayed by my great friend?
  'Another cause, which I must boldly own,
And not the least, for which I quit the town,
Is to behold it made the common-sewer,*
Where France does all her filth and ordure pour;
What spark of true old English rage can bear
Those, who were slaves at home, to lord it here?
We've all our fashions, language, compliments,
Our music, dances, curing, cooking thence;
And we shall have their poisoning too ere long,†
If still in the improvement we go on.   [view
What would'st thou say, great Harry, should'st thou
Thy gaudy fluttering race of English now,
Their tawdry clothes, pulvilios, essences;
Their Chedreux ‡ perruques, and those vanities,
Which thou, and they of old did so despise?
What would'st thou say to see the infected town
With the foul spawn of foreigners o'er run?
Hither from Paris, and all parts they come,
The spew and vomit of their gaols at home;
To court they flock, and to St. James's-square, .
And wriggle into great men's service there;
Footboys at first, till they, from wiping shoes,
Grow by degrees the masters of the house;

---

* The common-sewer of Paris and of Rome.—*London*.

† The recent death of the Duchess of Orleans, who was poisoned by her husband immediately after her return from her mission to England, is here pointed at. It was a current subject at the time, and is more than once alluded to by Dryden in his prologues; as in the prologue to the *Spanish Friar:*

  ' When murder's out what vice can we advance,
    Unless the new-found poisoning trick of France ?'

‡ So called from Chedreux, a celebrated maker of perruques in Paris. In Etherege's comedy of *The Man of Mode*, Sir Fopling Flutter boasts of his Chedreux periwig, of which Dryden gives a description in the epilogue. Dryden himself wore a Chedreux and a sword when he ate tarts with Mrs. Reeve in the Mulberry-garden.

Ready of wit, hardened of impudence,
Able with ease to put down either Haines,
Both the King's player,* and King's evidence;
Flippant of talk, and voluble of tongue,
With words at will, no lawyer better hung;
Softer than flattering court-parasite,
Or city trader, when he means to cheat,
No calling or profession comes amiss;
A needy monsieur can be what he please.†
Groom, page, valet, quack, operator, fencer,
Perfumer, pimp, Jack-pudding, juggler, dancer:
Give but the word, the cur will fetch and bring,
Come over to the Emperor, or King;
Or, if you please, fly o'er the pyramid,
Which Johnston and the rest in vain have tried.

'Can I have patience, and endure to see
The paltry foreign wretch take place of me,
Whom the same wind and vessel brought ashore,
That brought prohibited goods, and vices o'er?
Then, pray, what mighty privilege is there
For me, that at my birth drew English air?
And where's the benefit to have my veins
Run British blood, if there's no difference
'Twixt me and him, the statute freedom gave,
And made a subject of a true-born slave?

'But nothing shocks, and is more loathed by me,
Than the vile rascal's fulsome flattery;
By help of this false magnifying glass,
A louse or flea shall for a camel pass;
Produce a hideous wight, more ugly far
Than those ill shapes which in old hangings are,
He'll make him straight a beau garçon appear;

---

* Joe Haines, the actor, who went over to the church of Rome, and afterwards made his recantation in a white sheet on the stage.

    † Obsequious, artful, voluble, and gay,
      On Britain's fond credulity they prey. . . . . .
      All sciences a fasting monsieur knows,
      And bid him go to hell to hell he goes.—*London.*

Commend his voice and singing, though he bray
Worse than Sir Martin Marr-all in the play :
And, if he rhyme, shall praise for standard wit,
More scurvy sense than Prynne, and Vicars writ.*
  'And here's the mischief, though we say the same,
He is believed, and we are thought to sham ;
Do you but smile, immediately the beast
Laughs out aloud, though he ne'er heard the jest ;
Pretend you're sad, he's presently in tears,
Yet grieves no more than marble, when it wears
Sorrow in metaphor ; but speak of heat,
' O God! how sultry 'tis!' he'll cry, and sweat
In depth of winter; straight, if you complain
Of cold, the weather-glass is sunk again :
Then he'll call for his frieze campaign, and swear
'Tis beyond eighty, he's in Greenland here.
Thus he shifts scenes, and oftener in a day
Can change his face than actors at a play ;
There's nought so mean can 'scape the flattering
        sot,
Not his lord's snuff-box, nor his powder-spot ;
If he but spit, or pick his teeth, he'll cry,
' How everything becomes you! let me die,
Your lordship does it most judiciously!'
And swear 'tis fashionable if he sneeze,
Extremely taking, and it needs must please.
  ' Besides, there's nothing sacred, nothing free
From the hot satyr's rampant lechery ;
Nor wife, nor virgin-daughter can escape,
Scarce thou thyself, or son avoid a rape ;
All must go pad-locked ; if nought else there be,
Suspect thy very stables' chastity.
By this the vermin into secrets creep,
Thus families in awe they strive to keep.

---

* The 'voluminous' William Prynne, who is said to have written a
sheet for every day of his life ; and John Vicars, an enthusiastic con-
troversialist, whose writings abound in scurrility.

What living for an Englishman is there,
Where such as these get head, and domineer,
Whose use and custom 'tis, never to share
A friend, but love to reign without dispute,
Without a rival, full and absolute?
Soon as the insect gets his honour's ear,
And flyblows some of's pois'nous malice there,
Straight I'm turned off, kicked out of doors, dis-
        carded,
And all my former service disregarded.
    ' But leaving these messieurs, for fear that I
Be thought of the silk-weaver's mutiny,
From the loathed subject let us hasten on,
To mention other grievances in town:
And further, what respect at all is had
Of poor men here? and how's their service paid,
Though they be ne'er so diligent to wait,
To sneak, and dance attendance on the great?
No mark of favour is to be obtained
By one that sues, and brings an empty hand;
And all his merit is but made a sport,
Unless he glut some cormorant at court.
    ' 'Tis now a common thing, and usual here,
To see the son of some rich usurer
Take place of nobles, keep his first-rate whore,
And, for a vaulting bout or two, give more
Than a guard-captain's pay; meanwhile the breed
Of peers, reduced to poverty and need,
Are fain to trudge to the Bankside, and there
Take up with porters' leavings, suburb ware,
There spend that blood, which their great ancestor
So nobly shed at Cressy heretofore,
At brothel-fights, in some foul common-sewer.
    ' Produce an evidence, though just he be,
As righteous Job, or Abraham, or he
Whom Heaven, when whole nature shipwrecked was,
Thought worth the saving, of all human race;

Or t'other, who the flaming deluge 'scaped,
When Sodom's lechers angels would have raped;
' How rich he is?' must the first question be;
Next for his manners and integrity:
They'll ask, ' What equipage he keeps, and what
He's reckoned worth in money and estate,
Whether for shrieve he has been known to fine,
And with how many dishes he does dine?'
For look what cash a person has in store,
Just so much credit has he, and no more.
Should I upon a thousand Bibles swear,
And call each saint throughout the calendar
To vouch my oath, it wont be taken here;
The poor slight heaven and thunderbolts, they think,
And heaven itself does at such trifles wink.
　' Besides, what store of gibing scoffs are thrown
On one that's poor and meanly clad in town;
If his apparel seem but overworn,
His stocking out at heel, or breeches torn,
One takes occasion his ripped shoe to flout,
And swears 't has been at prison-gates hung out;
Another shrewdly jeers his coarse cravat,
Because himself wears point; a third his hat,
And most unmercifully shows his wit,
If it be old, or does not cock aright.
Nothing in poverty so ill is borne,
As its exposing men to grinning scorn,
To be by tawdry coxcombs jeered upon,
And made the jesting stock of each buffoon.
' Turn out there, friend!' cries one at church, ' the pew
Is not for such mean scoundrel curs as you;
'Tis for your betters kept;' belike some sot
That knew no father, was on bulks begot,
But now is raised to an estate and pride,
By having the kind proverb on his side;
Let Gripe and Cheatwell take their places there,
And Dash, the scrivener's gaudy sparkish heir,

That wears three ruined orphans on his back ;
Meanwhile, you in the alley stand, and sneak :
And you therewith must rest contented, since
Almighty wealth does put such difference.
What citizen a son-in-law will take,
Bred ne'er so well, that can't a jointure make ?
What man of sense, that's poor, e'er summoned is
Amongst the common council to advise ?
At vestry-consults when does he appear,
For choosing of some parish officer,
Or making leather buckets for the choir ?*
   "'Tis hard for any man to rise, that feels
His virtue clogged with poverty at heels ;†
But harder 'tis by much in London, where
A sorry lodging, coarse and slender fare,
Fire, water, breathing, everything is dear ;
Yet such as these an earthen dish disdain,
With which their ancestors, in Edgar's reign,
Were served, and thought it no disgrace to dine,
Though they were rich, had store of leather coin.
Low as their fortune is, yet they despise
A man that walks the streets in homely frieze ;
To speak the truth, great part of England now,
In their own cloth will scarce vouchsafe to go ;
Only, the statute's penalty to save,
Some few perhaps wear woollen in the grave.

---

   * After the fire of 1666, the Common Council passed an act obliging
the wards of the city to keep in readiness a certain number of leathern
buckets, ladders, hand-squirts, pickaxe sledges, and shod-shovels. By
the same act every alderman was compelled to furnish his quota of
buckets and hand-squirts.
   † Johnson's noble line—
      ' Slow rises worth by poverty depressed,'
casts Oldham's version into shadow. The picture given by Oldham
of the condition of poverty in London in the seventeenth century, con-
trasted with the ostentatious expenditure of the upper and middle
classes, throws a curious light on the miseries that lay under the
sensualities and dissipation of the time. The whole poem is interesting from its details of contemporary characteristics, and in this point
of view more curious than the *London* of Johnson.

Here all go daily dressed, although it be
Above their means, their rank, and quality;
The most in borrowed gallantry are clad,
For which the tradesmen's books are still unpaid;
This fault is common in the meaner sort,
That they must needs affect to bear the port
Of gentlemen, though they want income for't.
   ' Sir, to be short, in this expensive town
There's nothing without money to be done;
What will you give to be admitted there,
And brought to speech of some court minister?
What will you give to have the quarter-face,
The squint and nodding go-by of his Grace?
His porter, groom, and steward must have fees,
And you may see the Tombs, and Tower for less.
Hard fate of suitors! who must pay, and pray
To livery-slaves, yet oft go scorned away.
   ' Whoe'er at Barnet, or St. Albans, fears
To have his lodging drop about his ears,
Unless a sudden hurricane befal,
Or such a wind as blew old Noll to hell?
Here we build slight, what scarce outlasts the lease,
Without the help of props and buttresses;
And houses now-a-days as much require
To be ensured from falling, as from fire.
There, buildings are substantial, though less neat,
And kept with care both wind and water tight;
There, you in safe security are blessed,
And nought, but conscience, to disturb your rest.*
   ' I am for living where no fires affright,
No bells rung backward break my sleep at night;

---

* It appears from this passage that, although London was considerably improved by the widening of the streets when it was rebuilt after the fire, the new houses were slight and unsubstantial. They had the advantage, however, of being built of more durable materials than those they displaced. Stone and brick were first introduced by Alfred the Great, but were not generally adopted for many ages after.

I scarce lie down, and draw my curtains here,
But straight I'm roused by the next house on fire;
Pale, and half dead with fear, myself I raise,
And find my room all over in a blaze;
By this 't has seized on the third stairs, and I
Can now discern no other remedy,
But leaping out at window to get free;
For if the mischief from the cellar came,
Be sure the garret is the last takes flame.*
　'The moveables of Pordage were a bed
For him and 's wife, a basin by its side,
A looking-glass upon the cupboard's head,
A comb-case, candlestick, and pewter spoon
For want of plate, a desk to write upon;
A box without a lid served to contain
Few authors, which made up his Vatican;
And there his own immortal works were laid,
On which the barbarous mice for hunger preyed;
Pordage had nothing, all the world does know,
And yet should he have lost this nothing too,
No one the wretched bard would have supplied
With lodging, house-room, or a crust of bread.
　'But if the fire burn down some great man's house,
All straight are interested in the loss;
The court is straight in mourning sure enough,
The act, commencement, and the term put off;
Then we mischances of the town lament,
And fasts are kept, like judgments to prevent.
Out comes a brief immediately, with speed
To gather charity as far as Tweed.

---

* Fires were of frequent occurrence, and strict precautions were
taken to provide against them. The citizens were ordered to keep
their ashes in a secure part of their dwellings, at a distance from the
staircases, and to quench them with water every night before they
went to bed. Constables were appointed to inspect all houses twice
every year, and, upon a cry of fire, every householder was required to
place an armed man at his door, and to hang out a light if the fire
happened at night.

Nay, while 'tis burning, some will send him in
Timber, and stone to build his house again;
Others choice furniture; some rare piece
Of Rubens, or Vandyke presented is;
There a rich suit of Mortlack tapestry,
A bed of damask or embroidery;
One gives a fine scrutoire, or cabinet,
Another a huge massy dish of plate,
Or bag of gold: thus he at length gets more
By kind misfortune than he had before;
And all suspect it for a laid design,
As if he did himself the fire begin.
Could you but be advised to leave the town,
And from dear plays, and drinking friends be drawn,
A handsome dwelling might be had in Kent,
Surrey, or Essex, at a cheaper rent
Than what you're forced to give for one half year
To lie, like lumber, in a garret here.
A garden there, and well, that needs no rope,
Engine, or pains to crane its waters up;
Water is there through Nature's pipes conveyed,
For which no custom or excise is paid.
Had I the smallest spot of ground, which scarce
Would summer half a dozen grasshoppers,
Not larger than my grave, though hence remote
Far as St. Michael's Mount, I would go to't,
Dwell there content, and thank the Fates to boot.
  ' Here want of rest a-nights more people kills
Than all the college, and the weekly bills;
Where none have privilege to sleep, but those
Whose purses can compound for their repose.
In vain I go to bed, or close my eyes,
Methinks the place the middle region is,
Where I lie down in storms, in thunder rise;
The restless bells such din in steeples keep,
That scarce the dead can in their churchyards sleep;
Huzzas of drunkards, bellmen's midnight rhymes,
The noise of shops, with hawker's early screams,

Besides the brawls of coachmen, when they meet,
And stop in turnings of a narrow street,
Such a loud medley of confusion make,
As drowsy Archer on the bench would wake.
  'If you walk out in business ne'er so great,
Ten thousand stops you must expect to meet;
Thick crowds in every place you must charge through,
And storm your passage wheresoe'er you go;
While tides of followers behind you throng,
And, pressing on your heels, shove you along;
One with a board, or rafter, hits your head,
Another with his elbow bores your side;
Some tread upon your corns, perhaps in sport,
Meanwhile your legs are cased all o'er with dirt;
Here, you the march of a slow funeral wait,
Advancing to the church with solemn state;
There, a sedan and lacquies stop your way,
That bears some punk o'' honour to the play;
Now, you some mighty piece of timber meet,
Which tottering threatens ruin to the street;
Next, a huge Portland stone, for building Paul's,
Itself almost a rock, on carriage rolls;
Which, if it fall, would cause a massacre,
And serve at once to murder, and inter.
  'If what I've said can't from the town affright,
Consider other dangers of the night:
When brickbats are from upper stories thrown,
And empty chamber-pots come pouring down
From garret windows; you have cause to bless
The gentle stars, if you come off with piss;
So many fates attend, a man had need,
Ne'er walk without a surgeon by his side;
And he can hardly now discreet be thought,
That does not make his will ere he go out.*

---

* 'Prepare for death, if here at night you roam,
    And sign your will before you sup from home.'—*London.*
The parallel passages are both imitated from Juvenal; but in Oldham's
time the street dangers were more imminent.

'If this you 'scape, twenty to one you meet
Some of the drunken scourers* of the street,
Flushed with success of warlike deeds performed,
Of constables subdued, and brothels stormed,
These, if a quarrel or a fray be missed,
Are ill at ease a-nights, and want their rest;
For mischief is a lechery to some,
And serves to make them sleep like laudanum.
Yet heated, as they are, with youth and wine,
If they discern a train of flambeaux shine,
If a great man with his gilt coach appear,
And a strong guard of footboys in the rear,
The rascals sneak and shrink their heads for fear.
Poor me, who use no light to walk about,
Save what the parish, or the skies hang out,
They value not; 'tis worth your while to hear
The scuffle, if that be a scuffle, where
Another gives the blows I only bear;
He bids me stand; of force I must give way,
For 'twere a senseless thing to disobey,
And struggle here, where I'd as good oppose
Myself to Preston† and his mastiffs loose.
'Who's there?' he cries, and takes you by the throat;
'Dog! are you dumb? Speak quickly, else my foot
Shall march about your buttocks; whence d'ye come?
From what bulk-ridden strumpet reeking home?
Saving your reverend pimpship, where d'ye ply?
How may one have a job of lechery?'
If you say anything, or hold your peace,
And silently go off, 'tis all a case;
Still he lays on; nay well, if you 'scape so;
Perhaps he'll clap an action on you too
Of battery, nor need he fear to meet
A jury to his turn, shall do him right,
And bring him in large damage for a shoe
Worn out, besides the pains in kicking you.

---

* These disturbers of the peace furnished Shadwell with the subject
of a comedy.   † Keeper of the Bear-Garden in Hockley-Hole.

A poor man must expect nought of redress,
But patience; his best course in such a case
Is to be thankful for the drubs, and beg
That they would mercifully spare one leg,
Or arm unbroke, and let him go away
With teeth enough to eat his meat next day.
    'Nor is this all which you have cause to fear;
Oft we encounter midnight padders here,
When the exchanges and the shops are close,
And the rich tradesman in his counting-house
To view the profits of the day withdraws.
Hither in flocks from Shooter's Hill they come,
To seek their prize and booty nearer home:
'Your purse!' they cry; 'tis madness to resist,
Or strive, with a cocked pistol at your breast.
And these each day so strong and numerous grow,
The town can scarce afford them jail-room now.
Happy the times of the old Heptarchy,
Ere London knew so much of villany;
Then fatal carts through Holborn seldom went,
And Tyburn with few pilgrims was content;
A less, and single prison then would do,
And served the City and the County too.
    'These are the reasons, sir, which drive me hence,
To which I might add more, would time dispense
To hold you longer; but the sun draws low,
The coach is hard at hand, and I must go;
Therefore, dear sir, farewell; and when the town
From better company can spare you down,
To make the country with your presence blessed.
Then visit your old friend amongst the rest;
There I'll find leisure to unlade my mind
Of what remarks I now must leave behind;
The fruits of dear experience, which, with these
Improved, will serve for hints and notices;
And when you write again, may be of use
To furnish satire for your daring muse.'

THE EIGHTH SATIRE OF MONSIEUR BOILEAU, IMITATED.*

The Poet brings himself in, as discoursing with a Doctor of the University upon the subject ensuing.

OF all the creatures in the world that be,
  Beast, fish, or fowl, that go, or swim, or fly
Throughout the globe from London to Japan,
The arrantest fool in my opinion's man.
  'What?' straight I'm taken up, 'an ant, a fly,
A tiny mite, which we can hardly see
Without a perspective, a silly ass,
Or freakish ape?   Dare you affirm, that these
Have greater sense than man?'   Ay, questionless;
Doctor, I find you're shocked at this discourse.
  'Man is,' you cry, 'Lord of the Universe;
For him was this fair frame of nature made,
And all the creatures for his use and aid;
To him alone, of all the living kind,
Has bounteous Heaven the reasoning gift assigned.'
True, sir, that reason ever was his lot,
But thence I argue man the greater sot.
  'This idle talk,' you say, 'and rambling stuff
May pass in satire, and take well enough
With sceptic fools, who are disposed to jeer
At serious things; but you must make't appear
By solid proof.'   Believe me, sir, I'll do't:
Take you the desk, and let's dispute it out.
  Then by your favour, tell me first of all,
What 'tis which you grave doctors wisdom call?
You answer: ' 'Tis an evenness of soul,
A steady temper, which no cares control,
No passions ruffle, nor desires inflame,
Still constant to itself, and still the same;

* Written in October, 1682.

That does in all its slow resolves advance,
With graver steps than benchers when they dance.'
Most true; yet is not this, I dare maintain,
Less used by any, than the fool, called man.
    The wiser emmet, quoted just before,
In summer time ranges the fallows o'er,
With pains and labour, to lay in his store;
But when the blustering north with ruffling blasts
Saddens the year, and nature overcasts,
The prudent insect, hid in privacy,
Enjoys the fruits of his past industry.
No ant of sense was e'er so awkward seen,
To drudge in winter, loiter in the spring.
    But sillier man, in his mistaken way,
By reason, his false guide, is led astray;
Tossed by a thousand gusts of wavering doubt,
His restless mind still rolls from thought to thought;
In each resolve unsteady and unfixed,
And what he one day loathes, desires the next.
    'Shall I, so famed for many a truant jest
On wiving, now go take a jilt at last?
Shall I turn husband, and my station choose
Amongst the reverend martyrs of the noose?
No, there are fools enough besides in town,
To furnish work for satire and lampoon!'
Few months before, cried the unthinking sot,
Who quickly after, hampered in the knot,
Was quoted for an instance by the rest,
And bore his fate as tamely as the best,
And thought that Heaven from some miraculous
      side,
For him alone had drawn a faithful bride.
    This is our image just: such is that vain,
That foolish, fickle, motley creature, man:
More changing than a weathercock, his head
Ne'er wakes with the same thoughts he went to bed;
Irksome to all beside, and ill at ease,
He neither others, nor himself, can please;

Each minute round his whirling humours run,
Now he's a trooper, and a priest anon,
To-day in buff, to-morrow in a gown.*
    Yet, pleased with idle whimsies of his brain,
And puffed with pride, this haughty thing would fain
Be thought himself the only stay and prop,
That holds the mighty frame of nature up;
The skies and stars his properties must seem,
And turnspit angels tread the spheres for him;†
Of all the creatures he's the lord, he cries,
More absolute than the French King of his.
' And who is there,' say you, 'that dares deny
So owned a truth?' That may be, sir, do I.
    But to omit the controversy here,
Whether, if met, the passenger and bear,
This or the other stands in greater fear;
Or, if an act of parliament should pass
That all the Irish wolves should quit the place,
They'd straight obey the statute's high command,
And at a minute's warning rid the land;
This boasted monarch of the world, that awes
The creatures here, and with his beck gives laws;
This titular King, who thus pretends to be
The lord of all, how many lords has he?‡
The lust of money, and the lust of power,
With love and hate, and twenty passions more,
Hold him their slave, and chain him to the oar.
    Scarce has soft sleep in silence closed his eyes,
' Up!' straight says Avarice, ''tis time to rise.'
Not yet: one minute longer. ' Up!' she cries.
The Exchange and shops are hardly open yet.
' No matter: Rise!' But after all, for what?

---

    * This hour a slave, the next a deity.—POPE.

    † In pride, in reasoning pride, our error lies;
       All quit their sphere, and rush into the skies.
       Pride still is aiming at the blest abodes,
       Men would be angels, angels would be gods.—*Ib.*

    ‡ The lord of all things, yet a prey to all.—*Ib.*

'D'ye ask? go, cut the Line, double the Cape,
Traverse from end to end the spacious deep;
Search both the Indies, Bantam, and Japan;
Fetch sugars from Barbadoes, wines from Spain.'
What need all this?   I've wealth enough in store,
I thank the Fates, nor care for adding more.
'You cannot have too much; this point to gain,
You must no crime, no perjury refrain,
Hunger you must endure, hardship, and want,
Amidst full barns keep an eternal Lent,
And though you've more than Buckingham has spent,
Or Cuddon got, like stingy Bethel save,*
And grudge yourself the charges of a grave,
And the small ransom of a single groat,
From sword or halter to redeem your throat.'
And pray, why all this sparing?   'Don't you know?
Only to enrich a spendthrift heir, or so,
Who shall, when you are timely dead and gone,
With his gilt coach and six amuse the town,
Keep his gay brace of punks, and vainly give
More for a night, than you to fine for shrieve.
But you lose time; the wind and vessel waits,
Quick, let's aboard!   Hey for the Downs and Straits.'
    Or, if all-powerful money fail of charms
To tempt the wretch, and push him on to harms,
With a strong hand does fierce ambition seize,
And drag him forth from soft repose and ease;
Amidst ten thousand dangers spurs him on,
With loss of blood and limbs to hunt renown;
Who for reward of many a wound and maim,
Is paid with nought but wooden legs and fame,
And the poor comfort of a grinning fate,
To stand recorded in the next Gazette.
    'But hold,' cries one, 'your paltry gibing wit,
Or learn, henceforth, to aim it more aright;
If this be any, 'tis a glorious fault,
Which through all ages has been ever thought

---

* Alderman Cuddon and Sheriff Slingsby Bethel.

The hero's virtue and chief excellence;
Pray, what was Alexander in your sense?
A fool belike.' Yes, faith, sir, much the same;
A crack-brained huff that set the world on flame;
A lunatic broke loose, who in his fit
Fell foul on all, invaded all, he met;
Who, lord of the whole globe, yet not content,
Lacked elbow-room, and seemed too closely pent.
What madness was't, that, born to a fair throne,
Where he might rule with justice and renown,
Like a wild robber, he should choose to roam,
A pitied wretch, with neither house nor home,
And hurling war and slaughter up and down,
Through the wide world make his vast folly known?
Happy for ten good reasons had it been,
If Macedon had had a Bedlam then;
That there with keepers under close restraint,
He might have been from frantic mischief pent.

But that we mayn't in long digressions now
Discourse all Reynolds,* and the Passions through,
And ranging them in method stiff and grave,
Rhyme on by chapter and by paragraph;
Let's quit the present topic of dispute,
For More and Cudworth to enlarge about;
And take a view of man in his best light,
Wherein he seems to most advantage set.

''Tis he alone,' you'll say, ' 'tis happy he,
That's framed by nature for society;
He only dwells in towns, is only seen
With manners and civility to shine;
Does only magistrates and rulers choose,
And live secured by government and laws.'

---

* Dr. Reynolds, Bishop of Norwich, author, amongst numerous works, of a treatise *Of the Passions and Faculties of the Soul of Man*, 1640. In 1648, he was appointed Dean of Christ Church, Oxford, in the room of Dr. Fell, who was ejected; and in 1651 was himself ejected for refusing the engagement to be faithful to the Commonwealth. At the Restoration he was replaced in his deanery, made one of his Majesty's chaplains, and consecrated Bishop of Norwich.

'Tis granted, sir; but yet without all these,
Without your boasted laws and policies,
Or fear of judges, or of justices;
Whoever saw the wolves, that he can say,
Like more inhuman us, so bent on prey,
To rob their fellow wolves upon the way?
Whoever saw church and fanatic bear,
Like savage mankind one another tear?
What tiger e'er, aspiring to be great,
In plots and factions did embroil the State?
Or when was't heard upon the Libyan plains,
Where the stern monarch of the desert reigns,
That Whig and Tory lions in wild jars
Madly engaged for choice of shrieves and mayors?
The fiercest creatures we in nature find,
Respect their figure still in the same kind;
To others rough, to these they gentle be,
And live from noise, from feuds, from factions free.
    No eagle does upon his peerage sue,
And strive some meaner eagle to undo;
No fox was e'er suborned by spite or hire,
Against his brother fox his life to swear;
Nor any hind, for impotence at rut,
Did e'er the stag into the Arches put,
Where a grave dean the weighty case might state,
What makes in law a carnal job complete;
They fear no dreadful quo warranto writ,
To shake their ancient privilege and right;
No courts of sessions, or assize are there,
No Common-Pleas, King's-Bench, or Chancery-Bar;
But happier they, by nature's charter free,
Secure and safe in mutual peace agree,
And know no other law but equity.
    'Tis man, 'tis man alone, that worst of brutes,
Who first brought up the trade of cutting throats,
Did honour first, that barbarous term, devise,
Unknown to all the gentler savages;
And, as 'twere not enough t' have fetched from hell,
Powder and guns, with all the arts to kill,

Farther to plague the world, he must engross
Huge codes and bulky pandects of the laws,
With doctors' glosses to perplex the cause,
Where darkened equity is kept from light,
Under vast reams of nonsense buried quite.
'Gently, good sir!' cry you, 'why all this rant?
Man has his freaks and passions, that we grant;
He has his frailties and blind sides, who doubts?
But his least virtues balance all his faults.
Pray, was it not this bold, this thinking man,
That measured Heaven, and taught the stars to
    scan;
Whose boundless wit, with soaring wings, durst fly
Beyond the flaming borders of the sky;
Turned nature o'er, and with a piercing view
Each cranny searched, and looked her through and
    through?
Which of the brutes have Universities?
When was it heard that they e'er took degrees,
Or were professors of the faculties?
By law or physic were they ever known
To merit velvet, or a scarlet gown?'
   No, questionless; nor did we ever read
Of quacks with them, that were licentiates made,
By patent to profess the poisoning trade;
No doctors in the desk there hold dispute
About black pudding, while the wondering rout
Listen to hear the knotty truth come out;
Nor virtuosos teach deep mysteries
Of arts for pumping air, and smothering flies.
   But, not to urge the matter farther now,
Nor search it to the depth, what 'tis to know,
And whether we know anything or no;
Answer me only this, what man is there
In this vile thankless age, wherein we are,
Who does by sense and learning value bear?
'Wouldst thou get honour, and a fair estate,
And have the looks and favours of the great?'

Cries an old father to his blooming son;
'Take the right course, be ruled by me, 'tis done.
Leave mouldy authors to the reading fools,
The poring crowds in colleges and schools:
How much is threescore nobles?' Twenty pound.
'Well said, my son, the answer's most profound:
Go, thou knowest all that's requisite to know;
What wealth on thee, what honours haste to flow!
In these high sciences thyself employ,
Instead of Plato, take thy Hodder, boy;
Learn there the art to audit an account,
To what the King's revenue does amount;
How much the Customs and Excise bring in,
And what the managers each year purloin.
Get a case-hardened conscience, Irish proof,
Which nought of pity, sense, or shame can move;
Turn Algerine, Barbarian, Turk, or Jew,
Unjust, inhuman, treacherous, base, untrue;
Ne'er stick at wrong; hang widows' sighs and tears,
The cant of priests to frighten usurers;
Boggle at nothing to increase thy store,
Nor orphans' spoils, nor plunder of the poor;
And scorning paltry rules of honesty,
By surer methods raise thy fortune high.
'Then, shoals of poets, pedants, orators,
Doctors, divines, astrologers, and lawyers,
Authors of every sort, and every size,
To thee their works, and labours shall address,
With pompous lines their dedications fill,
And learnedly in Greek and Latin tell
Lies to thy face, that thou hast deep insight,
And art a mighty judge of what they write.
He that is rich, is everything that is,
Without one grain of wisdom he is wise,
And knowing nought, knows all the sciences;
He's witty, gallant, virtuous, generous, stout,
Well-born, well-bred, well-shaped, well-dressed, what
not?

Loved by the great, and courted by the fair,
For none that e'er had riches found despair;
Gold to the loathsomest object gives a grace,
And sets it off, and makes even Bovey please;
But tattered poverty they all despise,
Love stands aloof, and from the scarecrow flies.'

Thus a staunch miser to his hopeful brat
Chalks out the way that leads to an estate;
Whose knowledge oft with utmost stretch of brain
No higher than this vast secret can attain,
Five and four 's nine, take two, and seven remain.

Go, doctor, after this, and rack your brains,
Unravel Scripture with industrious pains;
On musty fathers waste your fruitless hours,
Correct the critics and expositors;
Outvie great Stillingfleet in some vast tome,
And there confound both Bellarmine and Rome;
Or glean the rabbies of their learnèd store,
To find what Father Simeon has passed o'er;
Then at the last some bulky piece compile,
There lay out all your time, and pains, and skill;
And when 'tis done and finished for the press,
To some great name the mighty work address,
Who, for a full reward of all your toil,
Shall pay you with a gracious nod or smile:
Just recompense of life too vainly spent!
An empty 'Thank you, sir!' and compliment.

But, if to higher honours you pretend,
Take the advice and counsel of a friend;
Here quit the desk, and throw your scarlet by,
And to some gainful course yourself apply;
Go, practise with some banker how to cheat,
There's choice in town, enquire in Lombard-street;
Let Scot and Ockam wrangle as they please;
And thus in short with me conclude the case,
A doctor is no better than an ass.

'A doctor, sir, yourself! Pray have a care,
This is to push your raillery too far.

14—2

But not to lose the time in trifling thus
Beside the point, come now more home and close.
That man has reason is beyond debate,
Nor will yourself, I think, deny me that;
And was not this fair pilot given to steer
His tottering bark through life's rough ocean here?'
 All this I grant; but if in spite of it
The wretch on every rock he sees will split,
To what great purpose does his reason serve,
But to misguide his course, and make him swerve?
What boots it Howard, when it says, " Give o'er
Thy scribbling itch, and play the fool no more,'
If her vain counsels, purposed to reclaim,
Only avail to harden him in shame?
Lampooned and hissed, and damned the thousandth
  time,
Still he writes on, is obstinate in rhyme;
His verse, which he does everywhere recite,
Put all his neighbours and his friends to flight;
Scared by the rhyming fiend, they haste away,
Nor will his very groom be hired to stay.
 The ass, whom nature reason has denied,
Content with instinct for his surer guide,
Still follows that, and wiselier does proceed:
He ne'er aspires with his harsh braying note
The songsters of the wood to challenge out;
Nor, like this awkward smatterer in arts,
Sets up himself for a vain ass of parts;
Of reason void, he sees, and gains his end,
While man, who does to that false light pretend,
Wildly gropes on, and in broad day is blind.
By whimsey led he does all things by chance,
And acts in each against all common sense.
Pleased and displeased with everything at once,
He knows not what he seeks, nor what he shuns;
Unable to distinguish good or bad,
For nothing he is gay, for nothing sad;

At random loves and loathes, avoids, pursues,
Enacts, repeals, makes, alters, does, undoes.*
　Did we, like him, e'er see the dog, or bear,
Chimeras of their own devising fear?
Frame needless doubts, and for those doubts forego
The joys which prompting nature calls them to?
And, with their pleasures awkwardly at strife,
With scaring phantoms pall the sweets of life?
Tell me, grave sir, did ever man see beast
So much below himself, and sense debased,
To worship man with superstitious fear,
And fondly to his idol temples rear?
Was he e'er seen with prayers and sacrifice
Approach to him, as ruler of the skies,
To beg for rain or sunshine on his knees?
No, never; but a thousand times has beast
Seen man, beneath the meanest brute debased,
Fall low to wood and metal heretofore,
And madly his own workmanship adore;
In Egypt oft has seen the sot bow down,
And reverence some deified baboon;
Has often seen him on the banks of Nile
Say prayers to the almighty crocodile;.
And now each day, in every street abroad,
Sees prostrate fools adore a breaden-god.
　'But why,' say you, 'these spiteful instances
Of Egypt and its gross idolatries?
Of Rome and hers, as much ridiculous?
What are these lewd buffooneries to us?
How gather you from such wild proofs as these,
That man, a doctor, is beneath an ass?
An ass! that heavy, stupid, lumpish beast,
The sport and mocking-stock of all the rest?

---

* Chaos of thought and passion, all confused,
　　Still by himself abused, and disabused—
　　Sole judge of truth, in endless error hurled,
　　The glory, jest, and riddle of the world.—POPE.

Whom they all spurn, and whom they all despise,
Whose very name all satire does comprise?'
　　An ass, sir? Yes: pray what should make us laugh?
Now he unjustly is our jeer and scoff.
But, if one day he should occasion find
Upon our follies to express his mind;
If Heaven, as once of old, to check proud man,
By miracle should give him speech again;
What would he say, d'ye think, could he speak out,
Nay, sir, betwixt us two, what would he not?
　　What would he say, were he condemned to stand
For one long hour in Fleet-street, or the Strand,
To cast his eyes upon the motley throng,
The two-legged herd, that daily pass along;
To see their old disguises, furs, and gowns,
Their cassocks, cloaks, lawn sleeves, and pantaloons?
What would he say to see a velvet quack
Walk with the price of forty killed on's back?
Or mounted on a stage, and gaping loud,
Commend his drugs and ratsbane to the crowd?
What would he think on a Lord Mayor's day,
Should he the pomp and pageantry survey?
Or view the judges, and their solemn train,
March with grave decency to kill a man?
What would he think of us, should he appear
In Term amongst the crowds at Westminster,
And there the hellish din and jargon hear,
Where Jeffreys* and his pack, with deep-mouthed notes,
Drown Billingsgate and all its oyster-boats?
There see the judges, sergeants, barristers,
Attorneys, counsellors, solicitors,

---

* Judge Jeffreys, who is clearly indicated here, (the name, in common
with several others, being left blank in the early editions) had not
attained his ultimate infamy when this poem was written; but he was
sufficiently notorious even then to justify the distinction conferred upon
him by the satirist. Shortly before, he had made himself very active in the
Duke of York's interest, and had succeeded in a cause respecting the
Post-office, of considerable importance to his Royal Highness's revenues.
He was knighted in 1680, and made chief justice and a baronet in 1681.

Criers and clerks, and all the savage crew
Which wretched man at his own charge undo?
If after prospect of all this, the ass
Should find the voice he had in Æsop's days;
Then, doctor, then, casting his eyes around
On human fools, which everywhere abound,
Content with thistles, from all envy free,
And shaking his grave head, no doubt he'd cry,
' Good faith, man is a beast as much as we!'

A SATIRE TOUCHING NOBILITY.

OUT OF MONSIEUR BOILEAU.*

'TIS granted, that nobility in man
 Is no wild fluttering notion of the brain,
Where he, descended of an ancient race,
Which a long train of numerous worthies grace,
By virtue's rules guiding his steady course,
Traces the steps of his bright ancestors.
 But yet I can't endure an haughty ass,
Debauched with luxury and slothful ease,
Who, besides empty titles of high birth,
Has no pretence to anything of worth,
Should proudly wear the fame which others sought,
And boast of honour which himself ne'er got.
 I grant, the acts which his forefathers did
Have furnished matter for old Hollinshed,
For which their scutcheon, by the conqueror graced,
Still bears a lion rampant for its crest;
But what does this vain mass of glory boot
To be the branch of such a noble root,

---

* Pope's obligations to Boileau have been to some extent traced by
his critics. That he was also indebted to Oldham, may be easily determined by a comparison between this fluent and spirited version of
one of Boileau's Satires, and the Fourth Epistle of the *Essay on Man*.

If he, of all the heroes of his line
Which in the register of story shine,
Can offer nothing to the world's regard,
But mouldy parchments which the worms have spared?
If sprung, as he pretends, of noble race,
He does his own original disgrace,
And swollen with selfish vanity and pride,
To greatness has no other claim beside,
But squanders life, and sleeps away his days,
Dissolved in sloth, and steeped in sensual ease?
    Meanwhile, to see how much the arrogant
Boasts the false lustre of his high descent,
You'd fancy him comptroller of the sky,
And framed by Heaven of other clay than I.
    Tell me, great hero, you that would be thought
So much above the mean and humble rout,
Of all the creatures which do men esteem?
And which would you yourself the noblest deem?
Put case of horse: No doubt, you'll answer straight,
The racer which has oftenest won the plate;
Who full of mettle, and of sprightly fire,
Is never distanced in the fleet career;
Him all the rivals of Newmarket dread,
And crowds of venturers stake upon his head.
But if the breed of Dragon, often cast,
Degenerate, and prove a jade at last,
Nothing of honour, or respect, we see,
Is had of his high birth, and pedigree;
But, maugre all his great progenitors,
The worthless brute is banished from the course,
Condemned for life to ply the dirty road,
To drag some cart, or bear some carrier's load.
    Then how can you, with any sense, expect
That I should be so silly to respect
The ghost of honour perished long ago,
That's quite extinct, and lives no more in you?
Such gaudy trifles with the fools may pass,
Caught with mere show, and vain appearances;

Virtue's the certain mark, by Heaven designed,
That's always stamped upon a noble mind.
If you from such illustrious worthies came,
By copying them your high extract proclaim;
Show us those generous heats of gallantry,
Which ages past did in those worthies see,
That zeal for honour, and that brave disdain,
Which scorned to do an action base or mean:
Do you apply your interest aright,
Not to oppress the poor with wrongful might?
Would you make conscience to pervert the laws,
Though bribed to do't, or urged by your own cause?
Dare you, when justly called, expend your blood
In service for your king's and country's good?
Can you in open field in armour sleep,
And there meet danger in the ghastliest shape?
   By such illustrious marks as these, I find,
You're truly issued of a noble kind:
Then fetch your line from Albanact, or Knute,
Or, if these are too fresh, from older Brute;
At leisure search all history to find
Some great and glorious warrior to your mind;
Take Cæsar, Alexander, which you please,
To be the mighty founder of your race:
In vain the world your parentage belie,
That was, or should have been, your pedigree.
   But, though you could with ease derive your kin
From Hercules himself in a right line,
If yet there nothing in your actions be,
Worthy the name of your high progeny,
All these great ancestors, whom you disgrace,
Against you are a cloud of witnesses;
And all the lustre of their tarnished fame
Serves but to light and manifest your shame.
In vain you urge the merits of your race,
And boast that blood, which you yourself debase;
In vain you borrow, to adorn your name,
The spoils and plunder of another's fame,

If, where I looked for something great and brave,
I meet with nothing but a fool or knave,
A traitor, villain, sycophant, or slave,
A freakish madman, fit to be confined,
Whom Bedlam only can to order bind,
Or, to speak all at once, a barren limb,
And rotten branch of an illustrious stem.
  But I am too severe, perhaps you'll think,
And mix too much of satire with my ink;
We speak to men of birth and honour here,
And those nice subjects must be touched with care.
Cry mercy, sirs!   Your race, we grant, is known:
But how far backwards can you trace it down?
You answer: For at least a thousand year,
And some odd hundreds, you can make't appear.
'Tis much.   But yet, in short, the proofs are clear;
All books with your forefathers' titles shine,
Whose names have 'scaped the general wreck of time;
But who is there so bold, that dares engage
His honour, that, in this long tract of age,
No one of all his ancestors deceased
Had e'er the fate to find a bride unchaste?
That they have all along Lucretias been,
And nothing e'er of spurious blood crept in,
To mingle and defile the sacred line?
  Cursed be the day, when first this vanity
Did primitive simplicity destroy,
In the blessed state of infant time, unknown,
When glory sprung from innocence alone;
Each from his merit only title drew,
And that alone made kings, and nobles too;
Then, scorning borrowed helps to prop his name,
The hero from himself derived his fame;
But merit, by degenerate time at last,
Saw vice ennobled, and herself debased;
And haughty pride false pompous titles feigned,
To amuse the world, and lord it o'er mankind.

Thence the vast herd of earls and barons came,
For virtue each brought nothing but a name;
Soon after, man, fruitful in vanities,
Did blazoning and armory devise,
Founded a college for the herald's art,
And made a language of their terms apart,
Composed of frightful words, of Chief, and Base,
Of Chevron, Saltier, Canton, Bend, and Fesse,
And whatsoe'er of hideous jargon else
Mad Guilliam and his barbarous volume fills.
   Then, farther the wild folly to pursue,
Plain downright honour out of fashion grew;
But to keep up its dignity and birth,
Expense and luxury must set it forth:
It must inhabit stately palaces,
Distinguish servants by their liveries,
And, carrying vast retinues up and down,
The duke and earl be by their pages known.
   Thus honour to support itself is brought
To its last shifts, and thence the art has got
Of borrowing everywhere, and paying nought.
'Tis now thought mean, and much beneath a lord,
To be an honest man, and keep his word,
Who, by his peerage and protection safe,
Can plead the privilege to be a knave;
While daily crowds of starving creditors
Are forced to dance attendance at his doors;
Till he, at length, with all his mortgaged lands
Are forfeited into the banker's hands.
Then, to redress his wants, the bankrupt peer
To some rich trading sot turns pensioner;
And the next news you're sure to hear, that he
Is nobly wed into the company,
Where for a portion of ill gotten gold,
Himself and all his ancestors are sold;
And thus repairs his broken family,
At the expense of his own infamy.

For if you want estate to set it forth,
In vain you boast the splendour of your birth;
Your prized gentility for madness goes,
And each your kindred shuns and disavows.
But he that's rich is praised at his full rate,
And though he once cried 'Small-coal!' in the street,
Though he, nor one of his e'er mentioned were,
But in the parish-book or register,
Dugdale,* by help of chronicle, shall trace
An hundred barons of his ancient race.

A SATIRE.

ADDRESSED TO A FRIEND THAT IS ABOUT TO LEAVE THE UNIVERSITY, AND COME ABROAD IN THE WORLD.

IF you're so out of love with happiness,
To quit a college life and learnèd ease,
Convince me first, and some good reasons give,
What methods and designs you'll take to live;
For such resolves are needful in the case,
Before you tread the world's mysterious maze.
Without the premises, in vain you'll try
To live by systems of philosophy;
Your Aristotle, Cartes, and Le Grand,
And Euclid too, in little stead will stand.
How many men of choice and noted parts,
Well fraught with learning, languages, and arts,
Designing high preferment in their mind,
And little doubting good success to find,
With vast and towering thoughts have flocked to town,
But to their cost soon found themselves undone,

---

* Sir William Dugdale, joint author with Dodsworth of the *Monasti-con Anglicanum*, the first volume of which was published in 1655, and the second in 1661. Oldham's allusion to him more especially refers to his *Baronage of England*, published in 1675 and 1676.

Now to repent, and starve at leisure left,
Of misery's last comfort, hope, bereft!
  ' These failed for want of good advice,' you cry,
' Because at first they fixed on no employ.'
Well then, let's draw the prospect, and the scene
To all advantage possibly we can.
The world lies now before you, let me hear
What course your judgment counsels you to steer;
Always considered, that your whole estate,
And all your fortune lies beneath your hat.
Were you the son of some rich usurer,
That starved and damned himself to make his heir,
Left nought to do, but to inter the sot,
And spend with ease what he with pains had got;
'Twere easy to advise how you might live,
Nor would there need instruction then to give.
But you, that boast of no inheritance,
Save that small stock which lies within your brains,
Learning must be your trade, and, therefore, weigh
With heed how you your game the best may play;
Bethink yourself awhile, and then propose
What way of life is fitt'st for you to choose.
  If you for orders and a gown design,
Consider only this, dear friend of mine,
The church is grown so overstocked of late,
That if you walk abroad, you'll hardly meet
More porters now than parsons in the street.
At every corner they are forced to ply
For jobs of hawkering divinity;
And half the number of the sacred herd
Are fain to stroll and wander unpreferred.
  If this, or thoughts of such a weighty charge,
Make you resolve to keep yourself at large,
For want of better opportunity,
A school must your next sanctuary be.
Go, wed some grammar-bridewell, and a wife,
And there beat Greek and Latin for your life;

With birchen sceptre there command at will,
Greater than Busby's self, or Doctor Gill;*
But who would be to the vile drudgery bound
Where there so small encouragement is found?
Where you, for recompense of all your pains,
Shall hardly reach a common fiddler's gains?
For when you've toiled, and laboured all you can,
To dung and cultivate a barren brain,
A dancing master shall be better paid,
Though he instructs the heels, and you the head.†

---

* Dr. Busby, the master of Westminster School, equally celebrated for his learning and his severity. He was living when this
poem was written. Dr. Gill, the son of the head master of St. Paul's
School, was at first usher under his father, and afterwards succeeded
him, but was dismissed at the end of five years, it is supposed for his
excessive use of corporal punishments. He subsequently set up a
school in Aldersgate-street, where he died in 1642. The most memorable incident connected with the career of Gill was that Milton, who
entertained high esteem and respect for him, was one of his scholars
at St. Paul's.

† Lloyd, who had passed with equal disgust through these ill-paid
drudgeries, describes the situation of the usher in nearly similar
terms :—

' Were I at once empowered to show
My utmost vengeance on my foe,
To punish with extremest rigor,
I could inflict no penance bigger
Than using him as learning's tool,
To make him usher of a school.
For, not to dwell upon the toil
Of working on a barren soil,
And labouring with incessant pains
To cultivate a blockhead's brains,
The duties there but ill befit
The love of letters, arts, or wit. . . . .
Oh ! 'tis a service irksome more
Than tugging at the slavish oar.
Yet such his task, a dismal truth,
Who watches o'er the bent of youth ;
And while, a paltry stipend earning,
He sows the richest seeds of learning,
And tills *their* minds with proper care,
And sees them their due produce bear,
No joys, alas! his toil beguile,
His *own* lies fallow all the while.'

The Author's Apology.

To such indulgence are kind parents grown,
That nought costs less in breeding than a son;
Nor is it hard to find a father now,
Shall more upon a setting-dog allow,
And with a freer hand reward the care
Of training up his spaniel, than his heir.
    Some think themselves exalted to the sky,
If they light in some noble family;
Diet, a horse, and thirty pounds a year,
Besides the advantage of his lordship's ear,
The credit of the business, and the state,
Are things that in a youngster's sense sound great.
Little the inexperienced wretch does know,
What slavery he oft must undergo,
Who, though in silken scarf and cassock dressed,
Wears but a gayer livery at best;
When dinner calls, the implement must wait,
With holy words to consecrate the meat,
But hold it for a favour seldom known,
If he be deigned the honour to sit down.
Soon as the tarts appear, Sir Crape, withdraw!
Those dainties are not for a spiritual maw;
Observe your distance, and be sure to stand
Hard by the cistern with your cap in hand;
There for diversion you may pick your teeth,
Till the kind voider* comes for your relief.
For mere board wages such their freedom sell,
Slaves to an hour, and vassals to a bell;
And if the enjoyment of one day be stole,
They are but prisoners out upon parole;
Always the marks of slavery remain,
And they, though loose, still drag about their chain.
    And where's the mighty prospect after all,
A chaplainship served up, and seven years' thrall?

------

* The basket, or tray, used for carrying away the relics of the
dinner. Dekker, observes Mr. Halliwell, applies the term to a person
who clears the table; the sense in which it here seems to be employed
by Oldham.

The menial thing, perhaps, for a reward,
Is to some slender benefice preferred,
With this proviso bound, that he must wed
My lady's antiquated waiting maid,
In dressing only skilled, and marmalade.*

Let others, who such meannesses can brook,
Strike countenance to every great man's look;
Let those that have a mind, turn slaves to eat,
And live contented by another's plate;
I rate my freedom higher, nor will I
For food and raiment truck my liberty.
But, if I must to my last shifts be put,
To fill a bladder, and twelve yards of gut,
Rather with counterfeited wooden leg,
And my right arm tied up, I'll choose to beg;
I'll rather choose to starve at large, than be
The gaudiest vassal to dependency.

---

* This picture of the condition of the domestic chaplain is referred
to by Mr. Macaulay as one of the authorities upon which he has founded
a still more elaborate sketch of that class of the clergy. The case was
sometimes even worse than it is represented by Oldham, who pensions
off the young Levite, and marries him to an 'antiquated waiting-maid.'
'With his cure,' says Mr. Macaulay, 'he was expected to take a wife.
·The wife had ordinarily been in the patron's service; and it was well
if she had not been suspected of standing too high in the patron's
favour.'—*Hist. of Eng.*, i. 328. Selden assigns a reason for the contumely
with which the Protestant clergy were treated. 'Ministers with the
Papists [that is their priests] have much respect; with the Puritans
they have much, and that upon the same ground, they pretend both of
'em to come immediately from Christ; but with the Protestants they
have very little, the reason whereof is, in the beginning of the Reformation they were glad to get such to take livings as they could procure
by any invitations, things of pitiful condition. The nobility or gentry
would not suffer their sons or kindred to meddle with the church, and
therefore at this day, when they see a parson, they think him to be
such a thing still, and there they will keep him, and use him accord-
ingly.'—*Table Talk.* Ar. *Minister Divine.*
These young house-priests were very appropriately called 'trencher-
chaplains,' and are frequently alluded to under that name by the
writers of the seventeenth century. Burton, in his *Anatomy of Melancholy*, thus speaks of them, confirming the scandal referred to by Mr.
Macaulay. 'If he be a trencher-chaplain in a gentleman's house, after
some seven years' service he may perchance have a living to the halves,
or some small rectory, with the mother of the maids at length, a poor

'T has ever been the top of my desires,
The utmost height to which my wish aspires,
That Heaven would bless me with a small estate,
Where I might find a close obscure retreat;
There, free from noise and all ambitious ends,
Enjoy a few choice books, and fewer friends,
Lord of myself, accountable to none,
But to my conscience, and my God alone:
There live unthought of, and unheard of die,
And grudge mankind my very memory.
But since the blessing is, I find, too great
For me to wish for, or expect of fate;
Yet, maugre all the spite of destiny,
My thoughts and actions are, and shall be, free.
A certain author, very grave and sage,
This story tells; no matter what the page.
  One time, as they walked forth ere break of day,
The wolf and dog encountered on the way:

---

kinswoman, or a crackt chambermaid to have and to hold during the
time of his life.' A writer in *Notes and Queries* explains the term ' to
the halves' as meaning inadequate, as we should say ' half and half
measures.' Bishop Hall gives a very curious sketch in his *Satires* of
these trencher chaplains :—

> ' A gentle squire would gladly entertaine
> Into his house some trencher-chapelaine,
> Some willing man, that might instruct his sons,
> And that would stand to good conditions.
> First, that he lie upon the truckle-bed,
> While his young master lieth o'er his head ;
> Second, that he do, upon no default,
> Never to sit above the salt;
> Third, that he never change his trencher twice ;
> Fourth, that he use all common courtesies,
> Sit bare at meals, and one half rise and wait;
> Last, that he never his young master beat
> But he must ask his mother to define
> How many jerks she would his breech should line;
> All these observed, he could contented be,
> To give five markes, and winter liverie.'

The custom of marrying off the domestic chaplain to the lady's
waiting-woman is alluded to by Beaumont and Fletcher in the *Woman
Hater*, Act iii., sc. 3.

OLDHAM.   15

Famished the one, meagre, and lean of plight,
As a cast poet, who for bread does write;
The other fat, and plump, as prebend was,
Pampered with luxury and holy ease.
     Thus met, with compliments, too long to tell,
Of being glad to see each other well :
'How now, Sir Towzer?' said the wolf, 'I pray,
Whence comes it that you look so sleek and gay,
While I, who do as well, I am sure, deserve,
For want of livelihood am like to starve?'
     'Troth, sir,' replied the dog, ''t has been my fate,
I thank the friendly stars, to hap of late
On a kind master, to whose care I owe
All this good flesh wherewith you see me now.
From his rich voider every day I'm fed
With bones of fowls, and crusts of finest bread;
With fricassee, ragout, and whatsoe'er
Of costly kickshaws now in fashion are,
And more variety of boiled and roast,
Than a Lord Mayor's waiter e'er could boast.
Then, sir, 'tis hardly credible to tell,
How I'm respected and beloved by all;
I'm the delight of the whole family,
Not darling Shock more favourite than I;
I never sleep abroad, to air exposed,
But in my warm apartment am inclosed;
There on fresh bed of straw, with canopy
Of hutch above, like dog of state I lie.
Besides, when with high fare and nature fired,
To generous sports of youth I am inspired,
All the proud shes are soft to my embrace,
From bitch of quality down to turnspit race;
Each day I try new mistresses and loves,
Nor envy sovereign dogs in their alcoves.
Thus happy I of all enjoy the best,
No mortal cur on earth yet half so blessed;
And farther to enhance the happiness,
All this I get by idleness and ease.'

'Troth,' said the wolf, ' I envy your estate;
Would to the gods it were but my good fate,
That I might happily admitted be
A member of your blessed society!
I would with faithfulness discharge my place
In any thing that I might serve his grace.
But, think you, sir, it would be feasible,
And that my application might prevail?'
   'Do but endeavour, sir, you need not doubt;
I make no question but to bring 't about;
Only rely on me, and rest secure,
I'll serve you to the utmost of my power,
As I am a dog of honour, sir:—but this
I only take the freedom to advise,
That you'd a little lay your roughness by,
And learn to practise complaisance, like me.'
   'For that let me alone, I'll have a care,
And top my part, I warrant, to a hair;
There's not a courtier of them all shall vie
For fawning and for suppleness with me.'
   And thus resolved at last, the travellers
Towards the house together shape their course.
The dog, who breeding well did understand,
In walking gives his guest the upper hand;
And as they walk along, they all the while
With mirth and pleasant raillery beguile
The tedious time and way, till day drew near,
And light came on; by which did soon appear
The mastiff's neck to view all worn and bare.
   This when his comrade spied, 'What means,' said he,
' This circle bare, which round your neck I see?
If I may be so bold ;'—' Sir, you must know,
That I at first was rough and fierce like you,
Of nature cursed, and often apt to bite
Strangers, and else, whoever came in sight;
For this I was tied up, and underwent
The whip sometimes, and such light chastisement;

15—2

Till I at length by discipline grew tame,
Gentle, and tractable, as now I am.
'Twas by this short, and slight severity
I gained these marks and badges which you see.
But what are they? Allons, monsieur! let's go.'
   ' Not one step farther, sir; excuse me now.
Much joy t'ye of your envied, blessed estate,
I will not buy preferment at that rate;
In God's name, take your golden chains for me;
Faith, I'd not be a king, not to be free.
Sir dog, your humble servant, so good bye!'

A SATIRE.

The person of Spenser is brought in, dissuading the author from the study of Poetry, and showing how little it is esteemed and encouraged in this present age.

ONE night, as I was pondering of late
   On all the miseries of my hapless fate,
Cursing my rhyming stars, raving in vain
At all the powers which over poets reign,
In came a ghastly shape, all pale and thin,
As some poor sinner who by priest had been,
Under a long Lent's penance, starved and whipped,
Or parboiled lecher, late from hothouse crept.
Famished his looks appeared, his eyes sunk in,
Like morning gown about him hung his skin,
A wreath of laurel on his head he wore,
A book, inscribed the *Fairy Queen*, he bore.
   By this I knew him, rose, and bowed, and said,
' Hail reverend ghost! all hail most sacred shade!
Why this great visit? why vouchsafed to me,
The meanest of thy British progeny?
Comest thou, in my uncalled, unhallowed muse,
Some of thy mighty spirit to infuse?

If so, lay on thy hands, ordain me fit
For the high cure and ministry of wit;
Let me, I beg, thy great instructions claim,
Teach me to tread the glorious paths of fame;
Teach me, for none does better know than thou,
How, like thyself, I may immortal grow.'
    Thus did I speak, and spoke it in a strain
Above my common rate and usual vein,
As if inspired by presence of the bard,
Who, with a frown, thus to reply was heard
In style of satire, such wherein of old
He the famed tale of *Mother Hubbard* told.
    'I come, fond idiot, ere it be too late,
Kindly to warn thee of thy wretched fate;
Take heed betimes, repent, and learn of me
To shun the dangerous rocks of poetry;
Had I the choice of flesh and blood again,
To act once more in life's tumultuous scene,
I'd be a porter, or a scavenger,
A groom, or anything, but poet here.
Hast thou observed some hawker of the town,
Who through the streets with dismal scream and
     tone,
Cries matches, small-coal, brooms, old shoes and boots,
Socks, sermons, ballads, lies, gazettes, and votes?
So unrecorded to the grave I'd go,
And nothing but the register tell who;
Rather that poor unheard-of wretch I'd be,
Than the most glorious name in poetry,
With all its boasted immortality;
Rather than he, who sung on Phrygia's shore,
The Grecian bullies fighting for a whore;
Or he of Thebes, whom fame so much extols
For praising jockeys and Newmarket fools.
    'So many now, and bad, the scribblers be,
'Tis scandal to be of the company;
The foul disease is so prevailing grown,
So much the fashion of the court and town,

That scarce a man well-bred in either's deemed,
But who has killed, been drunk, and often rhymed.
The fools are troubled with a flux of brains,
And each on paper squirts his filthy sense;
A leash of sonnets and a dull lampoon
Set up an author, who forthwith is grown
A man of parts, of rhyming, and renown.
Even that vile wretch, who in lewd verse each year
Describes the pageants and the good Lord Mayor,
Whose works must serve the next election day
For making squibs, and under pies to lay,
Yet counts himself of the inspired train,
And dares in thought the sacred name profane.*
    'But is it nought,' thou'lt say, 'in front to
       stand,
With laurel crowned by White, or Loggan's hand?†
Is it not great and glorious to be known,
Marked out, and gazed at through the wondering
      town,
By all the rabble passing up and down?'
So Oates and Bedloe have been pointed at,
And every busy coxcomb of the state;

---

* Jordan, who, in 1671, succeeded Tatham as 'city poet,' and continued to produce the annual pageants till 1682, when the usual show
was dropped, and not resumed till 1684, in consequence of the suspen-
sion of the charter of the city by Charles II. This Satire was published
in 1683. Notwithstanding the severity with which he is, justly upon
the main, treated by Oldham, Jordan had some merit as a writer of
pageants, especially in the after-dinner glorification, a part of the enter-
tainment in which he excelled all his predecessors. ' He is the most
humorous of city poets,' says Mr. Fairholt, ' and his songs, in some of
the pageants, are extremely good.' See *Lord Mayors' Pageants*, published by the Percy Society.

      † ' And in the front of all his senseless plays,
      Makes David Loggan crown his head with bays.'
                        DRYDEN.

David Loggan, a native of Dantzic, who settled in England before
the Restoration, was an engraver in high repute at this period. Robert
White was one of his pupils; and ' no man,' says Walpole, ' perhaps
exceeded him in the multiplicity of English heads.' Lists of the por-
traits they executed, collected by Vertue, will be found in Walpole's
Catalogue of Engravers.

The meanest felons who through Holborn go,
More eyes and looks than twenty poets draw.
If this be all, go, have thy posted name
Fixed up with bills of quack, and public shame,
To be the stop of gaping 'prentices,
And read by reeling drunkards, when they pass;
Or else to lie exposed on trading stall,
While the bilked owner hires Gazettes to tell,
'Mongst spaniels lost, that author does not sell.
   ' Perhaps, fond fool, thou soothest thyself in dream,
With hopes of purchasing a lasting name?
Thou think'st, perhaps, thy trifles shall remain,
Like sacred Cowley, or immortal Ben;
But who of all the bold adventurers,
Who now drive on the trade of fame in verse,
Can be ensured in this unfaithful sea,
Where there so many lost and shipwrecked be?
How many poems writ in ancient time,
Which thy forefathers had in great esteem,
Which in the crowded shops bore any rate,
And sold like news-books, and affairs of state,
Have grown contemptible, and slighted since,
As Pordage,* Flecknoe,† or the *British Prince?*‡
Quarles, Chapman, Heywood, Wither had applause,
And Wild, and Ogilby in former days;
But now are damned to wrapping drugs and wares,
And cursed by all their broken stationers. §
And so mayst thou, perchance, pass up and down,
And please awhile the admiring court and town,
Who after shalt in Duck-lane ‖ shops be thrown,

---

  * Samuel Pordage, a writer of wretched doggrel, and one of the swarm of verse-mongers that attacked the *Absalom and Achitophel* of Dryden.—See *ante,* p. 183.
  † The Irish priest immortalized by Dryden in his Satire on Shadwell.
  ‡ An epic poem by the Hon. Edward Howard.
  § The term by which booksellers and publishers were designated.
  ‖ Duck-lane, lying between Little Britain and Smithfield, and now called Duke-street, was as celebrated for book-stalls and second-hand book shops as Grub-street for starving authors.

To mould with Silvester,* and Shirley† there,
And truck for pots of ale next Stourbridge fair,
Then who'd not laugh to see the immortal name
To vile Mundungus made a martyr flame?
And all thy deathless monuments of wit,
Wipe porters' tails, or mount in paper kite?
   ' But, grant thy poetry should find success,
And, which is rare, the squeamish critics please;
Admit it read, and praised, and courted be
By this nice age, and all posterity;
If thou expectest aught but empty fame,
Condemn thy hopes and labours to the flame.
The rich have now learned only to admire;
He, who to greater favours does aspire,
Is mercenary thought, and writes for hire.
Wouldst thou to raise thine, and thy country's fame,
Choose some old English hero for thy theme,
Bold Arthur, or great Edward's greater son,
Or our fifth Harry, matchless in renown;
Make Agincourt and Cressy fields outvie
The famed Lavinian shores, and walls of Troy;
What Scipio, what Mæcenas wouldst thou find,
What Sidney now to thy great project kind?
' Bless me! how great his genius! how each line
Is big with sense! how glorious a design
Does through the whole, and each proportion shine!
How lofty all his thoughts, and how inspired!
Pity, such wondrous thoughts are not preferred;'
Cries a gay wealthy sot, who would not bail,
For bare five pounds, the author out of jail,
Should he starve there, and rot; who, if a brief
Came out the needy poets to relieve,
To the whole tribe would scarce a tester give.

---

    * Joshua Silvester, the translator of Du Bartas.
   † James Shirley, the dramatist. These allusions are curious, as
showing the popular opinion entertained at this time of several writers
who had enjoyed celebrity in their own day, but were treated, under
the Restoration, with contempt, from which some of them have since
been rescued.

But fifty guineas for a punk—good hap!
The peer's well used, and comes off wondrous cheap;
A poet would be dear, and out o' th' way,
Should he expect above a coachman's pay!
For this will any dedicate, and lie,
And daub the gaudy ass with flattery?
For this will any prostitute his sense
To coxcombs void of bounty as of brains?
Yet such is the hard fate of writers now,
They're forced for alms to each great name to bow;
Fawn, like her lap-dog, on her tawdry Grace,
Commend her beauty, and belie her glass,
By which she every morning primes her face;
Sneak to his Honour, call him witty, brave,
And just, though a known coward, fool, or knave;
And praise his lineage and nobility,
Whose arms at first came from the Company.
    "Tis so, 'twas ever so, since heretofore
The blind old bard, with dog and bell before,
Was fain to sing for bread from door to door:
The needy muses all turned gipsies then,
And of the begging trade e'er since have been.
Should mighty Sappho in these days revive,
And hope upon her stock of wit to live,
She must to Creswell's* trudge to mend her gains,
And let her tail to hire, as well as brains.
What poet ever fined for sheriff? or who
By wit and sense did ever Lord Mayor grow?
    'My own hard usage here I need not press,
Where you have every day before your face
Plenty of fresh resembling instances.
Great Cowley's muse the same ill treatment had,
Whose verse shall live for ever to upbraid
The ungrateful world, that left such worth unpaid.
Waller himself may thank inheritance
For what he else had never got by sense.

_____

* Mother Creswell, a notorious personage.

On Butler who can think without just rage,
The glory, and the scandal of the age?
Fair stood his hopes, when first he came to town,
Met everywhere with welcomes of renown,
Courted, and loved by all, with wonder read,
And promises of princely favour fed;
But what reward for all had he at last,
After a life in dull expectance passed?
The wretch at summing up his misspent days
Found nothing left, but poverty and praise;
Of all his gains by verse he could not save
Enough to purchase flannel and a grave;
Reduced to want, he in due time fell sick,
Was fain to die, and be interred on tick;
And well might bless the fever that was sent,
To rid him hence, and his worse fate prevent.
  ' You've seen what fortune other poets share;
View next the factors of the theatre,
That constant mart, which all the year does hold,
Where staple wit is bartered, bought, and sold;
Here trading scribblers for their maintenance
And livelihood trust to a lottery-chance;
But who his parts would in the service spend,
Where all his hopes on vulgar breath depend?
Where every sot, for paying half-a-crown,*
Has the prerogative to cry him down?
Sedley indeed may be content with fame,
Nor care should an ill-judging audience damn;
But Settle, and the rest, that write for pence,
Whose whole estate's an ounce or two of brains,
Should a thin house on the third day appear,
Must starve, or live in tatters all the year.
And what can we expect that's brave and great,
From a poor needy wretch, that writes to eat?
Who the success of the next play must wait
For lodging, food, and clothes, and whose chief care
Is how to spunge for the next meal, and where?

---

* The price to the pit of the theatre.

‘Hadst thou of old in flourishing Athens lived,
When all the learnèd arts in glory thrived,
When mighty Sophocles the stage did sway,
And poets by the state were held in pay;
'Twere worth thy pains to cultivate thy muse,
And daily wonders then it might produce;
But who would now write hackney to a stage,
That's only thought the nuisance of the age?
Go, after this, and beat thy wretched brains,
And toil to bring in thankless idiots' means;
Turn o'er dull Horace, and the classic fools,
To poach for sense, and hunt for idle rules;
Be free of tickets, and the playhouses,
And spend thy gains on tawdry actresses.
   ‘All trades and all professions here abound,
And yet encouragement for all is found;
Here a vile empiric, who by licence kills,
Who every week helps to increase the bills,
Wears velvet, keeps his coach, and jade beside,
For what less villains must to Tyburn ride.
There a dull trading sot, in wealth o'ergrown
By thriving knavery, can call his own
A dozen manors, and, if fate still bless,
Expects as many counties to possess.
Punks, panders, bawds, all their due pensions gain,
And every day the great men's bounty drain;
Lavish expense on wit, has never yet
Been taxed amongst the grievances of state.
The Turkey, Guinea, India gainers be,
And all but the poetic company;
Each place of traffic, Bantam, Smyrna, Zante,
Greenland, Virginia, Seville, Alicant,
And France, that sends us vices, lace, and wine,
Vast profit all, and large returns bring in;
Parnassus only is that barren coast,
Where the whole voyage and adventure's lost.
   ‘Then be advised, the slighted muse forsake,
And Coke and Dalton for thy study take;

For fees each term sweat in the crowded hall,
And there for charters, and cracked titles bawl;
Where Maynard* thrives, and pockets more each year
Than forty laureats of the theatre.
Or else to orders, and the church betake
Thyself, and that thy future refuge make;
There fawn on some proud patron to engage
The advowson of cast punk and parsonage.
Or soothe the court, and preach up kingly right,
To gain a prebend or a mitre by't.
In fine, turn pettifogger, canonist,
Civilian, pedant, mountebank, or priest,
Soldier or merchant, fiddler, painter, fencer,
Jack-pudding, juggler, player, or rope-dancer;†
Preach, plead, cure, fight, game, pimp, beg, cheat, or
     thieve;
Be all but poet, and there's way to live.
  'But why do I in vain my counsel spend
On one whom there's so little hope to mend?
Where I perhaps as fruitlessly exhort,
As Lenten doctors, when they preach at court;
Not gamesters from the snares they once have tried,
Not fops and women from conceit and pride,
Not bawds from impudence, cowards from fear,
Nor seared unfeeling sinners past despair,
Are half so hard and stubborn to reduce,
As a poor wretch when once possessed with muse.
  'If, therefore, what I've said cannot avail,
Nor from the rhyming folly thee recall,
But, spite of all, thou wilt be obstinate,
And run thyself upon avoidless fate;

---

* Sir John Maynard, King's Sergeant, who is said to have made a larger income at the bar than any of his contemporaries.

† Such people were lavishly patronized by the nobility. Ladies of rank were in the habit of inviting jugglers and conjurers to their houses to amuse their company. Richardson, the fire-eater, was one of the most popular of these performers; and Jacob Hall, the rope-dancer, occupies so conspicuous a position in the social annals of the time, that he may be regarded as a sort of spurious historical character.

Mayst thou go on unpitied, till thou be
Brought to the parish, bridge, and beggary;
Till urged by want, like broken scribblers, thou
Turn poet to a booth, a Smithfield show,
And write heroic verse for Bartholomew;
Then slighted by the very Nursery,*
Mayst thou at last be forced to starve, like me.'

COUNTERPART TO THE SATIRE AGAINST VIRTUE.

IN PERSON OF THE AUTHOR.†

I

PARDON me, Virtue, whatsoe'er thou art,
   (For sure thou of the godhead art a part,   .
And all that is of him must be
     The very deity)

---

* The Nursery stood in Barbican. It was a theatre established
under letters patent for training boys and girls in the art of acting.
See DRYDEN'S *Poems*, Ann. Ed. ii. 28, *note*.

† Amongst the pieces published with the *Satires on the Jesuits* was
a Pindaric ode, entitled *A Satire against Virtue*, followed by some
verses designed as an apology for what might otherwise have appeared
to imply a serious attack on morality and religion. In these verses,
which he calls an epilogue, Oldham declares that he has been merely
acting in masquerade, and that the true aim of his satire is to expose
the vices of the age. He avows that his muse on this occasion had
intentionally spoken like one who, by converse with bullies, had grown
wicked, and 'learnèd the mode to cry all virtue down;' but that in
future, should he continue to write, he will adopt a more direct and
open course :—

   ' Though against virtue once he drew his pen,
   He'll ne'er for aught, but her defence again.
   Had he a genius and poetic rage,
   Great as the vices of this guilty age,   '
   Were he all gall, and armed with store of spite,
   'Twere worth his gains to undertake to write;
   To noble satire he'd direct his aim,
   And by't mankind and poetry reclaim;
   He'd shoot his quills, just like a porcupine,
   At vice, and make them stab in every line;
   The world should learn to blush.'

It must be confessed that the *Satire against Virtue* required, not an

Pardon, if I in aught did thee blaspheme,
    Or injure thy pure sacred name:
Accept unfeigned repentance, prayers, and vows,
The best atonement of my penitent humble muse,
The best that heaven requires, or mankind can
        produce.
All my attempts hereafter shall at thy devotion be,
Ready to consecrate my ink and very blood to thee.
Forgive me, ye blest souls that dwell above,
Where you by its reward the worth of virtue prove;
Forgive, if you can do't, who know no passion now
        but love.
    And you unhappy, happy few,
Who strive with life, and human miseries below,
        Forgive me too,
If I in aught disparaged them, or else discouraged you.

2

    Blessed Virtue! whose almighty power
    Does to our fallen race restore
All that in Paradise we lost, and more;
    Lifts us to heaven, and makes us be
    The heirs and image of the deity.
Soft gentle yoke! which none but resty fools refuse,
    Which before freedom I would ever choose.

---

explanation, for its purpose is obvious enough, but an apology, such as
Oldham had the good sense to publish along with it. In that apology
there is a sufficient justification for the exclusion of the piece from this
volume. If Oldham found it necessary to deprecate its coarseness at a
time when no language was considered too gross for satire, there is still
greater reason for rejecting it altogether in the present age. It may be
inferred from the above *Counterpart*, published amongst his *Remains*,
that had he lived to revise and collect his works, he would himself
have cast out a foolish poem which he earnestly regretted having
written. The satire itself comes strictly within Pope's censure. It
is mere bald Billingsgate, and falls flat from the dead weight of
its gratuitous extravagance. Oldham mistook his powers when he
attempted a masquerade of this kind, which requires to be sustained
by the play of covert wit. His strength was in the opposite direction; and he always succeeded best when he went straight to his
object.

Easy are all the bonds that are imposed by thee;
  Easy as those of lovers are,
 (If I with aught less pure may thee compare)
Nor do they force, but only guide our liberty.
 By such soft ties are spirits above confined;
 So gentle is the chain which them to good does bind.
Sure card, whereby this frail and tottering bark we
  Through life's tempestuous ocean here; [steer
  Through all the tossing waves of fear,
  And dangerous rocks of black despair.
Safe in thy conduct, unconcerned we move,
  Secure from all the threatening storms that blow,
  From all attacks of chance below,
And reach the certain haven of felicity above.

3

Best mistress of our souls! whose charms and beauties
  And are by very age increased,   [last,
 By which all other glories are defaced.
 Thou'rt thy own dowry, and a greater far
 Than all the race of womankind e'er brought,
 Though each of them like the first wife were fraught,
 And half the universe did for her portion share.
That tawdry sex, which giddy senseless we
 Through ignorance so vainly deify,
Are all but glorious brutes when unendowed with thee.
  'Tis vice alone, the truer jilt, and worse,
  In whose enjoyment though we find
 A flitting pleasure, yet it leaves behind
  A pain and torture in the mind, [remorse,
And claps the wounded conscience with incurable
Or else betrays us to the great trepans of human kind.

4

 'Tis vice, the greater thraldom, harder drudgery,
 Whereby deposing reason from its gentle sway,
 That rightful sovereign which we should obey,
  We undergo a various tyranny,
And to unnumbered servile passions homage pay.

These with Egyptian rigour us enslave,
And govern with unlimited command;
   They make us endless toil pursue,
   And still their doubled tasks renew,
To push on our too hasty fate, and build our grave,
Or which is worse, to keep us from the promised
     land.
   Nor may we think our freedom to retrieve,
   We struggle with our heavy yoke in vain:
     In vain we strive to break that chain,
     Unless a miracle relieve;
   Unless the Almighty wand enlargement give,
   We never must expect delivery,
Till death, the universal writ of ease, does set us free.

5

Some, sordid avarice in vassalage confines,
   Like Roman slaves condemned to th' mines;
These are in its harsh Bridewell lashed and punishèd,
  And with harsh labour scarce can earn their bread.
   Others, ambition, that imperious dame,
   Exposes cruelly, like gladiators, here
     Upon the world's great theatre.
Through dangers and through blood they wade to fame,
To purchase grinning honour and an empty name,
   And some by tyrant lust are captive led,
     And with false hopes of pleasure fed;
   'Till, tired with slavery to their own desires,
Life's o'ercharg'd lamp goes out, and in a snuff expires.

6

Consider we the little arts of vice,
   The stratagems and artifice
Whereby she does attract her votaries:
   All those allurements, and those charms,
     Which pimp transgressors to her arms,
   Are but foul paint, and counterfeit disguise,
   To palliate her own concealed deformities.
And for false empty joys betray us to true solid harms.

In vain she would her dowry boast,
Which clogged, with legacies, we never gain,
But with invaluable cost;
Which got, we never can retain,
But must the greatest part be lost,
To the great bubbles, age or chance, again.
'Tis vastly over-balanced by the jointure which we make,
In which our lives, our souls, our all is set at stake.
Like silly Indians, foolish we
With a known cheat a losing traffic hold;
Whilst led by an ill-judging eye,
We admire a trifling pageantry,
And merchandize our jewels and our gold,   [pery.
For worthless glass and beads, or an exchange's frip-
If we a while maintain the expensive trade,
Such mighty impost on the cargo's laid,
Such a vast custom to be paid,   [out,
We're forced at last like wretched bankrupts to give
Clapped up by death, and in eternal durance shut.

7

What art thou, Fame, for which so eagerly we strive?
What art thou, but an empty shade
By the reflection of our actions made?
Thou, unlike others, never followest us alive;
But, like a ghost, walkest only after we are dead.
Posthumous toy! vain after-legacy!
Which only ours can be,
When we ourselves no more are we!
Fickle as vain! who dost on vulgar breath depend,
Which we by dear experience find
More changeable, more veering than the inconstant
wind.
What art thou, gold, that cheat'st the miser's eyes?
Which he does so devoutly idolize;
For whom he all his rest and ease does sacrifice?
'Tis use alone can all thy value give,
And he from that no benefit can e'er receive.

OLDHAM.   16

Cursed mineral! near neighbouring hell begot,
Which all the infection of thy damned neighbourhood
　　　hast brought;
　　Thou bawd to murders, rapes, and treachery,
　　And every greater name of villany;
From thee they all derive their stock and pedigree;
Thou the lewd world with all its crying crimes dost
　　store,
And hardly wilt allow the devil the cause of more.
　　And what is pleasure, which does most beguile,
　　That syren which betrays us with a flattering
　　　smile?
　　We listen to the treacherous harmony,
　　Which sings but our own obsequy,
　　The danger unperceived till death draws nigh;
Till, drowning, we want power to 'scape the fatal enemy.

8

　　How frantic is the wanton epicure,
　　Who a perpetual surfeit will endure,
　　Who places all his chiefest happiness
　　　In the extravagancies of excess,
　　Which wise sobriety esteems but a disease!
　　O mighty envied happiness to eat!
　　Which fond mistaken sots call great!
　　Poor frailty of our flesh! which we each day
Must thus repair for fear of ruinous decay!
　　Degrading of our nature, where vile brutes are fain
　　　To make and keep up man!
　　Which, when the paradise above we gain,
Heaven thinks too great an imperfection to retain!
　　By each disease the sickly joy's destroyed;
　　　At every meal it's nauseous, and is cloyed,
　　Empty at best, as when in dream enjoyed;
　　When, cheated by a slumbering imposture, we
　　Fancy a feast, and great regalios by;
　　　And think we taste, and think we see,
　　And riot on imaginary luxury.

9

Grant me, O Virtue, thy most solid lasting joy;
  Grant me the better pleasures of the mind,
Pleasures, which only in pursuit of thee we find,
    Which fortune cannot mar, nor chance destroy.
  One moment in thy blessed enjoyment is
Worth an eternity of that tumultuous bliss,
      Which we derive from sense,
Which often cloys, and must resign to impotence.
Grant me but this, how will I triumph in my happy
  Above the chances and reverse of fate;   [state,
    Above her favours and her hate.
  I'll scorn the worthless treasures of Peru,
    And those of the other Indies too;
I'll pity Cæsar's self, with all his trophies and his fame,
And the vile brutish herd of epicures contemn,
And all the under-shrievalties of life not worth a name;
    Nor will I only owe my bliss,
    Like others, to a multitude,
Where company keeps up a forcèd happiness;
    Should all mankind surcease to live,
    And none but individual I survive,
Alone I would be happy, and enjoy my solitude.
    Thus shall my life in pleasant minutes wear,
    Calm as the minutes of the evening are,
    And gentle as the motions of the upper air;
    Soft as my muse, and unconfined as she,
When flowing in the numbers of Pindaric liberty.
    And when I see pale ghastly death appear,
That grand inevitable test which all must bear,
  Which best distinguishes the blessed and wretched
      here,
I'll smile at all its horrors, court my welcome destiny,
  And yield my willing soul up in an easy sigh;
  And epicures that see shall envy and confess
That I, and those who dare like me be good, the
    chiefest good possess.

UPON THE MARRIAGE OF THE PRINCE OF ORANGE WITH THE LADY MARY.

I

AS when of old, some bright and heavenly dame
  A god of equal majesty did wed;
Straight through the court above the tidings spread,
Straight at the news the immortal offspring came,
And all the deities did the high nuptials grace;
    With no less pomp, no less of grandeur, we
        Behold this glad solemnity,
        And all confess an equal joy,
And all expect as godlike and as great a race.
    Hark how united shouts our joys proclaim,
Which rise in gratitude to Heaven, from whence they
        came;
Gladsome, next those which brought our royal exile home,
    When he resumed his long usurpèd throne.
    Hark how the mighty vollies rend the air,
    And shake at once the earth and utmost sphere!
        Hark how the bells' harmonious noise
        Bear concert too with human joys!
    Behold those numerous fires, which up and down
Threaten almost new conflagration to the town,
Well do these emblems, mighty Orange, speak thy
        fame,
Whose loudness, music, brightness, all express the same;
'Twas thus great Jove his Semele did wed,
In thunder and in lightning so approached her bed.

2

Hail happy pair! kind Heaven's great hostages!
Sure pledges of a firm and lasting peace!
Call't not a match, we that low style disdain,
Nor will degrade it with a term so mean;
        A league it must be said,
Where countries thus espouse, and nations wed.

Our thanks, propitious Destiny!
Never did yet thy power dispense
A more plenipotentiary influence,
Nor heaven more sure a treaty ratify.
To you, our great and gracious monarch, too,
   An equal share of thanks is due, [and you.
Nought could this mighty work produce, but heaven
    Let others boast
  Of leagues, which wars and slaughter cost;
 This union by no blood cemented is,
Nor did its harmony from jars and discords rise.
 Not more to your great ancestor we owe,
 By whom two realms into one kingdom grow;
He joined but what nature had joined before,
Lands disunited by no parting shore:
 By you to foreign countries we're allied,
You make us continent, whom seas and waves divide.

3

How well, brave prince, do you by prudent conduct
  What was denied to mighty Jove, [prove
  Together to be wise and love!
In this you highest skill of choice and judgment show,
 'Tis here displayed, and here rewarded too;
Others move only by unbridled guideless heat,
But you mix love with policy, passion with state;
  You scorned the painter's hands your hearts should
    tie,
Which oft (and here they must) the original belie;
  For how should art that beauty undertake,
  Which Heaven would strive in vain again to make?
Taught by religion you did better methods try,
And worshipped not the image, but the Deity.
 Go, envied prince, your glorious bride receive,
 Too great for aught but mighty York to give:
She, whom if none must wed but those who merit her,
Monarchs might cease pretence, and slighted gods
   despair;

Think you in her far greater conquests gain,
Than all the powers of France have from your country
      ta'en;
In her fair arms let your ambition bounded lie,
And fancy there an universal monarchy!

4

And you, fair princess, who could thus subdue
What France with all its forces could not do,
      Enjoy your glorious prize,
Enjoy the triumphs of your conquering eyes:
From him, and the height of your great mind, look down,
      And with neglect despise a throne,
And think't as great to merit, as to wear a crown.
Nassau is all which your desires or thoughts can frame,
   All titles lodge within that single name;
A name which Mars himself would with ambition bear,
Prouder in that, than to be called the God of War.
To you, great madam, (if your joys admit increase,
If Heaven has not already set your happiness
      Above its power to raise)
    To you the zealous humble muse
   These solemn wishes consecrates and vows,
   And begs you'll not her offering refuse,
Which not your want, but her devotion shows.

5

   May your great consort still successful prove,
In all his high attempts, as in your love;
   May he through all attacks of chance appear
   As free from danger, as he is from fear;
   May neither sense of grief, nor trouble know,
   But what in pity you to others show;
May you be fruitful in as numerous store
Of princely births, as she who your great father bore;
   May Heaven, to your just merits kind,
Repeal the ancient curse on womankind;
   Easy and gentle, as the labours of the brain,
   May yours all prove, and just so free from pain;

May no rude noise of war approach your bed,
But peace her downy wings about you spread,
Calm as the season, when fair halcyons breed;
May you, and the just owner of your breast,
Both in as full content and happiness be blessed,
As the first sinless pair of old enjoyed,
Ere guilt their innocence and that destroyed;
Till nothing but continuance to your bliss can add,
And you, by Heaven alone, be happier made;
Till future poets, who your lives review,
When they'd their utmost pitch of flattery show,
Shall pray their patrons may become like you;
Nor know to frame a skilful wish more great,
Nor think a higher blessing in the gift of fate.

AN ODE FOR AN ANNIVERSARY OF MUSIC
ON ST. CECILIA'S DAY.*

I

BEGIN the song, your instruments advance,
      Tune the voice, and tune the flute,
      Touch the silent sleeping lute,
And make the strings to their own measures dance.
Bring gentlest thoughts, that into language glide,
Bring softest words, that into numbers slide;
      Let every hand, and every tongue,
      To make the noble concert throng.
Let all in one harmonious note agree
      To frame the mighty song,
For this is music's sacred jubilee.

2

Hark how the wakened strings resound,
      And break the yielding air,
The ravished sense how pleasingly they wound,
And call the listening soul into the ear;

---

* Set to music by Dr. Blow.

Each pulse beats time, and every heart
With tongue and fingers bears a part.
    By harmony's entrancing power,
When we are thus wound up to ecstasy,
    Methinks we mount, methinks we tower,
And seem to antedate our future bliss on high.

3

How dull were life, how hardly worth our care,
    But for the charm that music lends!
    How faint its pleasures would appear,
But for the pleasure which our art attends!
    Without the sweets of melody,
    To tune our vital breath,
    Who would not give it up to death,
And in the silent grave contented lie?

4

Music's the cordial of a troubled breast,
The softest remedy that grief can find;
The gentle spell that charms our care to rest,
And calms the ruffled passions of the mind.
    Music does all our joy refine,
    It gives the relish to our wine,
    'Tis that gives rapture to our love,
And wings devotion to a pitch divine;
'Tis our chief bliss on earth, and half our heaven above.

CHORUS.

Come then, with tuneful throat and string
The praises of our art let s sing;
    Let's sing to blest Cecilia's fame,
That graced this art, and gave this day its name;
    With music, wine, and mirth conspire
To bear a concert, and make up the choir.

TO MADAM L. E. UPON HER RECOVERY
FROM A LATE SICKNESS.

MADAM,

PARDON, that with slow gladness we so late
   Your wished return of health congratulate;
Our joys at first so thronged to get abroad,
They hindered one another in the crowd;
And now such haste to tell their message make,
They only stammer what they meant to speak.
   You, the fair subject which I am to sing,
To whose kind hands this humble joy I bring,
Aid me, I beg, while I this theme pursue,
For I invoke no other muse but you.
Long time had you here brightly shone below,
With all the rays kind Heaven could bestow;
No envious cloud e'er offered to invade
Your lustre, or compel it to a shade;
Nor did it yet by any sign appear,
But that you throughout immortal were;
Till Heaven (if Heaven could prove so cruel,) sent
To interrupt the growth of your content,
As if it grudged those gifts you did enjoy,
And would that bounty, which it gave, destroy.
'Twas since your excellence did envy move
In those high powers, and made them jealous prove,
They thought these glories, should they still have
    shined
Unsullied, were too much for woman-kind;
Which might they write as lasting as they're fair,
Too great for aught but deities appear.
But Heaven, it may be, was not yet complete,
And lacked you there to fill your empty seat;
And when it could not fairly woo you hence,
Turned ravisher, and offered violence.
   Sickness did first a formal siege begin,
And by sure slowness tried your life to win,

As if by lingering methods Heaven meant
To chase you hence, and tire you to consent.
But, thus in vain, fate did to force resort,
And next by storm strove to attack the fort;
A sleep, dull as your last, did you arrest,
And all the magazines of life possessed.
No more the blood its circling course did run,
But in the veins, like icicles, it hung;
No more the heart, now void of quickening heat,
The tuneful march of vital motion beat;
Stiffness did into all the sinews climb,
And a short death crept cold through every limb;
All signs of life from sight so far withdrew,
'Twas now thought Popery to pray for you.
There might you (were not that sense lost) have seen
How your true death would have resented been:
A lethargy like yours each breast did seize,
And all by sympathy caught your disease.
Around you silent imagery appears,
And nought in the spectators moves, but tears;
They pay what grief were to your funeral due,
And yet dare hope Heaven would your life renew.
    Meanwhile, all means, all drugs, prescribèd are,
Which the decays of health or strength repair,
Medicines so powerful they new souls would save,
And life in long-dead carcasses retrieve.
But, these in vain, they rougher methods try,
And now you're martyred that you may not die.
Sad scene of fate! when tortures were your gain,
And 'twas a kindness thought to wish you pain!
As if the slackened string of life run down,
Could only by the rack be screwed in tune.
    But Heaven at last, grown conscious that its power
Could scarce what was to die with you restore,
And loth to see such glories overcome,
Sent a post angel to repeal your doom;
Straight Fate obeyed the charge which Heaven sent,
And gave this first dear proof it could repent.

Triumphant charms! what may not you subdue,
When Fate's your slave, and thus submits to you!
She now again the new-broke thread does knit,
And for another clew her spindle fit;
And life's hid spark, which did unquenched remain,
Caught the fled light, and brought it back again.
Thus you revived, and all our joys with you
Revived, and found their resurrection too.
Some only grieved, that what was deathless thought,
They saw so near to fatal ruin brought.
Now crowds of blessings on that happy hand,
Whose skill could eager destiny withstand;
Whose learnèd power has rescued from the grave
That life, which 'twas a miracle to save;
That life, which were it thus untimely lost,
Had been the fairest spoil death e'er could boast. .
May he henceforth be god of healing thought,
By whom such good to you and us was brought;
Altars and shrines to him are justly due,
Who showed himself a god by raising you.

But say, fair saint, for you alone can know,
Whither your soul in this short flight did go?
Went it to antedate that happiness,
You must at last (though late we hope) possess?
Inform us, lest we should your fate belie,
And call that death which was but ecstasy.
The Queen of Love, we're told, once let us see
That goddesses from wounds could not be free;
And you, by this unwished occasion, show
That they like mortal us can sickness know.
Pity! that Heaven should all its titles give,
And yet not let you with them ever live.
You'd lack no point that makes a deity,
If you could like it too immortal be.

And so you are; half boasts a deathless state,
Although your frailer part must yield to fate.
By every breach in that fair lodging made,
Its blest inhabitant is more displayed;

In that white snow which overspreads your skin,
We trace the whiter soul which dwells within;
Which, while you through this shining hue display,
Looks like a star placed in the milky way.
Such the bright bodies of the blessèd are,
When they for raiment clothed with light appear;
And should you visit now the seats of bliss,
You need not wear another form but this.
Never did sickness in such pomp appear,
As when it thus your livery did wear,
Disease itself looked amiable here.
So clouds, which would obscure the sun, oft gilded be,
And shades are taught to shine as bright as he.
    Grieve not, fair nymph, when in your glass you trace
The marring footsteps of a pale disease;
Regret not that your cheeks their roses want,
Which a few days shall in full store replant,
Which, whilst your blood withdraws its guilty red,
Tells that you own no faults that blushes need.
The sun, whose bounty does each spring restore
What winter from the rifled meadows tore,
Which every morning with an early ray
Paints the young blushing cheeks of instant day;
Whose skill, inimitable here below,   [bow;
Limns those gay clouds which form heaven's coloured
That sun shall soon with interest repay
All the lost beauty sickness snatched away;
Your beams, like his, shall hourly now advance,
And every minute their swift growth enhance.
    Meanwhile, that you no helps of health refuse,
Accept these humble wishes of the muse;
Which shall not of their just petition fail,
If she (and she's a goddess) aught prevail.
    May no profane disease henceforth approach
This sacred temple with unhallowed touch,
Or with rude sacrilege its frame debauch;
May these fair members always happy be,
In as full strength and well-set harmony,

As the new foundress of your sex could boast,
Ere she by sin her first perfection lost;
May destiny, just to your merits, twine
All your smooth fortunes in a silken line;
And, that you may at Heaven late arrive,
May it to you its largest bottom give;
May Heaven with still repeated favours bless,
Till it its power below its will confess;
Till wishes can no more exalt your fate,
Nor poets fancy you more fortunate.

ON THE DEATH OF MRS. KATHARINE KINGSCOURT,

A CHILD OF EXCELLENT PARTS AND PIETY.

SHE did, she did—I saw her mount the sky,
  And with new whiteness paint the galaxy.
Heaven her methought with all its eyes did view,
And yet acknowledged all its eyes too few.
Methought I saw in crowds blessed spirits meet,
And with loud welcomes her arrival greet,
Which, could they grieve, had gone with grief away,
To see a soul more white, more pure than they.
  Earth was unworthy such a prize as this,
Only a while Heaven let us share the bliss;
In vain her stay with fruitless tears we'd woo,
In vain we'd court, when that our rival grew.
Thanks, ye kind powers! who did so long dispense
(Since you so wished her) with her absence thence:
We now resign, to you alone we grant
The sweet monopoly of such a saint;
So pure a saint, I scarce dare call her so,
For fear to wrong her with a name too low;
Such a seraphic brightness in her shined,
I hardly can believe her womankind.

'Twas sure some noble being left the sphere,
Which deigned a little to inhabit here,
And can't be said to die, but disappear.
Or if she mortal was, and meant to show
The greater skill by being made below,
Sure Heaven preserved her by the fall uncursed,
To tell how all the sex were formed at first.
Never did yet so much divinity
In such a small compendium crowded lie.
By her we credit what the learnèd tell,
That many angels on one point can dwell.
More damnèd fiends did not in Mary rest,
Than lodged of blessèd spirits in her breast;
Religion dawned so early in her mind,
You'd think her saint whilst in the womb enshrined;
Nay, that bright ray which did her temples paint,
Proclaimed her clearly, while alive, a saint.
Scarce had she learned to lisp religion's name,
Ere she by her example preached the same,
And taught her cradle like the pulpit to reclaim.
No action did within her practice fall
Which for the atonement of a blush could call;
No words of hers e'er greeted any ear,
But what a dying saint, confessed, might hear.
Her thoughts had scarcely ever sullied been
By the least footsteps of original sin.
Her life did still as much devotion breathe,
As others do at their last gasp in death.
Hence, on her tomb, of her let not be said,
So long she lived, but thus—So long she prayed !

PARAPHRASE UPON THE 137TH PSALM.

I

Ver. 1 FAR from our pleasant native Palestine,
            Where great Euphrates with a mighty
                current flows,

And does in watery limits Babylon confine,
Cursed Babylon! the cause and author of our woes;
    There, on the river's side,
    Sat wretched captive we,
  And in sad tears bewailed our misery;   [tide.
Tears, whose vast store increased the neighbouring
We wept, and straight our grief before us brought
A thousand distant objects to our thought.
  As oft as we surveyed the gliding stream,
  Loved Jordan did our sad remembrance claim;
  As oft as we the adjoining city viewed,
  Dear Sion's razèd walls our grief renewed;
We thought on all the pleasures of our happy land,
  Late ravished by a cruel conqueror's hand;
We thought on every piteous, every mournful thing,
That might excess to our enlargèd sorrows bring. ·
2 Deep silence told the greatness of our grief,
  Of grief too great by vent to find relief;
    Our harps, as mute and dumb as we,
    Hung useless and neglected by;
And now and then a broken string would lend a sigh,
  As if with us they felt a sympathy,
  And mourned their own, and our captivity;
The gentle river, too, as if compassionate grown,
  As 'twould its natives' cruelty atone,
As it passed by, in murmurs gave a pitying groan.

2

3 There the proud conquerors, who gave us chains,
  Who all our sufferings and misfortunes gave,
  Did with rude insolence our sorrows brave,
And with insulting raillery thus mocked our pains:
  ' Play us,' said they, ' some brisk and airy strain,
  Such as your ancestors were wont to hear
     . On Shilo's pleasant plain,
Where all the virgins met in dances once a year;
     Or one of those
Which your illustrious David did compose,

While he filled Israel's happy throne,
Great soldier, poet, and musician, all in one:
    Oft, have we heard, he went with harp in hand,
        Captain of all the harmonious band,
And vanquished all the choir with 's single skill alone.
4 Forbid it, Heaven! forbid it, thou great thrice hal-
            lowed name,
        We should thy sacred hymns defame,
        Or them, with impious ears, profane. ·
    No, no, inhuman slaves, is this a time
    (Oh! cruel and preposterous demand!)
    When every joy, and every smile's a crime,
A treason to our poor unhappy land,
        Is this a time for sprightly airs,
    When every look the badge of sorrow wears,
        And livery of our miseries,
Sad miseries that call for all our breath in sighs,
        And all the tribute of our eyes,
And moisture of our veins, our very blood in tears?
When nought can claim our thoughts, Jerusalem, but
        thou,   [throw?
Nought but thy sad destruction, fall, and over-

3

5 Oh, dearest city! late our nation's justest pride!
    Envy of all the wondering world beside!
Oh, sacred temple, once the Almighty's blessed abode,
    Now quite forsaken by our angry God!
        Shall ever distant time, or place,
    Your firm ideas from my soul deface?
        Shall they not still take up my breast,
As long as that, and life, and I shall last?
Grant Heaven (nor shall my prayers the curse with-
            stand)
        That this my learnèd, skilful hand,   [mand,
Which now o'er all the tuneful strings can boast com-
Which does as quick, as ready, and unerring prove,
As nature, when it would its joints or fingers move,

Grant, it forget its art and feeling too,
When I forget to think, to wish, to pray for you!
6 For ever tied with dumbness be my tongue,
When it speaks aught that shall not to your praise
      belong,   [song.
If that be not the constant subject of my muse and

4

7 Remember, Heaven, remember Edom on that day,
   And with like sufferings their spite repay,
Who made our miseries their cruel mirth and scorn,
   Who laughed to see our flaming city burn,
         And wished it might to ashes turn:
   'Raze, raze it,' was their cursèd cry,
   'Raze all its stately structures down,
And lay its palaces and temple level with the ground,
Till Sion buried in its dismal ruins lie,
Forgot alike its place, its name, and memory.'
8 And thou, proud Babylon! just object of our hate,
   Thou too shalt feel the sad reverse of fate,
         Though thou art now exalted high,
   And with thy lofty head o'ertop'st the sky,
   As if thou wouldst the Powers above defy;
   Thou, if those powers (and sure they will) prove just,
   If my prophetic grief can aught foresee,
   Ere long shalt lay that lofty head in dust,
And blush in blood for all thy present cruelty;
How loudly then shall we retort these bitter taunts!
How gladly to the music of thy fetters dance!

5

A day will come (oh, might I see 't!) ere long,
   That shall revenge our mighty wrong;
   Then blessed, for ever blessed, be he
   Whoever shall return 't on thee,
And grave it deep, and pay 't with bloody usury!
   May neither agèd groans, nor infant cries,
Nor piteous mothers' tears, nor ravished virgins' sighs,
   Soften thy unrelenting enemies;

OLDHAM.   17

Let them, as thou to us, inexorable prove,
   Nor age, nor sex, their deaf compassion move;
   Rapes, murders, slaughters, funerals,
And all thou durst attempt within our Sion's walls,
   Mayst thou endure, and more, till joyful we
Confess thyself outdone in artful cruelty.
9 Blessed, yea thrice blessèd, be that barbarous hand
   (O grief, that I such dire revenge commend!)
   Who tears out infants from their mothers' womb,
   And hurls them yet unborn unto their tomb;
   Blessed he who plucks them from their parents' arms,
   That sanctuary from all common harms,
Who with their skulls and bones shall pave thy streets
               all o'er,   [brains and gore.
And fill thy glutted channels with their scattered

PARAPHRASE UPON THE HYMN OF ST. AMBROSE.

AN ODE.

I

TO Thee, O God, we thy just praises sing,
   To Thee, we Thy great name rehearse:
We are Thy vassals, and this humble tribute bring
   To Thee, acknowledged only Lord and King,
Acknowledged sole and sovereign monarch of the uni-
   All parts of this wide universe adore,   [verse!
   Eternal Father! Thy Almighty power;
   The skies, and stars, fire, air, and earth, and sea,
   With all their numerous nameless progeny,
   Confess, and their due homage pay to Thee;
For why? Thou spak'st the word, and mad'st them
               all from nothing be.
   To Thee all angels, all Thy glorious court on high,
      Seraph and cherub, the nobility,

And whatsoever spirits be
Of lesser honour, less degree,
To Thee, in heavenly lays,
They sing loud anthems of immortal praise:
Still Holy, Holy, Holy Lord of Hosts, they cry;
This is their business, this their sole employ,
And thus they spend their long and blessed eternity.

2

Farther than nature's utmost shores and limits stretch,
The streams of Thy unbounded glory reach;
Beyond the straits of scanty time and place,
Beyond the ebbs and flows of matter's narrow seas
They reach, and fill the ocean of eternity and space.
Infused like some vast mighty soul,
Thou dost inform and actuate this spacious whole; ·
Thy unseen hand does the well-jointed frame sustain,
Which else would to its primitive nothing shrink again.
But most Thou dost Thy majesty display
In the bright realms of everlasting day;
There is Thy residence, there dost Thou reign,
There on a state of dazzling lustre sit,
There shine in robes of pure refinèd light;
Where sun's coarse rays are but a foil and stain,
And refuse stars the sweepings of Thy glorious train.

3

There all Thy family of menial saints,
Huge colonies of blessed inhabitants,   [hence,
Which death through countless ages has transplanted
Now on Thy throne for ever wait,
And fill the large retinue of Thy heavenly state.
There reverend prophets stand, a pompous goodly show,
Of old Thy envoys extraordinary here,
Who brought Thy sacred embassies of peace and war,
That, to the obedient, this, the rebel world below.
By them, the mighty twelve have their abode,
Companions once of the incarnate suffering God,

17—2

Partakers now of all His triumphs there,
As they on earth did in His miseries share.
Of martyrs next, a crowned and glorious choir,
        Illustrious heroes who have gained
Through dangers, and red seas of blood, the promised
        land,
And passed, through ordeal flames, to thy eternity in
        fire.
There, all make up the concert of Thy praise,
        To Thee they sing, and never cease,
Loud Hymns and Hallelujahs of applause;
An angel-laureat does the sense and strains compose,
    Sense, far above the reach of mortal verse,
    Strains, far above the reach of mortal ears,
And all, a Muse unglorified can fancy or rehearse.

4

Nor is this concert only kept above,
    Nor is it to the blessed alone confined;
    But earth, and all thy faithful here are joined,
And strive to vie with them in duty and in love;
And, though they cannot equal notes and measures raise,
Strive to return the imperfect echoes of thy praise.
    They through all nations own thy glorious name,
    And everywhere the great Three-One proclaim:
    Thee, Father of the world! and us, and Him,
    Who must mankind, whom Thou didst make, redeem;
Thee, blessèd Saviour! Thee, adored, true, only Son
    To man debased, to rescue man undone;
        And Thee, Eternal, Holy Power!
Who dost by grace exalted man restore
To all he lost by the old fall and sin before;
        You, blessed and glorious Trinity!
Riddle to baffled knowledge and philosophy,
Which cannot comprehend the mighty mystery
    Of numerous One, and the unnumbered Three!
Vast topless pile of wonders! at whose sight
    Reason itself turns giddy with the height,

Above the fluttering pitch of human wit,
And all, but the strong wings of faith, that eagle's
    towering flight.

5

Blessed Jesu! how shall we enough adore,
Or Thy unbounded love, or Thy unbounded power?
Thou art the Prince of Heaven, thou art the Almighty's
    heir,
Thou art the eternal offspring of the Eternal Sire:
  Hail Thou, the world's Redeemer! whom to free
  From bonds of death and endless misery,
    Thou thought'st it no disdain to be
  Inhabiter to low mortality;
    The Almighty thought it no disdain
  To dwell in the pure Virgin's spotless womb,   .
There did the boundless Godhead, and whole heaven
    find room,
And a small point the circle of infinity contain.
  Hail, ransom of mankind, all great, all good!
    Who didst atone us with Thy blood,
  Thyself the offering, altar, priest, and God!
  Thyself didst die, to be our glorious bail
From death's arrests, and the eternal flaming jail;
  Thyself thou gav'st, the inestimable price
To purchase and redeem our mortgaged heaven and
    happiness;
  Thither, when Thy great work on earth had end,
   When death itself was slain and dead,
  And hell with all its powers captive led,
  Thou didst again triumphantly ascend;
There dost Thou now by Thy great Father sit on high,
  With equal glory, equal majesty,
Joint ruler of the everlasting monarchy.

6

Again from thence, Thou shalt with greater triumph
    come,
  When the last trumpet sounds the general doom.

And, lo! Thou com'st, and, lo! the direful sound does
        make
  Through Death's wide realm mortality awake;
     And, lo! they all appear
      At Thy dread bar,
And all receive the unalterable sentence there.
Affrighted nature trembles at the dismal day,
  And shrinks for fear, and vanishes away;
Both that, and time, breathe out their last, and now
      they die,
And now are swallowed up and lost in vast eternity.
    Mercy, O mercy, angry God!
Stop, stop Thy flaming wrath, too fierce to be with-
     stood,
  And quench it with the deluge of Thy blood;
  Thy precious blood which was so freely spilt
  To wash us from the stains of sin and guilt;
  O write us with it in the book of fate,
  Amongst Thy chosen and predestinate,
Free denizens of heaven, of the immortal state.

7

  Guide us, O Saviour! guide Thy church below,
  Both way and star, compass and pilot Thou;
 Do Thou this frail and tottering vessel steer
    Through life's tempestuous ocean here,
    Through all the tossing waves of fear,
    And dangerous rocks of black despair.
Safe, under Thee, we shall to the wished haven move,
And reach the undiscovered lands of bliss above.
  Thus low, behold! to Thy great name we bow,
    And thus we ever wish to grow;
  Constant, as time does Thy fixed laws obey,
  To Thee our worship and our thanks we pay;
    With these, we wake the cheerful light,
    With these, we sleep and rest invite;   [days,
And thus we spend our breath, and thus we spend our
And never cease to sing, and never cease to praise.

8

While thus each breast, and mouth, and ear,
Are fillèd with Thy praise, and love, and fear,
Let never sin get room, or entrance there :
Vouchsafe, O Lord, through this and all our days,
    To guard us with Thy powerful grace :
Within our hearts let no usurping lust be found,
    No rebel passion tumult raise,
    To break Thy laws, or break our peace,
But set Thy watch of angels on the place,
And keep the tempter still from that forbidden ground.
    Ever, O Lord, to us Thy mercies grant ;
    Never, O Lord, let us thy mercies want ;
Ne'er want Thy favour, bounty, liberality,
        But let them ever on us be,
Constant as our own hope and trust on Thee.
On Thee, we all our hope and trust repose !
        O never leave us to our foes,
        Never, O Lord, desert our cause ;
        Thus aided and upheld by Thee,
We'll fear no danger, death, nor misery ;
Fearless we thus will stand a falling world,
With crushing ruins all about us hurled,   [defy.
And face wide gaping hell, and all its slighted powers

A SUNDAY-THOUGHT IN SICKNESS.

LORD, how dreadful is the prospect of death, at the remotest
distance !   How the smallest apprehension of it can pall the
most gay, airy, and brisk spirits !   Even I, who thought I could
have been merry in sight of my coffin, and drink a health with
the sexton in my own grave, now tremble at the least envoy of
the king of terrors.   To see but the shaking of my glass makes
me turn pale, and fear is like to prevent and do the work of my
distemper.   All the jollity of my humour and conversation is
turned on a sudden to chagrin and melancholy, black as despair,

and dark as the grave.   My soul and body seem at once laid out, and I fancy all the plummets of eternal night already hanging upon my temples.   But whence proceed these fears ?   Certainly they are not idle dreams, nor the accidental product of my disease, which disorders the brains, and fills 'em with odd chimeras.   Why should my soul be averse to its enlargement ?   Why should it be content to be knit up in two yards of skin, when it may have all the world for its purlieu ?   'Tis not that I'm unwilling to leave my relations and present friends : I'm parted from the first already, and could be severed from both the length of the whole map, and live with my body as far distant from them as my soul must when I'm dead.   Neither is it that I'm loth to leave the delights and pleasures of the world; some of them I have tried, and found empty, the others covet not, because unknown.   I'm confident I could despise 'em all by a greatness of soul, did not the Bible oblige me, and divines tell me, 'tis my duty.   It is not neither that I'm unwilling to go hence before I've established a reputation, and something to make me survive myself.   I could have been content to be still-born, and have no more than the register or sexton to tell that I've never been in the land of the living.   In fine, 'tis not from a principle of cowardice, which the schools have called self-preservation, the poor effect of instinct and dull pretence of a brute as well as me.   This unwillingness, therefore, and aversion to undergo the general fate, must have a juster original, and flow from a more important cause.   I'm well satisfied that this other being within, that moves and actuates my frame of flesh and blood, has a life beyond it and the grave; and something in it prompts me to believe its immortality.   A residence it must have somewhere else, when it has left this carcase, and another state to pass into, unchangeable and everlasting as itself, after its separation.   This condition must be good or bad, according to its actions and deserts in this life; for as it owes its being to some infinite power that created it, I well suppose it his vassal, and obliged to live by his law; and as certainly conclude, that according to the keeping or breaking of that law, 'tis to be rewarded or punished hereafter.   This diversity of rewards and punishments makes the two places, heaven and hell, so often mentioned in Scripture, and talked of in pulpits.   Of the latter my fears too cruelly convince me, and the anticipation of its torment, which I already feel in my own conscience.   There is, there is a hell, and damned fiends, and a never dying worm, and that sceptic that doubts of it, may find 'em all within my single breast.   I dare not any longer, with the atheist, disbelieve them, or think 'em the clergy's bugbears, invented as nurses do frightful names for their children, to scare 'em into quietness and obedience. How oft have I triumphed in my unconcerned and seared insensibility? How oft boasted of that unhappy suspected calm, which, like that of the Dead Sea, proved only my curse, and a treacherous ambush to those storms, which at present (and will for ever, I dread,) shipwreck my quiet and hopes? How oft have I rejected the advice of that bosom friend, and drowned its alarms in the noise of a tumultuous debauch, or by stupifying wine (like some condemned malefactor) armed myself against the apprehensions of my certain doom?

Now, now the tyrant awakes, and comes to pay at once all arrears of cruelty. At last, but too late, (like drowning mariners) I see the gay monsters which inveigled me into my death and destruction. Oh, the gnawing remorse of a rash, unguarded, unconsidering sinner! Oh, how the ghosts of former crimes affright my haunted imagination, and make me suffer a thousand racks and martyrdoms! I see, methinks, the jaws of destruction gaping wide to swallow me; and I (like one sliding on ice), though I see the danger, cannot stop from running into it. My fancy represents to me a whole legion of devils, ready to tear me in pieces, numberless as my sins or fears; and whither, alas! whither shall I fly for refuge? Where shall I retreat and take sanctuary? Shall I call the rocks and mountains to cover me, or bid the earth yawn wide to its centre, and take me in? Poor shift of escaping Almighty justice! Distracting frenzy! that would make me believe contradictions, and hope to fly out of the reach of him whose presence is everywhere, not excluding hell itself; for he is there in the effects of his vengeance. Shall I invoke some power infinite as that that created me, to reduce me to nothing again, and rid me at once of my being and all that tortures it? Oh no, 'tis in vain; I must be forced into being, to keep me fresh for torment, and retain sense only to feel pain. I must be dying to all eternity, and live ever, to live ever wretched. Oh that Nature had placed me in the rank of things that have only a bare existence, or, at best, an animal life, and never given me a soul and reason, which now must contribute to my misery, and make me envy brutes and vegetables! Would the womb that bore me had been my prison till now, or I stept out of it into my grave, and saved the expenses and toil of a long and tedious journey, where life affords nothing of accommodations to invite one's stay! Happy had I been if I had expired with my first breath, and entered the Bill of Mortality as soon as the world; happy if I had been drowned in my font, and that water which was to regenerate and give me new life, had proved mortal in another sense! I had then died without any guilt of my own, but what I brought into the world with me, and that too atoned for; I mean that which I contracted from my first parents, my unhappiness rather than fault, inasmuch as I was fain to be born of a sinning race: then I had never enhanced it with acquired guilt, never added those innumerable crimes which must make up my indictment at the grand audit.   Ungrateful wretch! I've made my sins as numerous as those blessings and mercies the Almighty bounty has conferred upon me, to oblige and lead me to repentance.   How have I abused and misemployed those parts and talents which might have rendered me serviceable to mankind, and repaid an interest of glory to their donor!   How ill do they turn to account which I have made the patrons of debauchery, and pimps and panders to vice!   How oft have I broke my vows to my great Creator, which I would be conscientious of keeping to a silly woman, a creature beneath myself!   What has all my religion been but an empty parade and show?   Either an useful hypocrisy taken up for interest, or a gay specious formality worn in complaisance to custom and the mode, and as changeable as my clothes and their fashion.   How oft have I gone to church (the place where we are to pay Him homage and duty) as to an assignation or play, only for diversion; or at best, as I must ere long (for aught I know) with my soul severed from my body?   How I tremble at the remembrance! as if I could put the sham upon Heaven, or a God were to be imposed on like my fellow-creature. And dare I, convicted of these high treasons against the King of Glory, dare I expect a reprieve or pardon?   Has He thunder, and are not all his bolts levelled at my head, to strike me through the very centre?   Yes, I dare appeal to thee, boundless pity and compassion!   My own instances already tell me, that Thy mercy is infinite; for I've done enough to shock long-sufferance itself, and weary out an eternal patience.   I beseech Thee by Thy soft and gentle attributes of mercy and forgiveness, by the last dying accents of my suffering Deity, have pity on a poor, humble, prostrate and confessing sinner; and Thou, great ransom of lost mankind, who offered'st thyself a sacrifice to atone our guilt, and redeem our mortgaged happiness, do Thou be my Advocate, and intercede for me with the angry Judge.

My prayers are heard, a glorious light now shone,
And, lo! an angel-post comes hastening down

From heaven; I see him cut the yielding air,
So swift, he seems at once both here and there;
So quick, my sight in the pursuit was slow,
And thought could scarce so soon the journey go.
No angry message in his look appears,
His face no signs of threatening vengeance wears;
Comely his shape, of heavenly mien and air,
Kinder than smiles of beauteous virgins are.
Such he was seen by the blessed maid of old,
When he the Almighty Infant's birth foretold.
A mighty volume in one hand is borne,
Whose opened leaves the other seems to turn;
Vast annals of my sins in scarlet writ,
But now erased, blot out, and cancelled quite.
Hark! how the heavenly whisper strikes mine ear,
Mortal, behold thy crimes all pardoned here! ·
Hail, sacred envoy of the Eternal King!
Welcome as the blessed tidings thou dost bring;
Welcome as heaven from whence thou cam'st but now;
Thus low to thy great God and mine I bow,
And might I here, O might I ever grow,
Fixed and unmoved, an endless monument
Of gratitude to my Creator sent!

THE END.

BELL'S ENGLISH POETS.

CHEAP RE-ISSUE,

In Fortnightly Volumes, on the 1st and 15th of every month, foolscap 8vo., handsomely bound in cloth,

1s. 3d. each,

OF

THE ENGLISH POETS,

WITH CRITICAL AND HISTORICAL NOTES, MEMOIRS, AND GLOSSARIES.

BY ROBERT BELL.

ORDER AND DATE OF PUBLICATION.

*** *If desired, Subscribers can obtain at once, through any Bookseller, the Volumes not yet issued of Chaucer's Works. The last Volume contains the Glossary.*

"The best-edited series of Poets in the language."—*Bookseller.*

"We need not dwell on the fulness, the taste, the accuracy, and the general excellence of Mr. Bell's editorial labours."—*Daily Telegraph.*

"Admirably produced, and most handy and natty in size and shape."—*Publishers' Circular.*

LONDON: CHARLES GRIFFIN & CO., STATIONERS' HALL COURT.